GUN WORK

THE FURTHER EXPLOITS
OF HAYDEN TILDEN

J. LEE BUTTS

BERKLEY BOOKS, NEW YORK

THE BERKLEY PUBLISHING GROUP
Published by the Penguin Group
Penguin Group (USA) Inc.
375 Hudson Street, New York, New York 10014, USA
Penguin Group (Canada), 90 Eglinton Avenue East, Suite 700, Toronto, Ontario M4P 2Y3, Canada
(a division of Pearson Penguin Canada Inc.)
Penguin Books Ltd., 80 Strand, London WC2R 0RL, England
Penguin Group Ireland, 25 St. Stephen's Green, Dublin 2, Ireland (a division of Penguin Books Ltd.)
Penguin Group (Australia), 250 Camberwell Road, Camberwell, Victoria 3124, Australia
(a division of Pearson Australia Group Pty. Ltd.)
Penguin Books India Pvt. Ltd., 11 Community Centre, Panchsheel Park, New Delhi—110 017, India
Penguin Group (NZ), 67 Apollo Drive, Rosedale, North Shore 0632, New Zealand
(a division of Pearson New Zealand Ltd.)
Penguin Books (South Africa) (Pty.) Ltd., 24 Sturdee Avenue, Rosebank, Johannesburg 2196,
South Africa

Penguin Books Ltd., Registered Offices: 80 Strand, London WC2R 0RL, England

This is a work of fiction. Names, characters, places, and incidents either are the product of the author's imagination or are used fictitiously, and any resemblance to actual persons, living or dead, business establishments, events, or locales is entirely coincidental. The publisher does not have any control over and does not assume any responsibility for author or third-party websites or their content.

GUN WORK

A Berkley Book / published by arrangement with the author

PRINTING HISTORY
Berkley edition / February 2010

ISBN: 978-0-425-23301-6

BERKLEY®
Berkley Books are published by The Berkley Publishing Group,
a division of Penguin Group (USA) Inc.,
375 Hudson Street, New York, New York 10014.
BERKLEY® is a registered trademark of Penguin Group (USA) Inc.
The "B" design is a trademark of Penguin Group (USA) Inc.

PRINTED IN THE UNITED STATES OF AMERICA

10 9 8 7 6 5 4 3 2 1

SHOT IN THE CABOOSE

Carl flashed a death-dealing grin. Hissed, "Them two snaky bastards in back're already dead where they stand. Just don't know it yet."

Brought my hands up as though surrendering to the circumstances. Stood, then edged sidewise into the aisle. Thought for sure everything was going right well, till the feller fired a shot into the seat back right in front of me. Big gob of dust, wood splinters, leather seat covering, and horsehair padding flew into the air, then rained down on everything within three feet of where I drew to a quick, unflinching stop.

Thunderous ear splitter of a pistol shot inside the confines of that coach came nigh on to being deafening. The thought suddenly flashed across my mind that the crazy bastards who'd just stormed into our midst might well kill us all . . .

For

My friend Diann Bellscamper:
Who rediscovered her past on the bookshelves of Wal-Mart.

And, of course, for

Carol
But for her dedication to my success, not a single word of
mine would have ever seen the light of day.

ACKNOWLEDGMENTS

Special thanks to Kimberly Lionetti for keeping the ball rolling. And to Sandy Harding at Berkley for taking the reins and lettin' 'er buck. Big sweeping wave of the sombrero to Linda McKinley for continuing to work for free in spite of numerous wounds suffered in a wrasslin' match with her pet mule. And a special nod to Diane Estes, who reads my stuff and without fail always tells me how good it is.

"Tut! I have done a thousand dreadful things
As willingly as one would kill a fly!"
>—Shakespeare, *Titus Andronicus,*
>Act V, Scene 1.

"Friar Barnardine: Thou hast committed . . .
Barabas: Fornication? But that was in another country.
And besides, the wench is dead."
>—Christopher Marlowe, *The Jew of Malta,*
>Act 4, Scene 1.

"Women are like tricks by sleight of hand,
Which to admire, we should not understand."
>—William Congreve, *Love for Love,*
>Act 4, Scene 3.

"How early murder is discovered!"
>—Shakespeare, *Titus Andronicus,*
>Act II, Scene 3.

PROLOGUE

AUTHOR'S NOTE TO THE READER

THE FOLLOWING FEW pages constitute a restored version of interview notes hand recorded by now-deceased former *Arkansas Gazette* reporter Franklin J. Lightfoot Jr. While the original rendering of this particular conversation is difficult to read at best, every possible effort has been made by the author to bring to life, for the reader, one of Mr. Lightfoot's later meetings with former Deputy U.S. Marshal Hayden Tilden.

Although it cannot be independently confirmed, it is believed that when this meeting took place Deputy Marshal Tilden had recently celebrated his ninetieth birthday. Tilden was, at that time, still considered one of the most stalwart former members of Judge Isaac C. Parker's cadre of two hundred valiant law enforcement officers. Men who had plied their dangerous, and often deadly, trade in the Indian Territories between 1875 and 1896.

The daunting task of renewing Mr. Lightfoot's scribbled observations for publication was accomplished by way of an in-depth study and use of the man's personal writing techniques. His methods are readily observable in other, more accessible question-and-answer sessions conducted with Marshal Tilden on any of a number of previous methodically chronicled occasions.

From all that can be legitimately determined, by way of thorough examination of the available record, this particular tale appears to have emerged from Mr. Lightfoot's impromptu interview with Deputy Marshal Tilden on April 17, 1949, at the Rolling Hills Home for the Aged in Little Rock, Arkansas.

For those readers who might harbor a special interest, all of the prolific Mr. Lightfoot's carefully crafted, wonderfully detailed, day-by-day memoirs, notebooks, and other pertinent historical papers are open to the public for examination through prior arrangement with the Arkansas State Historical Society's Archives Division. Their offices are located on the grounds of the Old State House Museum at 300 West Markham Street in Little Rock, Arkansas.

FROM MR. LIGHTFOOT'S INTERVIEW, APRIL 17, 1949, AND NOTES

Stopped by to look in on my good friend Tilden. Raining to beat the band. Blue-black sky, thunder and pitchfork lightning abounded. Took a handful of Tilden's favorite cigars and four half-pint bottles of rye whiskey with me. From past discussions I've determined that the old lawman hides the contraband in secret places all over his room. Claims that he only indulges at late hours of the night when the nurses tend not to be on the prowl. Not sure I put much credence in his declarations of restraint.

Found the old man and his cat, the formidable General Black Jack Pershing, napping beneath the concealing limbs of a potted plant on the retirement home's sunporch. As always, the yellow-striped, notch-eared feline awakened as soon as I took a seat. Imperial-acting beast presented me with a sneering, disdainful glare that revealed a broken front tooth. Immediately jumped out of Tilden's lap and prissed away with its fuzzy tail hiked in the air. Near as I'm able to ascertain, the cat refuses to have contact with anyone other than Tilden. Well, with the possible exception of nurse Heddy McDonald. Tilden and the cat appear much taken with the girl.

For a man of such advanced years—he's eighty-nine or ninety now, I think (have always felt he lies about his age, so he could be older) Tilden's robust appearance still amazes me. Tall, muscular, and only a bit stooped, the man sports a leonine mane of steel-gray hair, droopy moustache, a stubbled beard that gives him a rugged unshaven appearance, still has most of his own teeth, and looks at least twenty years younger than his true age (whatever that might be) would indicate.

Evidently women tend to agree with this observation. I've noticed he's a particular favorite with many of the youngest and prettiest nurses. Seems as though attractive young women are often nearby anytime I stop in for a visit, including the stunning Miss McDonald. The old man appears to genuinely enjoy female company. He once told me that the average young woman tended to be far better company than any of the smartest men he'd ever met.

Took my usual seat and opened the conversation with, "Hope you're feeling well today, Hayden."

"Well as can be expected, I suppose, Junior. 'Course when you get to be nigh on ten years older than Methuselah, it's hard to tell most of the time."

"Have any particular aches, pains, or complaints?"

"Not really. Just the general everyday, run-of-the-mill ninety-year-old-guy stuff. Lack of serious female companionship, good drinking whiskey, and a decent smoke tend to make me dull-witted. The companionship's the one that weighs on me the most."

"Can't help you with a woman. Although it does appear to me that you hardly lack for company in that area."

"Well, all these cute little nurses and candy stripers are

okay, but ain't exactly what you'd call *serious* when it comes to the real, low-down, man-woman thing."

Ignored his shaded inferences and offered him the loot. "Please take these by way of apology for my failings when it comes to supplying you with *serious* female companionship. Make sure they're properly stored away from Chief Nurse Leona Wildbank's prying, officious eyes. Sure she'll joyfully confiscate the entire boodle if you don't get it all stashed in your secret places as soon as possible."

"Well, by God, Junior. That's mighty nice of you. Gold-label rye whiskey and cee-gars. Damn right, I'll take them. You keep an eye down the hall for marauding nurses whilst I hide these puppies on my person till I can make it back to my room."

"Well, get to hiding. Right now the coast is pretty much clear. Don't see anyone coming our way."

"Stuff it all inside my shirt and pants pockets. Squirrel everything away, in my most confidential spots, later tonight. Wouldn't do to go running down to my room right now. Inquisitive little gals get right suspicious when one of the inmates goes and does anything out of the ordinary, like getting in a hurry, you know. Really do appreciate this, Junior."

"You're quite welcome. Figured you might regale me with another of your stories by way of reciprocation."

"Oh, hell, yes. That's easy enough. Pretty cheap payment for this kind of booty. Be more than happy to oblige."

"Want you to think about something while you're working to stash all that loot."

"Go on ahead, but keep your eyes peeled. Don't want to go and let any of the nurses catch us. Sure would hate to have all this fine stuff you brought confiscated before I can at least enjoy some of it."

"Was wondering, Hayden. Have you ever found yourself involved in a difficult and deadly situation that caused you to think you just might not survive?"

"Whiskey bottle's not sticking out of my shirt is it, Junior?"

"No, sir."

"See any of them cigars I shoved into my pants pockets?"

"No, sir. Think you're safe. Nothing showing that I can detect. You just look a mite lumpy's all."

"Well, lumpy's okay. Damn near all us ninety-year-olds look kind of lumpy somewhere. Old-age curse, you know. Really do appreciate you thinking of me, son. Hell, you're just about the only person left in the entire world as makes such efforts on my behalf and, by Godfrey, I'm genuinely grateful for it."

"Assure you, old friend, it's my great pleasure."

"Uh, now, what was the question again? Brain's still a bit foggy from my recent nap. Your query's already slipped away from me." He leaned over, winked, and gave me a conspiratorial pat on the knee. "Soon as I get some of this rye in me though, bet I'll be thinking a whole bunch better."

"Difficult and deadly situation. Thought you might not survive. That kind of stuff. Remember?"

"Ah. Yeah. Well, let's see. Involved in a damned bunch of them kind of circumstances over the years, don't you know. More than one of them just like you described. Some downright awful."

"I'd like to know about the fear factor as well, if you're willing to talk about it, that is."

"Ah, the fear factor. Well, see, anytime somebody gets to shooting at you there's always a chance you might not survive. Chance for an accident tended to prove right worrisome for me. Been my experience that there's more dead men in the ground what got killed by pure accident than there are them what died by a well-aimed, deliberately placed two-hundred-fifty-five-grain pistol bullet, delivered from the business end of a Colt's pistol."

"Uh-huh. I see. But that doesn't exactly answer my question about fear."

"Hmmmm. Yeah, fear. Being afraid. Well, gotta understand, there's a hell of a difference between coming to the heart-thumping realization that the outcome of a blistering confrontation involving gunfire might not go well and heart-pounding, piss-your-pants, bug-eyed fear."

"Okay. Let me see if I can be a bit clearer. Might work better for you if I put it this way. Have you, personally, ever feared for your own safety during the course of a gunfight?"

"Hmm. Not as I can recall at the moment. But, like I said, anytime the fur started to fly, always knew there was a chance I might not walk away from the scrap without a new leak or two here and there."

"Must admit I've cheated a bit on you, Hayden. Some recent research at the courthouse in Fort Smith indicates that you and Deputy Marshal Carlton J. Cecil took part in a somewhat infamous gun battle down at Wagon Wheel in the Nations. That right?"

"Uh-huh. Yeah. That was a bad one all right. Hadn't thought much about that particular dustup in a spell. Seems as how a man does tend to forget them bloody scrapes that he survives. Feller never forgets the ones where he gets hit though. Getting shot does hone a feller's memory to a right sharp point."

"Remember enough about the Wagon Wheel fight so that you can you tell me about it?"

"Suppose so. Sure. Just give me a second or two while I work on collecting my scattered thoughts."

Tilden stared into the distance. Appeared almost as though he fell into a trance. After about a minute, the old man seemed to relax from head to toe. No more than ten seconds later he turned, locked me in one of his squint-eyed, thousand-yard stares, and started the tale.

"See, me and Carlton J. Cecil were on our way back to Fort Smith. Herding half a dozen prisoners at the time. If my cankered memory still serves, had a child rapist, pair of whiskey-peddling sons of bitches, feller who murdered his parents over two dollars and an apple pie, guy we caught trying to pass some of the worst counterfeit money I've ever seen, and a doubled-up evil skunk named Potsy Tally."

"Tally the worst of them?"

"Oh, yeah. Worst by far. In that bunch anyway. See, he had three brothers that made him look like a Baptist Sunday school teacher's grandmother."

"The brothers known for violent behavior?"

"Well, if cutting a feller's head and private parts clean off with a dull handsaw qualifies as violent behavior, guess you could say as how them boys could have easily been certified as a pretty vicious bunch. 'Course when they went and beat the same man's brains out with the pointy end of a claw hammer, well, that's the part that kind of sealed their reputations with me."

"Jesus. They sawed a man's privates off with a handsaw? Beat his head in with a claw hammer? Makes me squirm all over just thinking about such a horror."

"Ain't that the truth. But let's be sure and get it straight. Didn't say they beat his head in. Said they beat his brains out. There's a hell of a difference."

"Yes. Suppose you're right. Got any idea why they did it?"

"Said as how they didn't like him."

"Didn't like him? That was it?"

"Seemed like enough for them boys. Maybe if they'd of liked him just a little bit more, would of only sawed his nuts off."

"Jesus. Look, as I understand the situation, you arrived in Wagon Wheel while searching for the Tally boys. And then what happened?"

"Well, let me see, now. Right nice little town, as I recall. Primitive, but nice enough for that part of the Nations. 'Bout forty miles southwest of Tishomingo. Heart of the Chickasaws' territory. Bad men liked the area. Really rugged. Damned rough, I guess you could say. Anyway, had our prisoners headed for Tishomingo so we could lock 'em up in the jail them Chickasaws built into their brand-new, solid-brick courthouse. Figured on letting some of those Chickasaw light-horse lawmen watch our pack of skunks whilst me and Carl took a break. Once we'd rested up, planned to point our band north, then head on out to Fort Smith."

"What, in particular, drew you to Wagon Wheel? You could've stopped just about anywhere else along the way."

"True, but me and Carl both had an axle dragging. We'd

chased Potsy Tally for so long, once we finally caught up with the low-life piece of seeping scum, the pursuit had pert near wore us both slap out. Remember Carlton saying as how his dauber was a dragging in the dirt."

"You were tired and the town of Wagon Wheel proved the nearest place to rest up."

"Ain't easy chasing skunks like Potsy while you're toting five other stripe-backed stink sprayers around, too. Remember Carlton saying he felt like he'd just pumped a railroader's hand car all the way to Yuma, Arizona. Besides, it's tougher than eating boiled boot heels when you're trying to control six men that know they're gonna hang by the neck until dead, dead, dead, soon as they get back to civilization. Threats and violence tend to be the order of the day."

"Carlton complained a lot."

"Yes, he did."

"According to you, that is."

"How else?"

"As I understand it, during that period in the Nations, towns like Wagon Wheel rarely had a jail. What'd you do with the prisoners once you arrived?"

"Carl chained the whole bunch of them to a big ole cottonwood tree right in the middle of the puny town's central square."

"All of them? All six?"

"Well, all of them except Tally. That man couldn't get along with anybody. Just look him in the eye, and he'd jump on you like ugly on an armadillo. Didn't take much to figure as how he'd end up stringing barbed wire in Hell, sooner or later. Son of a bitch fought with the other prisoners so much we decided to split him out from the rest of them."

"So, what'd you do with him?"

"Who?"

"Tally. Remember. You said you didn't chain him to the tree."

"Oh, yeah, well, Carlton shackled his sorry behind to the hitch rack in the street outside a café. Nice joint. Checkered curtains on the windows. Remember as how the joint had a sign over the door proclaimed it as EARLINE'S CAFÉ. Ain't that amazing? Had forgot the name of the place till just now."

"Glad it came to you when it did."

"Yeah. And that Earline was a good-looking woman. Being as how that was a year or two before either of us would've got ourselves hitched, me and Carl both took special note of the lady while sitting at the table next to the front window."

"You were seated near the café's front window?"

"Uh-huh. Don't want to hear 'bout Earline?"

"Not right now."

"I see. Yeah, sitting by the window. Needed a spot where we could watch our prisoners. Given the least chance, them sneaky sons a bitches could get away from you quicker than a body could spit."

"Really?"

"Oh, hell, yeah. Caught an ole boy named Hollis White-side over in the Sans Bois Mountains once. Bigger than a skint moose. Slipped his manacles. Jumped me and Carl in the middle of the night on our trip back to Fort Smith. Happened about ten or fifteen miles outside Eufala in the Creek Nation."

"Did he run?"

"Run? Hell, no. Told you. He went and jumped us. Beat the unmerciful bejabbers out of both of us. Was well on the way to killing the pair of us. Had a choke hold on me. Had a foot in the middle of Carl's chest. But then, about the time I was ready to pass over to Glory, a God-sent miracle occurred."

"A miracle? A real, honest-to-goodness miracle?"

"Yeah. See, somehow, that little redheaded scamp Carlton managed to get a bone-gripped bowie knife of his loose from one of his boots. Ran eight inches of Damascus steel all the way through the foot that Whiteside wasn't using to try and push Carl's breastbone through his spine and into the ground beneath."

"Sweet Mary."

"Yeah. Was kind of funny though. Once Carl was able to poke through Hollis's foot, oversized bastard yelped like a stomped-on tomcat. Grabbed at the knife's hilt, went to hop-pin' 'round like one of them whirling dervishes. Clumsy son of a bitch fell down right in the middle of our campfire. Rolled back and forth in the flames like some kind of complete idiot. Sparks went to flying ever which a-way. His clothes went to blazing. Watched in pure, dumbfounded amazement. Got to thinking as how, maybe, he was trying to cook his stupid self, or something. That's when Carl shot him."

"Shot him?"

"Four times."

"Four times?"

"You know, said the exact same thing myself. Said, 'Damn, Carl, did you have to shoot the ignorant bastard four times?' Carl was reloading when he said, 'Damn right. Wanted to make sure the big son of a bitch was good and dead. Might shoot him again, just for the hell of it, by God.'"

"Let's get back to the men you had chained to the tree and hitch rail in Wagon Wheel."

"Oh, yeah. Well, we weren't torturing them or anything like that, Junior. As a matter of pure fact, first thing we did was make arrangements for all those boys to get something to eat. And that was before we even bothered with our own hunger. Soon as they got served, that's when we strolled on into Earline's and ordered up some grub for ourselves. So hungry we finished off a damned fine feed in record time."

"Feeling better by then, I take it."

"Yep. Feeling right peppy when we stepped outside to have a smoke before we headed our prisoners on their way toward Tishomingo. About then, five men came storming up directly across Wagon Wheel's only thoroughfare. They were slinging dirt clods and dust here and yonder. Whooping, hol-lering, and yelping like a bunch of kicked dogs. Made a hell of a racket."

"Did you recognize any of them?"

"'Course I did. Three of them were Potsy's more-than-worthless brothers. Butch, Leroy, and Clem. Knew all those boys on sight. But I couldn't put a name to either of the other two scruffy-looking skunks."

"Sounds like a bad situation that was about to get worse."

"Well, just could've been. But only if me and Carl had forgot to carry our scatterguns along with us when we went inside Earline's place to eat."

"So, you had your shotguns in hand?"

"Yep. Pockets filled with shells, too."

"And then what happened?"

"Ah, yeah. Now try to picture this, Junior. We took our stand right behind where ole Potsy was chained up, on the boardwalk outside Earline's front door. Those bastards twirled their mounts around, then jumped off them. Spread out in a shoulder-to-shoulder line and hoofed it our direction before a body even had a chance to think twice."

"You could tell they meant business."

"No doubt in my mind what they intended. Bet they weren't twenty feet away when Butch, oldest and meanest of them Tally boys, went to reaching and grabbing for iron. He managed to get one pistol loose. Sent a blue whistler our direction that knocked my hat off. Brand-new Stetson. Hadn't got a month's worth of wear out of it. 'Course, rest of that bunch of churnheads took his lead and grabbed for their weapons as well."

"Which one of you lawmen returned fire first?"

"Not sure. Think it might have been Carlton."

"Carlton?"

"Yeah. Man never was much for messing around when it came to killing bad men. He'd drop the hammer on one of them faster than lickety-split."

"So you think Carl fired first?"

"Was a long time ago, Junior, but seems like Carl touched off both barrels of that ten-gauge blaster of his and took out the whole right side of ole Butch's line of would-be killers. Knocked down a couple or three of them boys as was already firing at us. Half an eye blink later, I cut loose. My God, sounded like the thunderous wrath of God had come down on that street. Sweet merciful Jesus, we dropped a curtain of buckshot on them ole boys that would've killed an entire company of Yankee cavalry."

"Was my understanding this was a gunfight. Your rendition makes it sound like something closer to an execution."

"Well, don't go and get all misty-eyed and feeling sorry for them bastards, Junior. They started the whole dance and were as game as it gets. Sons a bitches went down shooting. Three of them ended up on their knees after our initial volley. They peppered the whole front of Earline's place with pistol fire. Hot lead, splintered wood, and broken glass filled the air all around me and Carl like buzzing bees."

"Any place to hide?"

"Not much of one. Ended up rolling around on our bellies and backs behind a water trough next to the hitch rail. Those three remaining shooters did their level best to turn that trough into a screen door. Bullets pounded those water-soaked boards like someone had taken to beating on them with a ball-peen hammer. Have to admit, caught in that hailstorm of lead proved one of the very few times I actually got to wondering about my safety and future prospects of staying alive."

"What about Potsy Tally?"

"Ah. Sad tale there. Genuinely pitiful situation. Man came to a bad end. Real bad. See, unfortunately for ole Potsy, his chains didn't give him enough room to maneuver his way to safety."

"Don't tell me."

"Glanced over at the man just about the time a stray whistler, fired by one of his very own compadres, caught him in the right temple. Hell, could have been one of his own brothers killed the man, for all I know."

"God Almighty."

"Yeah. Big ole forty-five slug blew the poor sucker's head completely apart. Splattered most of his pea-sized brain all over Earline's boardwalk and café doors. Man's exploding skull bore a striking resemblance to a watermelon being blown up. Hair, skull bone, and brain matter sprayed all over creation. Can't imagine how it happened, but one of ole Potsy's eyeballs popped loose and hit me square in the chest. And, hell, I was stretched out on my back ten or fifteen feet away."

"Good God."

"Carlton saw what happened. Picked the eyeball off my chest. Held it up and yelled, 'Reckon he can still see us?' Then he turned the horrid thing around so it was looking at him, said, 'Can you see me, Potsy?' Then, you ain't gonna believe this, Carl laid that ghastly thing up on the edge of the water trough. Turned it around so it was looking toward the street at its friends. Then, Carlton went and busted out laughing, lying on his back in the dirt, right there in the middle of that hellish scene, laughing like a madman."

"That's just awful."

"Well, Junior, it's been my experience that people often do strange things when Death's lurking around looking for his next victim. Ain't any worse than when Carl shot Jackson Boosher."

"Hate to ask. What was so awful about shooting Jackson Boosher?"

"Caught up with ole Jackson in an outhouse. 'Course he was kind of preoccupied what with reading the Montgomery Ward catalogue and doing his business. Anyway, Carl riddled the place with a load of buckshot. Kicked the door down and Jackson was still sitting on the crapper when he died. Catalogue was opened to the women's corset section."

"Good God. Don't try to sidetrack me with something worse than flying eyeballs. Now, what'd you do about the men in Wagon Wheel who were still alive and shooting at you?"

"Rolled around behind that water trough, till we got our shotguns reloaded. Waited till some of the general blasting coming from the street calmed down a bit. Figured as how most of them ole boys was dead or dying. But just to make sure, we jumped up and hit them with four more barrels of hot lead."

"Four more barrels of ten-gauge buckshot?"

"Was a sight to behold, Junior. My God but the street around them poor bastards exploded in a cloud of flying dirt, rendered flesh, shredded clothing, and roiling clouds of spent, acrid-tasting gunpowder. Veritable cyclone of man-killing lead went through that crew of would-be bad men like a red-hot hay sickle. Our blasting hit them straight on. Storm of lead caused a vaporous spray of pinkish-red blood in the air. Looked like pink steam wafting off a fresh-stoked Baldwin engine—"

At this point one of the nurses, a striking, black-haired, blue-eyed young woman named Heddy McDonald, sashayed up and interrupted our conversation. She insisted that Tilden accompany her to his midday meal. Wouldn't take no for an answer. Think he was inclined to resist. But she tempted him with one of his favorite desserts—lime jello spiked with fruit salad and extra bits of banana and pineapple. Man's a born-again sucker for the stuff.

Tilden winked, ponderously hoisted himself out of his favorite chair, and shuffled away. I watched as he and the girl headed down the hall toward the cafeteria, arm in arm, like a pair of lovers. General Black Jack Pershing, the persnickety cat, appeared out of somewhere unknowable and trailed behind. At the dining hall's door, Tilden turned, big toothy grin on his weathered face, and waved.

Must admit I do spend way too much time worrying about the old marshal. He's as fine a gentleman as I've ever had the good fortune to call a friend. Know that sooner or later his age will catch up with him.

Additionally, I fear that, despite his gallant bluster, the old man's nights are likely filled with a legion of vengeance-seeking, bloodthirsty ghosts. Would bet the family manse, along with whatever in the way of inheritance might be forthcoming, that those phantoms come riding out of the gray-black miasma of his epic past right up to the old man's bedside every night. Not sure I would have anything like the will necessary to deal with such a frightening and terrifying possibility. Seriously doubt few men live, in these days of automobiles and worsted wool suits, who would, either.

Over the past two years or so I have heard him recite numerous tales of his violent and tumultuous past. Suppose it's a good thing Chief Nurse Leona Wildbank took the old man's pistols away from him. God help the ghost who approaches Hayden Tilden if he has a weapon in his hand.

Notes taken by my hand,

Franklin J. Lightfoot Jr.

1

"THE KNIFE, THURM. GIVE ME THE KNIFE."

AIN'T SURE EXACTLY when it went and happened, but I've done got so old it feels like I'm living on borrowed time and three of my payments, to the God that allows it, are way past due. If Carlton J. Cecil was still full of beans and kicking, he'd probably say something like, "Yeah, the Dead Sea wasn't even sick when Hayden Tilden got born. Man came into this world ten years before them gals found Moses floating down the Nile in a wicker basket. Yep, best thing you can say 'bout the man is that the spring's done gone out of his chicken."

Given as how I'm undeniably facing the very real prospect of shambling into the first year of my tenth decade pretty quick, seems I can't get through a week without some idiot asking me what I've learned over such a long, tumultuous, and blood-drenched life. Well, since random busybodies seem so interested, here are a few thoughts I've had on that particular subject.

Ain't gonna offer up any guarantees that my fractured ru-

minations on longevity will help anyone all that much, but
what follows is a bit of heartrending wisdom I wish had
come to me a lot earlier than it did. Pay attention, buckaroos
and buckarettes, because this is the important part of my
message. Here goes—no matter how hard a man tries he can
never escape his past.

Given that the modern mind can't remember anything longer than a few seconds, feel this bit of wisdom is so profound
it bears repeating. So, for the benefit of those so dumb they
think the Mexican border ought to pay rent, I'll phrase it in a
manner where even they can't miss the meaning. No matter
how hard you try, friends and neighbors, you'll never get free
of what you've done.

Sounds simple enough, doesn't it? But trust me, it's not.
In my nearly ninety years I've found that good works are
likely to go unnoticed, unrewarded, and quickly fade into the
fog of time and memory. Conversely, Lord help us, the bad
ones come back to haunt us. Truth is, just ain't no getting
away from who we were and what we might have done—
good, bad, or indifferent.

And worst of all, a body just never knows when one of his
ugliest, most carefully guarded of memories or secrets will
rear its Hydra-like head. Usually takes place when a feller
least expects it. As a general rule, mine typically come to me
in the middle of the night, when one of the old gummers down
the hall goes to screaming like a lunch whistle at a south
Arkansas sawmill.

I've been in this depot for prospective corpses several
years now. Still can't get a reasonable explanation from any
of the staff as to exactly what causes such midnight terrors.
Only way I can figure it is that those folks doing all the
screaming are witness to the events of their pasts. Pasts that
somehow come back to life. Truly does seem as how the
ghosts of long ago and far away like to visit more often as we
grow older.

And for their own unfathomable reasons, occurs to me
that visiting spirits usually tend to show their ugly faces between midnight and sunup. But not always. Take it from a

man who's studied the subject up close and personal, getting old is sometimes a damn sight more than a body can take— night or day.

Couple a weeks ago me and Black Jack were napping out on the sunporch. Snapped out of a wildly pleasant daydream about my dear Elizabeth. Heard people yelling and hollering down the hall toward the dayroom. Before a body could spit, sounded like furniture getting turned over, busted up, and dragged around. Then, glass went to breaking. Women started crying and members of the staff went to running up and down the hall.

Pushed the cat out of my lap and hobbled down that direction. Met one of the orderlies, big ole kid named Horace Bowman. He came huffing past me with blood streaming down the side of his face like somebody had hit him in the head with an ax. Next thing I knew, pair of the more brutish orderlies, kind of guys who looked like they lived under the front porch and you could roller skate on them, flew past me and darted through the dayroom door.

Edged up to the entry and peeked inside. Them big ole thuggish-looking boys had Thurmond Gaston pinned up in a corner, far side of the wrecked room. Thurmond waved a butcher knife the size of a meat cleaver back and forth at them, like he knew how to use it. In my personal opinion, there's just nothing more dangerous than a man determined to kill you and who has a knife handy.

One of the thugs, guy sporting a scar down his left cheek from hairline to chin, yelled, "Gimme the goddamned knife, old bastard."

Wild-eyed and crazy-looking, Thurmond grinned like a thing insane. "Come git it, you son of a bitch. Carve you up like a Sunday chicken."

Given the rarity and oddity of such events here at Rolling Hills, got to admit, I was shocked right down to the soles of my slippers. Shocked and amazed. Hadn't expected anything like a knife fight when I checked in. Body just doesn't anticipate such an event in an old folks home, now, would you?

Argument between Thurmond and Scarface went on for a

good five minutes and wasn't going anywhere. Strolled over to the action about the time Scarface's partner, feller named Buddy Johnson, got froggy. He took a jump Thurmond's direction. Came away with one hand sliced open all the way to the bone. Stupid jackass went running out of the dayroom, slinging blood all over hell and yonder. Howled like a kicked dog till I couldn't hear him anymore.

Purple-faced and bug-eyed, Scarface spotted me and said, "Get the hell outta here, Tilden. Got a dangerous situation here, old man. You could get badly hurt."

Guess I reverted back to my lawdog ways. Made a kind of peacemaking, shushing motion at Thurmond. Real friendly-like, I said, "It's okay, Thurm." Then I glanced over at Scarface. "Now, listen carefully, you ugly son of a bitch. Want you to back the hell out of here. Leave me and Thurmond alone for a few minutes. I'll find out what the problem is and take care of him."

"Don't make me kick your ass, too," Scarface growled.

"Do what I said, or trust me, you'll regret it." Tone of my voice must've finally got through to the bullyboy. Knew he was only trying to do his job, but hell, he was doing it badly.

Watched as the ugly jerk backed his way toward a door jammed full of goggle-eyed nurses and other staff. Turned to Thurmond. Said, "What's the problem, Thurm?"

Still held that big ole blade out like he meant business. "Problem?"

"Yeah, what's the problem?"

Man went to shaking all over, like he suffered from the final throes of a horrible tropical disease. "Problem? Yes, the problem. Man I know for dead won't leave me alone."

Well, shit. Knew exactly what he meant. Ghost of Carlton J. Cecil stopped by my room damn nigh every other night. Tried to keep my voice calm, even, friendly. "Dead feller, huh?"

Could see the confusion in his eyes. "Yeah. Keeps showing up. Here, the sunporch, cafeteria. Won't give me any peace. Can't even eat my tapioca 'thout the son of a bitch creepin' up on me. Just keeps coming back. Told him, last night, I'd kill 'im again if he bothered me one more time."

Some of the spunk appeared to drain out of Thurmond once he'd got it off his chest.

"That's why you've got the knife?"

"Yeah. Snuck it outta the kitchen. And just be damned, the maggot-riddled son of a bitch showed up again. Just wouldn't listen. Come up on me whilst I was readin' the newspaper. Hopped outta my seat and went to cuttin' on 'im. Know what he did?"

"No, Thurm. What'd he do?"

"Laughed at me. Said he'd see me in Hell soon."

"You know the man?"

"The ghost?"

"Yeah, the ghost."

"Uh-huh. No. Not sure. Maybe. Don't matter. Think I kilt him off again anyway. Or maybe not. Get 'im next time though."

About then I heard a police siren outside. Said, "Look, Thurm, why don't you give me the knife. I'll stay here with you, and we'll run the dead son of a bitch off together, if he comes back. Okay?"

Commotion at the door. Knew the law had arrived. Anxious cops would soon fill the room up. If pistols came out, figured anything could happen. Poor old brain-addled Thurm just might get shot to pieces.

"The knife, Thurm. Give me the knife. I'll stay with you."

Of a sudden, the man looked like a cheap umbrella in a rainstorm. He kind of collapsed into the corner. Dropped that big ole blade on the floor at my feet. I grabbed it up and pitched it across the room. Second or so later, red-faced trio of boys in blue stormed up behind me. They snatched Thurm up like a kid's raggedy doll. Man didn't say a word when they dragged him away. Just kind of whimpered.

Heddy McDonald came running up. Beautiful gal took my arm, escorted me into the hall, and pointed me back toward the dayroom. "I'm so glad you took a hand in the matter. Would have been awful if Mr. Gaston had been hurt or killed."

"Yes. Yes, it would've."

"Good thing I got here when I did," she added. "Was able to make those policemen understand which of you they'd been called to corral."

"Mighty thoughtful, darlin'. Sure wouldn't want to spend the night in the hoosegow for slicing and dicing some of Rolling Hills' nurses."

"Oh, Mr. Gaston won't spend any time in jail. He's being ushered downstairs to the med room in the basement. Have a call in to Baptist Hospital for Dr. F. Scott Bryles to rush over and medicate him a bit. After a day or two of rest, I'm sure he'll be fine. Thank God none of our other patients were injured."

Strolled up to the sunporch door. Turned to Heddy and said, "Sounded to me like Thurm might've pulled something like this before."

A pained look of deep sadness etched its way around the girl's beautiful eyes. She squeezed my hand. "Of course, you're right. This wasn't Mr. Gaston's first bout of oddly aggressive behavior. Poor man suffers from advanced hardening of the arteries, Hayden. Disease is characterized by loss of memory, confusion, lack of good judgment, and social grace. Anxiety, depression, and anger. Sad state of affairs. Very sad. Horrible end to a good man's life."

"Maybe what happened didn't have anything to do with hardening of the arteries. Maybe he really did see a ghost, or maybe his past finally just caught up with him."

Heddy smiled. Let out a muted chuckle. "Ghost, or not. Past, or whatever. Few days of sedation should cure the problem."

"Well, might be near the end, but he's not gone yet. Maybe he'll get better."

Now while I said it, didn't for a second believe a single syllable. Hid out on the sunporch couple of nights later. Sneaking a smoke and a sip of rye. Must've been around one thirty or two o'clock in the morning. Cat perked up in my lap. Then, those body-collecting cockroaches, with the squeaky white shoes, came scurrying down the hall pushing a wobble-wheeled gurney.

They crept into ole Thurm's room like a crew of masked thieves. Few minutes later, whizzed back past my hidey-hole with him all wrapped up in a sheet. Man's bloodless face was pasty white. Lips were black. Dead-eyed stare. Never saw him again.

You ask me, didn't have nothing to do with arteries hardening, or anything medical at all. Nope, a ghost from the man's past got him. Sure as pissants can't pull boxcars.

2

". . . DIED OF THE CONSUMPTION . . ."

MIGHT AS WELL get comfortable, folks. Gonna tell you a little story designed to further illustrate an old man's unsupported nightly ramblings about life and the past. See, six or eight months ago the wardens here at Rolling Hills took to dragging a hundred-year-old projector into the dayroom on Wednesday nights and running picture shows.

Bullet-headed, muscle-bound orderly name of Elton Slater works that clattering piece of machinery. Elton's about half as smart as a bag of stink bugs, but it appears he's the only guy on staff with brains enough to keep the contraption spinning all its squawking wheels and them pulleys what make that *kaflutta-kaflutta-kaflutta* sound. Borders nigh on to impossible for me to understand, because the man's just about half smart enough to put dents in a steel marble with a rubber hammer.

Anyway, Chief Nurse Leona Wildbank has all the working nurses, candy stripers, and a troop of other kindhearted volunteers wheel us inmates out of our individual cells, about seven o'clock on "movie" night. Before the lights go out and the film cranks up, they serve us cold drinks, candy bars, and popped corn.

Now it's damned difficult to eat popped corn when you're almost ninety and ain't exactly got all of your teeth. But, Lord, I do love the stuff, especially if it's drowning in an ocean of hot, melted butter and salty goodness. So, in spite of the fact that I've retained about enough of my choppers to fool most folks, I take a paper bag of that wonderful stuff and just spend the evening sucking on it, one kernel at a time.

Will confess here that I never had the opportunity to indulge in such mindless entertainment, back when I still carried a pistol on each hip, another at my back, a Winchester model 1876 hunting rifle, and a sawed-off shotgun when things got real serious. Back in them blood-spattered days, I chased killers, thieves, bootleggers, and whores all over the Indian Nations for Judge Isaac C. Parker—man known far and wide for quick trials and quicker hangings. 'Course I guess to be completely accurate, the motion picture business, as mass entertainment, didn't get going real good till after I'd left the U.S. Marshals Service and was toting a badge as a city law bringer down in Sunset, Texas, back in the 1920s.

And you know, in spite of my best guesswork and feelings on the subject beforehand, I have to admit it's got to where I kind of enjoy these weekly diversions. Seems as how sitting in the dark, sucking on popped corn and watching one of those flicker shows, has the power to take my near century-old, cankered mind off the fact that I had to give up so much of my personal freedom just to live in this goddamned place.

Best part of the whole Wednesday-night-picture-show experience and all was when I met up with Martha Frances Harrison. Seems the pair of us had committed ourselves to Rolling Hills at about the same time. Pretty sure we just kind of drifted together because neither of us knew anyone else living here back then.

Truth is, ain't many men as reside in one of these homes for the terminally aged to begin with. Reason's simple enough,

really. See, on average, the women outlive us gummers, gee-
zers, and old coots by decades. Seems us guys tend to croak
faster than Satan can open Hell's front gates and invite us to
come on in.

As a consequence of our collective rapid departure from
this life, any of us ole farts sporting half a functioning brain,
and can walk and chew gum at the same time, can have his
choice of female companionship in one of these waiting
rooms for the hereafter. And trust me when I tell you that,
even though such a situation sounds good on the surface, this
particular proposition can be a damned iffy sucker, given
how crazy some women can get as the years chip away at
them. Good many females get crazier than Thurmond Gaston
ever thought about being.

Much to my delight, Martha Frances has proven a god-
send. She's perky, good-looking as hell, and sports a hazel-
eyed gaze that has the power to make a man want to slap his
grandma—if the old gal was still alive, that is. She still has
her own hair, or most of it, and is about as well-built as any
seventy-year-old woman I've ever seen. Gal's stacked up like
a brick Montgomery Ward reading room.

Sitting there by myself, as usual, when Martha Frances
strolled up one night. Primly took the seat next to mine.
Dipped a dainty, scarlet-nailed, diamond-laden bunch of fingers into the paper bag of popped corn sitting in my lap. For
a second there, felt like a lightning bolt shot up my britches
leg, then burned a hole the size of a barrel lid through the seat
of my cotton drawers. Rest of the night, I had this buzzing
sensation in my ears, kind of like being shot at by a whole
gang of Indian Nation brigands out to kill me deader than
Hell in a Baptist preacher's front parlor.

Then, she rubbed a shoulder against mine, turned, and
whispered into my ear. Could feel the heat and warmth of her
when she said, "Mind if I sit with you, good-looking?"

Now, I tried my level best to sound suave, sophisticated, and
debonair, when I said, "Why, no, darlin'. Right pleased to have
the company." Hell, I might be older than Methuselah's great-
grandpappy, but my mama didn't raise any blithering idiots.

Lightning struck again when Martha Frances got tired of the popped corn and kind of leisurely slid her hand up my leg. Sweet hoobie joobus. Pretty sure if I had reached out and touched ole Elton's kafluttering movie machine, I'd of blown out every circuit breaker in the building.

After the show she slipped into my room—a direct violation of one of Chief Nurse Leona Wildbank's most stringent rules. Spent the night together. Of course, given how old we both are, not much of anything happened. But it felt right nice to have someone share my bed again, for a change.

Truth is, about the only thing we did was lay there in the dark and talk. Talked almost all night. Told that woman things I never thought I'd ever admit to anyone. Felt right good to unburden myself, you want to know the truth. And after that first night of sneaking around, we did the same thing every chance we got, and by God, I don't regret a minute of it.

We've gone and kept such close company seems as how most people here at Rolling Hills have pretty much decided we're some kind of an item or other. And, hell, must confess that I've taken to accompanying her out on bingo nights, too, and any other place I can think to meet her. And most days, the pair of us, along with General Black Jack Pershing, hijack the best corner out on the sunporch so we can sit together, talk, remember our pasts, and relax.

Big ole cat even likes the woman. And that's quite a considerable accomplishment for an independent soul like Black Jack. 'Cause up till now I've not found anybody else other than me that he'll even tolerate. Well, he liked Carlton J. Cecil okay I suppose, but as you're well aware, that redheaded scamp passed away nigh on a year ago.

Hate to even think about it, but I miss the hell out of ole Carl, and I'm still mad at him for up and dying the way he went and done, the son of a bitch. Know I told him more times than I can count that I just might kill him myself, but I never meant it. Not a single word.

Given my blood-saturated past, have to say as how everything went along so swimmingly after I met Martha it's a wonder the law hasn't arrested me for having way more fun than a body ought to be allowed, while still wearing his underpants. Leastways up till last night, that is.

See, Martye, oh, forgot to mention, she likes me to call her Martye. Says it makes her feel younger. Anyhow, Martye showed up at my door, strolled in, grabbed my hand and rubbed up against me, then said, "Great movie tonight, Hayden. One of my favorite actors is starring in this picture—Henry Fonda. You're going to love it. Given your lawman's background I figure this one's just your cup of tea."

As we wobbled out the door of my room, then headed on down the hall, I grinned and said, "And what might tonight's feature flick be about, darlin'?"

She held tight to my arm. "Why, it's a western."

Stopped me dead in my tracks. Held the gal at arm's length and stared into those hazel pools. "Now I know we've never discussed this before, but I hate western movies. Haven't seen one of them yet that wasn't a total rasher of bullshit."

"Hayden Tilden. Such language."

"Sorry, darlin', just slipped out."

"You're forgiven. And why is it that you feel western movies are a rasher of—well, you know?" she said, then went to pulling on me till I finally gave up and followed along.

"Aw, hell, Martha Frances, I love a good musical, drama, or comedy. I can even sit through one of them silly-assed things what has so-called *monsters* in 'em, and that's a fact. But singing cowboys, horses smarter'n most of the old fogies here at Rolling Hills, pistols that shoot twenty-five times, and fringed shirts with big yeller flowers stitched all over 'em just ain't anything close to what I can recall of the West I lived in."

She batted those bluey-greeny peepers at me and cooed, "Trust me, you'll like this one. Guarantee it. Story of a man you might have known at some point."

"Who? Who could I have possibly known that those Hollywood types would make a movie about him?"

"Gentleman named Wyatt Earp, as I recall."

Bet I hadn't heard that name in more'n fifty years. Stopped again. Must've looked something along the lines of shocked and amazed. "Wyatt Earp? You sure about this, girl? No doubt. Somebody's gone and made an actual motion picture show about Wyatt Earp?"

Have to admit that, deep down, I felt more than a twinge of jealousy knowing that Earp had managed to pull off such a feat. You might remember that my prolific biographer, Franklin J. Lightfoot, and me took a trip out to the land of fruits and nuts once ourselves. Thought we'd sold some of them movie-making weiners on the idea of cranking out a picture show about me.

Appears that what they paid us some pretty good money for was what they call an "option." Never claimed any skill as a lawyer, so near as I've been able to figure it, an "option" ain't nothing more than a half-assed promise to think about doing something, someday, maybe, perhaps. Whole experience was a real disappointment. And yet, a taciturn Wyatt Earp had pulled it off. Just thinking about it made me want to gag.

Well, Martha latched onto my arm even harder, gave me a mighty tug. Kept me moving toward the dayroom, as she said, "I put in a personal request for this very motion picture more than a month ago, just especially so you could see it, Hayden Tilden. Had begun to think Elton wouldn't have any luck getting a copy for us, but he did. Well, surprised me when I found out that Elton had proven a man of his word. He managed to ferret one out, and tonight you get to see it."

Two hours later we sat in the darkest corner of the sunporch and sipped on a couple of frosty RC Colas Martha Frances had cadged for us from somewhere. Couldn't really see her face when she patted my hand and said, "Well, I'm waiting. Are you ever going to tell me what you thought of this evening's entertainment?"

Coughed, squirmed in my seat, then said, "Lot better than them damned singing cowboy oaters, that's for sure. Liked that part where Earp kilt all them Clantons. Sorry, murdering bastards. Got no use for back-shooting scum like them boys."

Sounded a bit piqued when she said, "Well, I thought it very romantic."

Fished a panatela out of my jacket pocket, stoked it to life, then blew an invisible smoke ring at the ceiling. "That's the problem, darlin'. You could call the West of my experience a lot of things, but romantic sure as hell ain't one of them."

"You mean the events depicted in the movie didn't happen."

"Oh, I suppose some of them actually happened, but not like what you saw tonight."

Could hear the growing indignity in her voice when she said, "Well, Mr. Smarty-Pants Know-It-All, name me one thing you saw that wasn't true."

Grinned to myself. Of course she couldn't see me. "That's an easy one. Fact is, nobody ever shot Doc Holliday dead at the O.K. Corral, like they done in tonight's piece of well-made, but highly fictionalized, entertainment."

"Is that so?"

"Yes, it is very much so, Martye."

"And you know this for a fact?"

"Absolutely. Truth is, the man died of the consumption six years after the gunfight. Croaked in a sanatorium in Glenwood Springs, Colorado. Passed over, lying in bed with his boots off. Rumor has it he raised his head up right at the end, stared at his nekkid feet, and said, 'This is funny.' Top of that, while ole Doc might have, at some point, known a *Mexican* gal named Chihuahua, truth is when the real tale took place he was keeping company with a soiled dove everybody knew as Big Nose Kate."

Could feel Martha Frances kind of huff and puff a bit before she snapped, "Just a bit of writer's license, that's all. Still say I liked the romance."

"More like misplaced obsession, you ask me."

"Obsession? What obsession are you talking about, Hayden?"

Should've tiptoed around that one a bit, but didn't. "Well, in that piece of imaginary illusion we just witnessed, Clementine was obsessed with Doc. Chihuahua was obsessed with

Doc. Doc was obsessed with dying. Wyatt was obsessed with Clementine. Just a big ole circle of romantically misplaced obsessive behavior, you ask me. Except for ole man Clanton. But come to think on it, he was obsessed with Wyatt, too. But I don't think his feelings involved romance of any kind. 'Course I could be wrong 'bout that. Did sometimes get lonely out there on the trail."

"Why, you're kidding, of course?"

"'Course."

"And you never saw a similar kind of conduct during your days as a deputy U.S. marshal riding the rough country of the Indian Nations, I suppose."

Near a minute of silence slipped between us. Puffed on my cigar a time or two before I said, "Guess you could say I saw a bit of it, a time or two. 'Course, them as I'm aware of almost always led to murder."

Martha Frances grabbed my knee like a starving hawk grabbing a ground squirrel. Could feel those bloodred talons biting into my leg. "Tell me, Hayden Tilden. You've been somewhat reticent with many parts of your past. Open with some, I must admit, but restrained with others. Now, tell me what you know of obsession."

Had the distinct feeling she didn't, for a second anyhow, realize what she was asking. "Sure you want to hear it? It's a tale of murder, betrayal, and blood. Not the kind of thing most ladies of good character want to know about. And it's all true. Not a single word of romantic fiction involved."

Her grip on my knee tightened. "Well, go ahead. Tell me a story of obsession, murder, blood, and betrayal."

Leaned back into my chair. Screwed myself deeper into the cushions. Took another puff from the panatela, then said, "All right. Best strap in though, darlin'. Got the feelin' you just might not like the ending to this tale."

3

"HOBBLED AROUND LIKE A ONE-LEGGED CRIPPLE."

LETHAL DOSE OF gun smoke and quick death I'll talk about tonight started when Nate Swords and me drew our mounts to a halt atop a tree-shaded knoll outside the barely existent town of Lone Pine—over in the Chickasaw Nation. Rugged, primitive village occupied a grassy cup of land along the foothills of the Arbuckle Mountains out in the Wildhorse River country. Place was rougher than a box of petrified corncobs. Raw-edged, remote, and given to entertaining desperate men. Men who were often on the run.

Entire settlement didn't amount to much more than half a dozen canvas-roofed, board-and-batten shacks and a few raggedy-looking tents. Handmade signs decorated a few of the buildings, but most had no identifiers on them at all. Whole shebang was strung out in a straight line, right in front of us, along the far side of a rutted thoroughfare that ran up from the river and headed northwest toward Chickasha.

Way me and Nate figured it, the rugged community had but one purpose in existing. No doubt in our minds that the denizens of Lone Pine worked like sweaty field hands to introduce every form of strong spirits, rotgut whiskey, jig juice, ole skull popper, or hundred-fifty-proof coffin paint imaginable to the Nations' constantly shifting population of Indian and white, thieves and killers. And perhaps, depending on availability, they sometimes provided female companionship for them fellers as might have the wherewithal to pay for it.

Nate hiked a leg over his saddle horn. Pulled the makings and set to building himself a hand-rolled. As he worked tobacco and paper, he said, "Hope the sons a bitches are down there, Hayden. Don't know 'bout you, but I'm tired of chasin' the murderous skunks. We've been on the track now for nigh on three weeks. Been hot on their worthless tails all the way from Van Buren, to McAlester's Store, to here. Got blisters on my rump the size of a crop of coconuts."

Couldn't help but smile. Had come to recognize that when Nate went to getting himself prepared for the possibility of dodging blue whistlers, he just might go on a comical rip on any subject he could bring to mind. Swept my Stetson off. Pulled a bandanna and wiped out the inside of the hat, then let it hang down my back on a leather thong.

"What in the wide, wide world do you know about coconuts, Nate?" I said.

"Well, by God, know I like 'em fried. Yessir, just ain't nothin' I can think of matches the culinary goodness of a fried coconut."

"Fried? Coconuts? Sweet Jesus. Just where in the Sam Hill did you ever even so much as see a coconut, anyway?"

Man didn't miss a beat. He was on one of his yarn-spinning rolls and ran with it. Flashed a crooked grin my way, from beneath a straw-colored moustache, then laid the freshly rolled cigarette between his lips. He fired the smoke to life, flicked a smoldering match aside, then said, "Found 'em in the produce section of your wife's grocery store and mercantile in Fort Smith. Right next to them little yeller things called lee-mons. Yessir, bought me a couple a fryin'-sized coconuts not more'n a week 'fore we started on this raid."

"That a fact?"

"Damned sure is. Know you think I'm just tellin' a tall one, but you can check with your missus when we get back to town. Seen her that day. Waved, said howdy, exchanged pleasantries, by God."

"Which of Elizabeth's mercantile operations are you talking about?"

"She got more'n one?"

"Most like half a dozen, when last I counted."

"Well, place I'm talkin' 'bout's the bustlin' enterprise located on the corner of Towson and Rogers. Brick front. Substantial-looking. Feller might mistake it for a bank, he ain't paying strict attention."

"Ah. Yes. Elizabeth's largest and, perhaps, best-stocked emporium. Inherited it from her father when he passed on. Well, and you claim to have fried the aforementioned coconuts. That's what you said, isn't it?"

Fleeting bit of playful confusion crinkled around the corner's of Nate's slate-gray eyes. Looked right thoughtful when he leaned an elbow onto his knee, then hooked a thumb over the grip of one of the Colt pistols he carried strapped high on his hip in the old-fashioned, butts forward, Wild Bill Hickok manner.

"You bet. Fried them little boogers to mouthwaterin' crispiness," he said, after less than five seconds of thought.

"Now, I want to get this straight. No confusion. You're telling me that you fried a coconut?"

"Bet your boots, Deputy Marshal Tilden. You ain't never had a fried coconut, don't know what you're missin'."

In a move to keep from laughing out loud, maybe even gasping for breath to the point of falling off Gunpowder's broad, muscular back and perhaps breaking my neck in the tumble, pulled my long glass, then snapped it out to the third segment. Scanned everything I could lay an eye on in the disreputable burg not five hundred yards away. In spite of myself, though, let a snicker slip out while eyeballing the place.

Under my breath, said, "Fried coconuts. Sweet merciful Jesus, save me."

"Well, I did, by God," Nate chirped.

Squinted into the end of the glass, said, "That before or after you removed the hairy, outer shell?"

"Uh, after, a course. Cain't go fryin' no coconut with the hairy shell still on it. Any cook worth spit knows that. Leastways, that's what my sainted, white-haired ole mama and grandma taught me."

"What kind of grease you use?"

"Bacon grease, of course. Best kind. Gotta be fresh though. Nothing rancid. 'S why I always brown up a big ole slab a maple-flavored goodness 'fore I start in on fryin' my coconuts."

"Ah, of course. And what other dishes did you have with your fried coconuts, might I be so bold as to inquire?" Let the glass down and laid it across my thigh. Turned to watch Nate in the hope I could get his story to show some cracks.

Self-satisfied smile creased his handsome face. Then, like a man reciting the constituents of a complex chemical experiment, he said, "Cornbread, black-eyed peas, and collard greens."

"Cornbread, black-eyed peas, collard greens, and a fried coconut? That's one hell of a meal. And that's your story, is it?"

Swords swelled up in his saddle. His back stiffened and he got right regal when he said, "Damned right, and I'm stickin' to it. 'Course, I forgot to mention the smashed taters."

"Smashed taters?"

"Yep. Mama always said as how you don't never serve fried coconuts 'thout some smashed taters to kinda take some of the tart of'n 'em."

"Tart? Coconuts?"

"Absolutely. 'S why I stopped boilin' 'em. Couldn't get the tart out of 'em."

Had to strain quite a bit to keep from busting a gut. Didn't want to offend Nate. Snapped the glass down to its shortest length. Shoved it back into the battered, army-surplus, leather carrying case, and dropped it into my saddlebag. Gritted my teeth and went to checking the loads in my pistols.

Nate took the hint and set to scrutinizing his weapons, too.

Flipped the loading gate open on my belly gun, rolled the cylinder around. Stared at each shell as it passed, then said, "Don't care for boiled coconuts with your collard greens, huh?"

"Hate 'em. Damned things make me colicky, if'n I eat 'em boiled. Gut gets to hurtin' so bad I sometimes cry like a baby. Boil 'em and they leave you with a definite aftertaste, too. Sticks with a body for hours. Kinda like a mouthful of prairie bitterweed. Enough to make a starvin', Texas longhorn steer spit it out."

"Aftertaste. Kind of like bitterweed."

"Yep."

"Must really like them fried then?"

"Only thing's better, you ask me, is fried armadiller."

"Fried armadillo. Sweet Jesus."

Man grinned like a raccoon trying to wash a loaf of fresh-baked bread in a fast running creek. "Tasty. Ain't kiddin' a bit, Tilden. Really tasty. Fry up some coconuts along with an armadiller, and you've got yourself one helluva meal, my friend."

Returned the last of my three pistols to the holster at my back. Slipped the Winchester out of the boot. Jacked a shell into the breech, then laid it across my saddle just behind the horn.

Touched Gunpowder's side with a spur, started easing down the knoll. Nate followed. When he got up close I said, "Three droopy-looking nags tied at the hitch racks outside that false-front building in the middle, yonder—one with the sign over the door proclaiming it as BLACK'S. Bet a year's pay those animals belong to the boys we're looking for, Nate."

Out of the corner of my eye, saw him stand in his stirrups and rub his back. Settled in and said, "Sure as hell hope so. Horse of mine's about to wear me down to a nub."

"Bring these boys to book, we'll drag them over to Tishomingo. Lock them up in the Chickasaws' brand-new combination courthouse and jail."

"Works for me."

"And you know, I've been thinking, Nate. We get these ole boys back to Fort Smith, you're gonna have to invite Elizabeth and me over for one of those coconut and armadillo sit-downs."

"Sounds good, if these three bastards are willing to go back. But if'n they ain't, we get finished sending the egg-suckin' sons a bitches to Satan, Tilden, we'll for sure 'nuff do 'er. Might even cook up a couple a opossums for you, too. Only bake a opossum on extra special occasions, you know."

"Baked opossums? You're for sure kidding now, right?"

"Oh, no. Nice fat opossum's tastiest of the three of 'em, you ask me. Makes my mouth water just thinkin' 'bout cookin' up a juicy opossum. Good piece of opossum haunch is a meal fit fer a king, by God."

He went silent after that. Seriousness of the situation pimpled to a puss-filled head closer we got to our destination. Quickly put a damper on our ricochet into jocularity, fried coconuts, and downright silliness.

Headed straight for the centermost structure in Lone Pine. Hadn't gone far when I detected the tinny sound of music wafting from the rickety building's front entrance.

Drew our mounts to a stop on the far side of a muddy, rutted trace that ran a meandering course up from the river into a stand of trees off to the north. Couldn't have stepped down much more than sixty feet from the front entrance of an illegal whiskey-vending operation that sounded like it was chugging along full tilt. Position gave us a far better ear on the rinky-tink piano melody coming from inside.

Tied the animals to a spindly cottonwood. Only living tree within a hundred feet located on our side of the rudimentary thoroughfare.

Thumbed the hammer back on the Winchester. Made sure the hammer thongs on all my pistols were hanging loose, then glanced over at Nate and asked, "Should we call them out, or go inside and brace them where they sit?"

My hard-eyed partner rested his short-barreled ten gauge on one shoulder, scrunched his face up, then said, "Let's go in and surprise 'em. Stupid bastards can't possibly know they're about to take a fall. Desperate as these boys are, we call 'em out, announce our presence, bet they'll hide next to the doorway and go to blastin' at us right where we stand." He glanced around, then added, "And there sure as hell ain't no place to hide out here in the street. 'Cept maybe behind the horses."

Said, "Sounds good to me. Get up close to them, maybe they'll think twice about being foolish enough to draw down on us."

Then, we headed for the bloodred batwing doors of Black's.

Bit to my left and half a step behind me, Nate said, "Get a chance, Tilden, I'm gonna cook you up some of my world-famous snappin' turtle stew. Throw in a couple a catfish heads, few raw turnips, some alligator meat, and, boy how-dee, you got a real lip smacker goin'."

Couldn't do much but shake my head and grin.

No boardwalk in Lone Pine. Set of rickety-looking steps, made from rough-cut, unplaned boards, led into Black's front entrance. We stood on the top tread, gazed over the café doors, and scanned the pitiful interior of the place.

Under his breath Nate hissed, "Wish Carlton J. Cecil coulda come with us. Always like havin' that redheaded devil with a pistol along anytime we have to put lead in the air."

"Me, too," I said. "Always feel a bunch safer when Carl's around. Man can thumb a pistol faster than a chicken can peck seed from a metal pie plate."

My partner grunted, as though someone had pulled all the hair out of his nose at the same time, then said, "Guess by now he's probably already got that carbuncle on his rump lanced. Sweet mama. Heard tell as how that thing was the size of a grown man's fist. Makes me cringe just thinkin' 'bout it."

Whispering, I said, "It's a big one all right. Maybe the biggest I've ever seen. Went by to check on him day we rode out. Man was having trouble standing. Barely able to walk out onto the porch and wave good-bye. Hobbled around like a one-legged cripple."

Interior of Black's joint amounted to little more than a single, oblong wooden-and-canvas box, of about twenty by thirty feet. Rough-cut pine boards came up about three feet off the floor, like wainscoting in a house. Shabby, patched, canvas roof and half walls let in sunlight like a worn-out flour sifter. Three poles in the middle of the room held up the roof. Five tables scattered around the room. Only two were occupied. Three fellers sitting at the one closest to the door. Men we wanted took up space in the far corner. Bar, comprised of a single plank board atop two barrels, stood on the left, just inside the door.

Pushed the batwings aside with the barrels of our weapons and stepped inside. Heard the hammers of Nate's shotgun snap back, as we stepped over the roadhouse's threshold.

Nate headed left and attempted to wave the bartender into silence. Man, who bore a striking resemblance to a rake handle sporting a moustache the size of a wharf rat, snapped to attention behind one of the barrels. Went to waving his bar rag at us, then called out, "Wait just a damned minute, now. Just, by God, wait a minute."

Sounded like spit on a hot stove lid when Nate said, "Shut the hell up, you ignert son of a bitch."

Fellers at the table by the door hopped up and disappeared through the batwings like windblown steam.

Eyeballed our prey at the ramshackle table near an idle potbellied stove in the hangout's far corner. None of them appeared to have taken notice of our arrival. Given the number of empty bottles atop their table and on the floor, would have surprised me if any of the drunken trio would have noticed Gabriel blowing his horn for the Second Coming.

Flicked a quick, corner-of-the-eye glance over at Nate. He had a finger pressed against his lips and was shaking his head at the bug-eyed bartender. Whiskey wrangler had his hands up, kept shooting horrified looks from Nate to me, and vibrated like a plucked banjo string.

No more than ten feet from the far end of the bar, Black's piano player, eyes closed, head back like he was entertaining the king of France, tinkled away at his keyboard. Swayed back and forth on his wobbly bench like a weeping willow in a light breeze. Man was serious into his music.

Motioned Nate on around to my left toward the battered, upright music box. For no reason I could imagine, the ivory tickler's eyes suddenly popped open like a pair of cheap, paper window shades. He went to blinking and glanced around like a man who'd just woke up and didn't recognize his surroundings. Spotted us and stopped playing. His pale, stubble-covered face went scarlet. Veins popped out on his neck. Then, he hopped up and unceremoniously wobbled through a door in the wall right next to his twangy-sounding instrument.

Eased my way to the center of the room, next to one of the poles holding the canvas roof up. Couple of dust devils wafted off my boots. Tiny twisters twirled across the floor in front of me like a pair of intoxicated dancers, hit the stove and flew all to pieces. Ended up four or five steps away from the three drunks in the corner. Was close enough to them that no matter what happened knew I wouldn't miss whoever I picked to die first.

4

"WELL, WE MIGHTA KILT THAT WOMAN . . ."

BROUGHT MY WINCHESTER to bear on the trio. Addressed the man sitting on the backside of the table when I called out, "Okay, Mort, you boys best throw all your iron on the floor. Then get up real slow. Keep your hands where I can see 'em when you do it."

Mordecai Staine, who'd spent the whole time I approached them staring at the scarred tabletop, as though on the verge of drifting off to sleep or maybe passing slap out, snapped his head back with all the speed of a man sitting on the bottom of a deep, cold lake. With agonizing, near-paralytic slowness, he pushed back in his chair, then shoved a sweat-stained, wide-brimmed Stetson to the back of his head with one finger.

Brothers Darius and Dolphus swayed to their feet. Hands hovering over still holstered, well-used pistols, they backed into the tent saloon's far corner. Took a stand on either side of their eldest.

Mordecai's bloodshot, rheumy-eyed gaze wobbled around the room till it landed on me. "Jus' be got damned," he said.

"If'n it ain't Deppidy Marshal Hayden by-God Tilden, I'll shit in my hat, then eat it. Whachoo doin' all the way out here on the back side a nowhere, Deppidy Tilden? Mus' be sumthin' important for Isaac Parker's personal, hand-picked killer to show up way'n the hell out here. Brung another badge-totin' killer with you, too, I see."

Moved the Winchester, ever so slightly, and leveled the muzzle up on Mordecai's breastbone. Figured the heavy-grain bullet would go plumb through him at that range. Blow a big chunk of heart and lung onto the wooden half wall and flapping canvas at his back.

"My partner and I've come to arrest you fellers, Mort," I said. "Take you boys back to Fort Smith, where you'll dangle from a piece of Maledon's oiled Kentucky hemp at the Gates of Hell gallows down in the hollow next to the courthouse. Once you've stood trial and Judge Parker sees fit, of course."

Darius, gaunt, ghostly pale, and sporting the appearance of an advanced consumptive, coughed into his off hand. Fingers draped over his pistol grip twitched when he hissed, "We ain't done nothin', you law-bringin' son of a bitch. Why you Parker boys wanna go botherin' us? Why doanchu just hike it on outta here and leave us to our drinkin'."

Dolphus, whose eyes seemed just a mite too far apart in his wide, childlike face, let out a strange, eerie, hacking cackle. Said, "Yup. Why'er you Parker boys goin' and botherin' us? We ain't done nuthin'. Jus' hike it on outta here. Leave us to, uhhhh, well, you know, like Darius done said."

Felt rather than saw Nate, as he moved a step and a half along the wall, and a mite closer to the action. Sounded like a cornered wolf growling when he said, "Stupid questions you're askin', boys. You know exactly why we're here."

Dolphus flashed an idiotic grin. "I don't," he said, then giggled into the back of a filth-encrusted hand. "I don't be knowin' why you 'uns is here."

"Shut up, Dolphus," Mordecai snarled.

Dolphus ducked, as though someone had slapped him on the back of the head, then whimpered, "Well, I don't."

Could hear the growing irritation in Nate's voice when he

snarled, "You sons a bitches can't rob a Van Buren bank, then go and murder women and children in the process of gettin' away, and think you can escape punishment for your evil deeds. Now, if you don't wanna end up deader'n rotten tree stumps, best get to doin' like Tilden said. Two-finger them pistols outta their holsters and drop 'em on the floor."

"An' what if we don't?" Darius snapped back, then went into another fit of croupy coughing. Wiped a blood-flecked spew from his lips, and said, "Personally, I don't believe you sons a bitches got the *huevos* to do nothin'. Case you didn't notice, they's three of us. Ain't but two of you."

"Yeah, wha' if'n we doan do what y'all want? Yeah, an' them *huevos*, too," Dolphus said through a spray of slobbers. Then, he glanced at his oldest brother for approval. Drool ran down the man's chin and dropped onto the front of a never-washed, band-collared shirt the color of a year-old cow flop.

Sounded like a crosscut saw ripping through oak logs when Nate growled, "Any of you woman-killin' bastards get feisty, I'm gonna splatter the three of you all over the ceiling and wall. I touch this ten gauge off and there won't be enough left of you to run through Granny's favorite food mill."

Mordecai raised both hands from the table, as though to shush his idiot brothers. Accidentally tipped a half-empty bottle over in the process. Liquid leaked onto the tabletop, then ran over the edge and dribbled onto the dust-covered floor.

From behind us the witless bartender shouted, "Ain't nothin' illegal goin' on here, deputies. These fellers brung all that liquor with 'em. I didn't sell 'em nothin'. Just provided a place to sit, some glasses, a little music, a bit of privacy, and the possibility of some female companionship—long as they showed me they weren't violent."

"Told you to shut the hell up, mister," Nate shouted over one shoulder.

Drink slinger wouldn't let it go. "Cain't arrest me for nothin'. Didn't do nothin'. Swear it. 'Sides, I cain't spend no more time in that dungeon of a jail in Fort Smith."

"Damnation, are you deef as a rotten fence post? Hear me tell you to shut it?" Nate yelled.

Bartender sounded some desperate when he yelped, "Damn near addled my thinker mechanism last stretch I served in that viper's pit. Place is fulla murderers, thieves, and them what has their lock nuts cross threaded. Ain't goin' back there, you hear me. Ain't goin' back."

Over my own shoulder I said, "We're not here for you, you mouthy son of a bitch. So, why don't you just dance your ignorant self on out into the street and wait till we're finished with these fellers."

Slower than a five-hundred-pound pig in January, Mordecai Staine pushed out of the chair and brought himself erect. Seat caught on the back of one of his legs and made a squawking sound as it skittered on the rough-cut floor.

Mordecai ceremoniously placed both hands on the buckle of his pistol belt, then said, "Well, we mighta kilt that woman, that's fer damned sure an actual fact, lawdog. But if'n we done the foul deed, it were definitely accidental. As I recall, she just happened to come outta that Van Buren hardware store at the exact wrong moment." Of a sudden he appeared to lose his train of thought, but then blurted out, "Don't know nothin' 'bout no kid, though."

To my dismay, could tell that, in spite of hours at the bottle, all three of the Staine boys had begun to sober up. Realization as how bony-fingered Death had waltzed into Black's carrying a shotgun and rifle had begun to settle in on them like the worst kind of bloody nightmare they could think up.

Darius approved of his older brother's version of their murder and outlawry with a sage nod.

Dolphus giggled, did a kind of kid's jig, then set to watching his brothers for the right cue. Vigorously went to nodding as well, as though he'd heard something floating on the dust-laden air the rest of us had missed.

"Yup. Yup. Yup. Uh-huh. Uh-huh. Woman 'uz accidental kilt. Patch-assed kid, too. Didn't mean it whence I hit 'im with my pistol barrel. Jus' got in the way. Jus' got in the way. He'n his mammy both. Yup. Yup. Yup. Uh-huh. Uh-huh."

"Shut up, you blatherin' idiot," Darius snapped, then dabbed at his lips with a filthy bandanna.

Dolphus took half a step backward as if someone had slapped him across the face. Puckered up like he might bust out bawling, then said, "Best be a watchin' yer smort mouth, Darius. Mama finds out you gone and call't me an idiot, she'll whup yer stupid ass with one a Papa's razor strops. Laugh myself silly whilst I watch you git blistered, by God."

Dolphus never took his eyes off us. Didn't bother to look at his brother. "Mama's deader'n a rotten hoe handle, you stupid gob of walking dung. And Papa's been worm dirt for nigh on twenty year. So, shut the hell up. Hard for me to think with you yammerin'."

In a gesture of apparent peacemaking, Mordecai raised one hand. Couldn't help but notice that he bore the look of a man much put upon. Once his brothers had fallen silent again, barely heard him when he said, "Give it a rest, boys. Gotta take care of these lawdogs first. Let's get to killin' 'em, then you can kill hell outta each other, if'n that's what you want."

Swear 'fore Jesus, those loony bastards fixed their gazes on me and Nate like three diamondback rattlers that had just cornered a pair of fat field mice. Trust me when I tell you, there's no single thing I can think of to match the feeling that runs up and down your sweaty spine when you find it necessary to acknowledge that desperate, whisky-addled, and perhaps crazy men plan to go down shooting.

"Don't do it, Mort," I called out. "Best back off a notch. Come on back to Fort Smith with us. It's either that, or all of you'll die where you sit."

A twisted, weird, bloodthirsty grin etched its way across each of the Staine boys' unwashed, unshaven faces at the exact same instant. Struck me as likely their fierce glowers of shared insanity was the last thing that poor woman saw just before she and her child died in a dusty Van Buren street.

An obviously half-brained Dolphus actually smiled at me as though someone had just handed him a bowlful of ice-cold, seedless, cubed watermelon. Not certain the man had any idea what was about to go down though. Instant later, the finger of Mordecai's right hand twitched. His convulsive movement sent the level of lethal tension in the room right through the canvas roof like a July 4th whizbang.

As if agreed on by some unknowable method of communication that Nate and I didn't have the perverted power to hear, Mordecai made a grab for the brace of Remington .44-40s dangling from his paunchy waist.

Split second later, his stupid brother Darius did the same.

The gape-mouthed, brain-numbed Dolphus appeared oblivious to what was happening. Of a sudden, the scene started moving amazingly fast and damned slow at the same time.

Dolphus continued to grin like the village idiot when I touched off the round that caught Mordecai dead center. Bullet bored through the big bone in the man's chest, blasted out his back, and splattered a gob of blood and bone the size of a three-pound cannonball all over the wall behind him.

Amazed hell out me that, in spite of the death-dealing blow, ole Mort still managed to keep himself upright, get his strong-side pistol barrel free of the lip of its holster, and fire at least two wild shots into the top of the table. Then, the man began to collapse in on himself like a newspaper house sitting out in a rainstorm.

Knew full well that Mordecai Staine was on the way to being dead when he started sagging. Quickly turned my attention on Darius. Jacked another round into the Winchester about the same instant Nate cut loose with both barrels of that amputated ten-gauge popper of his.

My partner held the monstrous blaster hip high. His carefully placed discharge sent a murderous cloud of heavy-gauge, buzzing buckshot pellets that slapped into Darius just above his pistol belt. Same bedsheet sized veil of gray death nailed the drooping Mordecai right in the top of his anvil-thick head. Canvas and pine wall behind those two boys rattled and shook like a field of dry corn in a cyclone as those pieces of shot not stopped by their bodies flew past and sizzled through cloth and wood.

Bottles atop the Staine brothers' table shattered and flew

into thousands of glittering shards that sliced into all three of those skunks like tiny, flying, glass knives. Blistering curtain of lead hit them in a wave, as if they'd been swarmed by a nest of teased hornets. Darius and the near-dead Mordecai let out individual screeches of shocked pain that hit the ear as though they'd all come from a single man.

Instantaneous spray of blood, bone, rendered flesh, and chewed-up clothing filled the air in a misted spray of gory steam. Unnerving blast knocked the brothers backward, into a wooden section of the wall, as if God himself had reached down from Heaven and slapped the hell out of them. Their limp bodies bounced off the sap-dripping pine boards and dropped to the floor, one atop the other, in a gore-stained heap.

Thunderous report from Nate's weapon ran ahead of a shock wave of roiling dust that wafted across the joint's filthy floor. Powdery grit swelled and rose up all around us in the manner of water on a storm-tossed lake. Only took about half a second for the inside of Black's roadhouse to assume something akin to the look and smell of a place where a herd of buffalo had stampeded through.

Staggered, clearly stunned and amazed by the unfolding events, and bleeding from numerous minor wounds caused by the flying glass, a wide-eyed Dolphus Staine stared at his fallen brothers in stunned wonderment. After several seconds of gaping at the corpses, he glanced down at the blood leaking onto his shirt front and sleeves, then turned on me.

"Whachu lawmen's went and done? You done went an' kilt my brothers, that's what. Got Ammighty, that's what, fer sure. Well, by God I'm gonna . . ."

Surprised hell out of me then, and still amazes me today, how quick with a pistol that half-brained son of a bitch was. I saw the weapon flash into his hand. And though I didn't want it, he forced me to drop the hammer on a round that hit him in the right elbow, as he brought the shooter up to fire. Man yelped like a kicked dog.

Levered another hot round into the Winchester's receiver, as Dolphus's weapon fell to the floor and bounced near his foot.

To this very instant, I couldn't testify in one of Judge Parker's court trials as to where the second handgun came from. Heard Nate yell out a warning, but I'm not sure whether I blinked when Dolphus pulled the weapon from a holster at his back, and I just flat missed it, or maybe, at the time, I had it figured as how he was done and didn't pay strict enough attention, or what. But he for damned sure came up with another pistol from somewhere. Ripped off a blue whistler that hissed so close to my ear I could feel the heat and smell the bullet as it zipped past, kept going, and punched a hole in the wall behind me.

Still trying my level best just to cripple the lamebrain when my second slug caught him in the left hip just above his pants pocket. Heavy chunk of lead knocked the man around on his heels like a drunken ballet dancer. He ricocheted off the wall. Then, still half twirling, half stumbling, he managed to rip off another shot my direction. Behind me, at almost the exact same instant, I heard Nate yelp, and a sound like someone had hit a handful of the keys on the piano with a closed fist.

Off balance, and about to go to one knee, Dolphus fired a third time. Sent a slug into the boards not two inches in front of my right foot. Geyser of stinging splinters flew up and caught me in the thigh. That's when I had to completely give up on any chance of taking him alive.

Brought the rifle to my shoulder. Snapped off a final shot. Bullet hit the crazed bastard above the right eye. It bored through his skull, knocked his hat off, and flung a glob of brain matter on the wall atop the gory mess already put there by Nate's blasting of his brothers.

Dolphus went limp. Dropped like a hundred-pound sack of seed thrown from a freight wagon. Made a final, odd, wheezing sound, rolled onto one side, and, I swear before Jesus, still managed to thumb off a final, closing, wild shot that blew the toe off his own foot.

Then, an ear ringing silence fell around me as if someone had tossed a winter blanket over the entirety of Black's scabrous roadhouse. Acrid-tasting, spent, black powder hung in the air along with the sickly sweet, coppery smell and taste of freely flowing blood. Squinted into the roiling cloud of gun smoke. With one hand, I kept the Winchester leveled on the pile of wasted humanity in the corner. With the other, reached down and pawed at the stinging leg wound.

Still picking at my prickly, splintery injury when I heard Nate say, "Cain't damned believe it, Tilden. That bug nutty son of a bitch put a hole in me."

Jerked my head around and saw my friend sitting in the middle of the floor, back propped against the piano. Legs outstretched, it appeared as though he'd gone down hard. A clawlike hand covered an oozing wound in his right side, just above his pistol belt.

Hobbled over to him, knelt down, stiff-legged, and laid the Winchester on the floor. "Got to let me get a look at your new vent, Nate," I said, then pulled his grasping, blood-dripping fingers aside.

He grinned, then said, "Don't think she's all that bad, Hayden. But she's damn sure leakin' right smart and burns like the dickens."

Jerked the tail of his shirt out of his pants. Puckered, black-rimmed hole in the fleshy part of the boy's side was as big around as my thumb. Pulled him toward me and yanked the shirt up in the back. Pleased to find that the bullet had gone all the way through. Knew he'd be fine soon as I saw what had transpired. Have to admit, though, he was lucky, real damned lucky.

Patted his shoulder and said, "Well, you can talk with God tonight and thank him, Nate. Bullet doesn't appear to have hit anything important. Couple inches lower, though, you would've spent the rest of your life on a cane. We'll know for sure by tomorrow morning just how bad it really is. Gonna be sore as hell no matter what, but I think you'll most likely survive. Still and all, probably ought to get your bony behind back to civilization and to a doctor quick as we can."

He grunted and nodded as though heavily drugged.

"Need to plug this ugly sucker up first, Nate. Best flush it out with some whiskey 'fore we go and do that though."

Used the rifle as a crutch. Yanked myself erect. Hobbled back to the Staine boys' bullet- and shot-riddled table. Single, half-filled bottle of hundred-fifty-proof scamper juice had managed to survive all the gunfire. Can't imagine how half a dozen of Nate's buckshot pellets hadn't rendered it to smithereens, but as often happens during catastrophic gun work, something as delicate as a whiskey bottle had managed to survive the deadly onslaught.

Leg had begun to hurt pretty good when I limped my way back over to where a wild-eyed, bloody-fisted Nate Swords still sat. Groaned when I knelt, then pushed him onto his back. Grabbed a dirty pillow off the piano bench and stuffed it beneath his head.

"Have to trust me on this one, Nate. Seen it done a time or two. Even used it myself once, or twice. Works pretty good, if we manage to do it right. But be aware, this is gonna burn a bit no matter how we go about it."

Turned the bottle up and poured the amber-colored liquid directly into the hole in his side. 'Course, I'm certain it hurt him a lot worse than I had let on it might. He screeched like a trapped panther. Sat bolt upright. Then passed right out and flopped back down. Poured a second round in him. Shoved the bottle neck into the hole. Kept an eye on the opening in his back. Soon as the whiskey-tinted blood started flowing onto the floor, I jerked the bottle out of the wound and set to plugging him up as best I could.

Know it only amounted to a bit less than a week, but the time we spent in Lone Pine felt like a month. Nate was on his back in what went for a hotel in the unpleasant burg for most of those long, dreary days.

While he rested, I made all the necessary arrangements to bury the Staine brothers. Hired a couple of local boys to dig the holes. Gave the bartender at Black's the Staine boys' horses and gear in payment for building some coarse coffins and supervising their burial. Pretty rough stuff all the way around.

We finally set out for Fort Smith on the eighth or ninth day, as I recall.

Being as Nate was still pretty tender, took our time getting back to a spot where we could flag down a northbound M.K. & T. passenger train. Neither of us felt worth a damn, tell the pure truth. Got to admit, by the time we finally made it home, the pair of us were still in right sorry shape. At first Nate was worse off than me. But he cured up mighty fast. Couple of days and he got to hopping around like a cornered rabbit. Amazing what youth and a good dose of piss and vinegar can accomplish.

Elizabeth insisted that we put him up at our place. She fixed him a room and fussed over him like he was a small child. Glad we kept him over. 'Cause, as time dragged by, he proved mighty fine company and provided way more of a helping hand than we had any right to have expected.

5

". . . Skulls Stove in With a Double-Bit Ax."

OVER THE MANIFOLD and turbulent years I spent riding for Judge Parker, figure as how bad men, and a few bad women, too, managed to put half a dozen or so bullets in my leathery hide. Can't recall a single one of those wounds that proved as problematic as the patch of splinters Dolphus Staine gouged out of the floor of Black's roadhouse that ended up in my leg, as a consequence of a wild pistol shot.

All the way back to Fort Smith, I conscientiously treated the lesion with a daily whiskey and carbolic bath. Picked all the timber out of the wound. Leastways, all I could see. Just didn't matter one whit. Damned thing still managed to fester, get angry-looking as hell, and fill up with some god-awful-looking puss.

When I finally got home, had to spend a week in bed. Ran a horse-killing fever and sweated like a tied pig. Elizabeth said as how I hallucinated like a certifiable eccentric. Gal claimed, and I have no reason to disbelieve her, that more than once I went and talked with folks not present. Worst of all, a time or two, she said I even expressed the desire for immediate death. Poor girl had to give up her days down at the bank and care for me the whole time.

Was a godsent miracle Nate recovered enough to lend the woman a hand during her trials and tribulations. Grateful as hell he was there to help her with getting me up and around when she needed him. Amazing to me that a man with a hole in his side, and back, the size of a Yankee quarter, recovered as quick as he did. Still puzzles the hell out of me that I ended up sick as the proverbial dog because of a fistful of splinters from a pine board, and he got better.

Truth be told, most folks now don't remember, but it was easy to die back in them days. Man could dodge bullets every week of his life, catch a cold, and pass on from the pneumonia within a week. Simplest scratch might prove fatal. Spiders, scorpions, even something as simple as a bee sting could have ended a man's life as quickly as a body would blow out a lamp before lying down in his bed. Come down with a fever, like I done from a fistful of wood splinters, and your fate very definitely hung in the balance as surely as if you'd fallen headfirst into a well. Can't imagine what might've transpired if it hadn't been for my dear Elizabeth. But I am sure if it hadn't been for her, I might not be here today.

'Course when my feverish spell finally passed, I got that beautiful gal's standard lecture that always ended with her shaking an angry finger in my face and saying, "We're one of the most prosperous families in the whole of northwest Arkansas, Hayden Tilden. Have more money in the bank than Croesus. You don't have to go chasing murderous skunks all over the Indian Nations who will kill you for the cost of a plug of tobacco."

No point arguing with the woman. And besides, she already knew that no matter what she said, I wasn't about to change anyway.

Eventually, got to spend most of my forced leisure time relaxing out on the veranda of my house. Still think of those slow-moving days, spent with Nate and Carlton, with great affection. See, almost every morning, bit after ten o'clock, Judith Cecil drove ole sore-tailed Carl from their little house in town to my place on the bluff overlooking the Arkansas River.

They'd roll up out front with Carl perched atop a fringed, silk pillow looking as if he could barely stand it. He crawled down out of that buggy like a man made of leaded cut glass. Crept up my steps. Flopped into an empty chair and barely moved all day long.

Three of us often spent pretty much the whole afternoon just watching travelers pass on the road that ran by my house on its way to Van Buren. On the whole, most folks were right friendly. We'd wave and they'd wave back.

Have to admit, though, us ole boys must've been a pretty sorry-looking bunch. Me hobbling around like a Barbary pirate on my sore leg. Nate all doubled over like a humpback, limping from here to there babying the hole in his side. Carlton shambling around, one hand attached to his lacerated behind as if he feared a piece might fall off or something. Spent the better part of three weeks sitting in our rocking chairs whittling, spitting, smoking, telling all kinds of lies about our past exploits, and griping over the state of our various hurts.

Thanks be to a benevolent God, the insidious tortures of an idle life didn't last very long. After nigh on four lazy weeks of profound loafing, beating Nate or Carl at checkers two or three times a day, or generally dawdling around and wasting daylight, admit that I felt right pert and more than ready for something to happen—anything. And sure enough, it did.

Come a beautiful morning, as I recall it. Come on just the right combination of blue sky and puffy white clouds that day. Temperature proved bearable, long as a body didn't move around too much. Still and all, one of our seeming endless days of less than productive indolence. And, as usual, the three of us broke-down lawmen were stationed in our rocking chairs. We'd camped out in a moving wedge of comfortable shade soon as Carl arrived and went to rocking like certifiable maniacs. Sipped at tall, cold glasses of Elizabeth's fresh-squeezed lemonade and pretty much indulged in the joyful contemplation of another week as thumb twiddlers.

Then, of a sudden, Carl stopped his rocking. Snatched an ash-laden, smoldering hand-rolled from between twitching lips. Rose and adjusted his royal-colored pillow a bit, then pointed out a cloud of dust coming up the road from Fort Smith.

"Looks like you might have some more visitors on the way, Hayden," Carl said.

Nate climbed out of his chair, strolled over to the veranda's waist-high railing. Took a seat with his back to one of the porch pillars. "Can't be absolutely certain from this distance, but that looks like Judge Parker's chief bailiff, Tilden," he said.

"You mean Mr. Wilton?" I asked.

Nate nodded.

"Think he's right, Hayden," Carl said, leaned with his elbows on his knees for a second, then stood and eased up to a spot near Nate.

Arms crossed over his chest, Carl glanced back, shrugged, squinted hard, then held his arms out and turned his hands up at me as though asking a silent question. Knew from his wordless reaction, he felt Wilton might have a job for the Brotherhood of Blood, and Carl was wondering what we'd do about telling Nate. Still hadn't brought Swords in our secret society, and that was my fault.

Turned my attention away from Carl and watched as the rider neared. Made up my mind, right then and there, the time was about as right as it was going to get. Figured if Judge Parker had a new mission for us, might as well talk with Nate and determine if he wanted a place in the Brotherhood. Carl and I had discussed such an action when the three of us went down to Waco looking for John Henry Slate. But Billy Bird's terrible death still weighed heavy on my mind at the time, and I just had no stomach for thoughts of replacing him.

George Wilton got in no rush to get to us. Appeared to me

as how he was genuinely enjoying the opportunity to get out of Parker's courthouse for a spell. Man proved quite a sight in the saddle—tall, straight-backed, well-dressed, dignified. Animal he'd chosen for the short jaunt from downtown Fort Smith was a prancer. Black as coal from nose to tail. Fire breather of a stallion. Kind of mount that looked like it just might take off and fly. Sizzle through the air like a bolt of lightning, if given its head.

Ever since my confidential agreement with Judge Parker to act as his personal manhunter and, as he put it, "the sword in my mighty right hand in the Nations," George Wilton had acted the part of go-between. Man took care of all my assignments and let me know, in no uncertain terms, whether the judge wanted the men he sent me after to come back dead or alive. All too often past assignments had ended with the admonition to kill them, kill them all. Knew as soon as Nate spotted Wilton coming toward the house that something requiring my deadly services was very likely in the works.

Wilton reined his midnight-colored steed to a halt, stepped down, then looped the reins over my hitch rack. For all his poise and flamboyance in the saddle, George Wilton proved exactly the opposite when afoot. A large man, his legs appeared too short for a heavy, stout upper body—small, spindly, and ill suited for his rather bulky girth. Looked to me like a man who, as he grew older, had gained considerable weight—from the waist up. Know it sounds like an odd circumstance, but it did happen to some men back in those bygone days. Wasn't unusual for men of prominence to have a kind of walking, barrel-like appearance.

With some obvious difficulty, Wilton climbed the steep set of steps to my expansive covered porch. He swept a spotless, gray, felt hat off and extended his hand when I stood.

"Hayden, so good to see you looking well," he said and smiled, then acknowledged Carl and Nate with a nod and equally gracious tilt of the head.

Offered him the seat Carl had so recently vacated and a glass of the lemonade. In the manner of a fussy old maid, Wilton built himself something of an elaborate nest before finally becoming comfortable in the seat next to mine. Once settled in, he ceremoniously lit a cigar the color of his horse and the size of an ax handle. Daintily shook the still smoldering lucifer to death and dropped it into the glass ash tray atop the table between our chairs.

He blew a smoke ring the size of wagon wheel, flashed a toothy grin, then said, "You gentlemen appear to have recovered nicely. Sincerely hope you're all feeling as well as you look."

"Doing fine, thank you," I said. Waved at my friends and added, "Figure we should be ready for something new by way of missions any day now."

"Good, very good. Glad to hear your collective recovery has gone well," he said, then took another deep drag on the massive stogie. Unlike most who favored cigars, Wilton inhaled the potent smoke, held it in his lungs for a second or so, then expelled it in a long thin stream. And in the same manner I'd noticed about his ride, he appeared to genuinely enjoy himself.

After a moment of self-imposed silence, he harrumphed a time or two before saying, "In point of fact, Marshal Tilden, you've hit upon the precise purpose of my visit today. Wanted to check in on Judge Parker's most stalwart trio of deputies, of course. Make sure you were all on the mend, as it were. But I'm also here to offer the three of you a mission that should prove just the type of undertaking you might want to consider, given you're all nearing the end of a somewhat lengthy convalescence."

Though oblique in the extreme, I recognized the hidden message from Judge Parker that it was time for us to get back to work. Offered a slight nod of the head, so as to encourage Wilton to continue. Happened to notice, for the first time, that the man's hair had begun to go gray. The color of onyx, when first we met, it now formed a halolike frame for his handsome, ebony face.

As if in deep contemplation, he sat in silence for a few more seconds. Took the time to examine the ash at the end of his smoke. Inhaled another long, satisfying puff, then said,

"Are you aware of the terrible triple murder that took place up in Dutch Crossing some months ago?"

Had to shake my head, but said, "Seems I did hear something about some horrible killings up that way. But must admit I've no definitive knowledge of the crime."

Nate stood, leaned a shoulder against the porch pillar, shoved both hands into the waist of his pants, then said, "I've heard about the carnage you're talkin' 'bout, sir. Way I got the story, authorities found the butchered bodies of a man, woman, and their young son. If memory serves, was a farm family name of Cassidy."

Wilton nodded. "Indeed. Indeed. Cassidy."

Nate scratched his head and continued. "Seems as how local authorities found the bullet-riddled body of Mr. Matthew Cassidy out in one of his sorghum fields. Then they discovered the corpses of his wife and son inside their house. Heard tell as how the woman and child died from havin' their skulls stove in with a double-bit ax."

Wilton chewed his cigar and nodded.

"Near as anyone could tell," Nate continued, "the heartless killers ran for the wildest parts of the Nations and haven't been heard of since. Last bit of information on the subject coming my direction indicated that no one had, as yet, even determined who did the killings."

While listening to Nate's rendition of the brutal particulars of the Cassidy family's sad departure from this earthly vale of tears, Wilton blew several large smoke rings and watched them drift toward the ceiling of the porch. He puffed a final bluish-gray circle from between pursed lips, then said, "Correct in most every particular, Deputy Marshal Swords. However, you did leave out one important piece of pertinent factual information. One that you might not have even known."

"How so?" Nate said.

Wilton's face twisted into a sad grimace. "There was a second child. A girl of about seventeen years, perhaps eighteen, or maybe even older."

Nate shuffled as though embarrassed. "You're entirely

right, sir. No such information as that has come to me on the subject."

"Well," Wilton continued, "she disappeared sometime right before, or right after, the horrific killings of her other family members took place. As triple murders are a rarity within Judge Parker's jurisdiction, we have communicated with a number of law enforcement offices in neighboring states in an effort to find the girl. In truth, our fear has always been that she had likely met the same fate as the rest of her family and her body was yet to be located."

"Don't have any suspects at all in these killings?" Carl said.

Wilton rubbed a closely shaven chin with the back of his free hand. "Suspicion has fallen on the Coltrane brothers."

"Sweet Jesus," Nate muttered.

"Jesse, Benny, and Leroy Coltrane? Thought they were bank and train robbers. Never heard tell of them ole boys murdering farmers for no apparent reason," Carlton said.

Wilton shifted in his seat, as though seeking a more comfortable position. "We think the Coltrane boys robbed the Winslow branch of the Elk Horn Bank earlier on the same day as the murders."

"That's only about five miles up the road from Dutch Crossing," Carl offered.

"Exactly," Wilton said.

"And prosecutors believe the missing girl is a material witness to the murders of her family," I offered.

A quick, gloomy smile flickered across Wilton's darkly handsome face. "Yes. A state's witness that we sorely need to convene a grand jury, given that your friend Barnes Reed dragged Benny Coltrane in yesterday afternoon."

"Are you and Judge Parker completely convinced that the Coltrane brothers had a hand in the Cassidy murders?" Carlton said.

"According to Deputy Marshal Reed, a loose-mouthed Benny admitted as much. Bragged about his part in the sorry deed all the way in from the Jack Fork Mountains where Barnes ran him down."

"Why'd Barnes drag Benny all the way back here in the first place?" Nate said. "Personally got no use for them bastards as would cold-bloodedly kill women and kids. Been me, I just mighta shot hell outta the son of a bitch soon as he admitted his heinous behavior. Might've cost me a few dollars, just like it did when me'n Hayden whacked the Staine boys. But such a deed would've also saved Judge Parker and the people the trouble of putting the sorry skunk on trial."

A near-undetectable smile danced across Wilton's lips. Physical sign of his approval for Nate's feelings on the matter passed so quickly I felt certain neither of my friends even saw it.

I said, "Benny's capture isn't the only reason you came by today though, is it, Mr. Wilton?"

Parker's chief bailiff eyeballed a bit of fallen ash decorating the front of his otherwise spotless vest. Frowned, flicked at the unwanted ornament with stubby fingers, then stared into the distance as though lost in thought.

"You are correct, Hayden," he said, after some seconds of silence. "This morning word came from the city marshal of Fort Worth, by way of telegram. Seems a young woman claiming to be Daisy Cassidy strolled into his office yesterday afternoon seeking protection from men that she maintained had murdered her family, abducted her, dragged her to Fort Worth's infamous Hell's Half Acre, and forced her into a life of depravity and prostitution."

"Jesus. 'S quite a tale," Carl muttered and shook his head disgust.

"Any ideas on how Miss Cassidy managed to get all the way to a well of perdition like Hell's Half Acre?" I said.

Wilton fiddled with the knifelike crease along one leg of his pants. "Not really. In spite of a number of wild rumors, nothing of any substance. Presently we can do little but guess at the hidden developments behind such events."

"And you want us to go to Fort Worth, retrieve the unfortunate Miss Cassidy, and bring her back so she can testify against the Coltrane boys," Nate said.

"Yes. Given what little we know at the moment, it appears

the missing Miss Cassidy is the only person who might provide the pertinent testimony necessary to send the whole Coltrane family to an appointment with George Maledon and his Gates of Hell gallows."

While Wilton's answer was directed at Nate, his narrow, riflelike gaze bored in on me as he spoke. Man didn't have to add anything else, really. Completely understood the unspoken message he'd been commissioned to deliver. Knew exactly what Judge Parker expected of us without further elucidation and so did Carlton. The Coltrane brothers were already dead and just didn't know it.

"If memory serves," Wilton continued, "the three of you already have an affable relationship with Fort Worth's city marshal, Sam Farmer. That rapport should serve you well in this instance as well."

Carl let out a derisive snort. I knew what was coming before he even spoke.

"Met him when we went down there and brought the Doome brothers, Maynard Dawson, Charlie Storms, and Cotton Rix to book," Carlton said. "Man didn't like deputy U.S. marshals from Arkansas much when we first introduced ourselves. Took to us about like you'd expect Satan to take to holy water. But, over time, feel like he came to think right highly of us. Ain't that about right, Hayden?"

Couldn't help but grin. Given that Carl had threatened the man with a bloody ass whipping within minutes of meeting him, and Nate had pulled his pistols on some of Farmer's policemen, it still amazed me that the man had come to have a genuine fondness for the three of us by the time we vacated his town.

Nodded and, my gaze still locked into Wilton's, said, "Think it would be safe to say we left Fort Worth on good terms with Marshal Farmer and his staff when we last visited."

"Good," Wilton said, then ponderously got to his feet. He snatched a sizable manila envelope from his suit jacket's inside pocket. Handed the thick packet to me. "Usual travel documents. Extra cash and such. Tickets on tomorrow's noon departing M.K. & T. passenger train to Fort Worth. Should you need anything else, Hayden, your wired requests will be acted upon immediately."

Tapped the packet against the back of my hand. "I'm certain everything's in order, Mr. Wilton. We'll do our best."

He slapped me on the shoulder, said, "You always do, Marshal Tilden. Just be careful. Jesse and Leroy Coltrane are not men to be taken lightly. Get Miss Cassidy back here as quickly as possible, by whatever means you deem necessary."

We watched as he headed for the steps, but stopped on the top tread and turned. Shook his cigar at me for emphasis. Said, "You might want to have a talk with Benny Coltrane before you leave. Suggest a meeting this afternoon, if possible. I'll locate Barnes Reed and you can all talk to Benny at the same time."

Carl had an enormous grin on his face when he said, "No problem locating Barnes. If that man's in town, bet the family fortune he's down at the Napoli Café, as we speak. Ole Barnes has a sweet tooth worse'n any kid I've ever seen. Gets within a city block of a cherry, apple, or chocolate pie and, Lord God, you'd need a Sharps Big .50 to keep him away from it."

With some difficulty, Wilton hoisted his cumbersome self onto the black's back. Before he turned the animal back toward town, he pulled a turnip-sized gold watch from his vest pocket. Called out, "Ten thirty right now, gentlemen." He snapped the cover shut and shoved the big ticker back into its hiding place. "I'll have Benny brought up from the general population and lodged in the holding cell in the U.S. marshal's office. Marshal's out of town. You can conduct your interview with him there. Should have it all set up and read for you by two o'clock this afternoon."

With that he tipped his hat, spurred the black into a trot, threw a wave of the hand over his shoulder, and sped away.

6

". . . HAVE TO STUDY UP TO BE A HALF-WITTED IDIOT."

DRAGGED ELIZABETH'S FANCY-DANCY, Sunday-go-to-meetin' cabriolet out of the barn for the ride into town. Figured there was no reason to torture our still-on-the-mend bodies with a horseback jaunt until absolutely necessary.

Arrived at the courthouse steps almost the same instant as Barnes Reed. In spite of a sore, aching rump, Carl hopped out of the still-rolling coach and grabbed the bearlike Reed's paw of a hand.

Prior to me and Carl meeting up, and our subsequent search for the murderous Martin Luther Big Eagle, he and Barnes had ridden many a hard trail together. Barnes accompanied us on our search for Smilin' Jack Paine. Though he never said it, I sometimes felt that Carl missed Barnes a lot more than he was willing to admit and would seek out the man's company again should anything wayward ever happen to me.

The massive, black deputy marshal, wide as a New Hampshire barn door and covered in a layer of thick ropey muscles beneath clothing that strained to hold him all in, grabbed Carl and embraced him like a long-lost brother. Barnes looked, for all the world, like he could single-handedly throw a buckboard across Red Rock Canyon. Watching him embrace Carl put me in mind of a bantam rooster being hugged by a grizzly bear.

After several seconds of laughing and good-natured back slapping, Barnes pushed Carl to arm's length, then said, "By God, it's mighty good to see you, my friend. Why you hobblin' 'round like some kinda old man? Spotted you comin' outta Tilden's coach, swear 'fore sufferin' Jesus, thought you'd aged a hunnert years since last I seen you."

Carl instinctively rubbed his hip, dismissively waved Barnes's question aside and said, "Minor problem. Gettin' better by the minute. Good to see you, Barnes. Missed the hell outta your coffee. Tilden's mighty fine company out on the scout, but the man can't cook coffee grounds worth a damn."

Reed threw his ursine head back and roared with delight. Turned and grabbed my hand in his. "Damned pleased to see both you fellers. Sorry we ain't had the chance to work together in a spell."

Nodded toward Nate. Said, "This here's our newest running buddy, Barnes. Kind of fell in with us when Billy Bird passed."

Swords looked embarrassed. Nodded and shuffled his feet.

Waved him to my side. Said, "Nate, say hello to Judge Parker's most prolific lawdog. Meet Barnes Reed. Barnes is feared by bad men from the Mississippi all the way to Trinidad, Colorado. From the Canadian border to the Rio Grande. Go to fightin' the law, you don't want Barnes Reed coming after you."

Carl whacked his old compadre on the shoulder. "Judge Parker wants 'em brought in alive, this here's the man he sends out to get 'em."

Sheepish grin on his face, Nate stepped forward and shook Reed's hand. "No need for an introduction, Hayden. Can't be a deputy marshal working the Nations that hasn't heard of Mr. Reed. 'S my great pleasure and honor to finally meet you, sir."

Barnes bobbed his head up and down, shot me a happy glance, and winked. "See you boys been trainin' this young man right," Reed said, then laughed so loud my ears hurt.

Grabbed our old friend by the elbow and pointed him toward the courthouse door. As we made our way up the steep, white steps, said, "Hear tell as how you recently dragged Benny Coltrane back."

As Barnes pushed the courthouse door open, he said, "'S a fact all right. Ran 'im to ground 'bout twenty miles west of Tuskahoma, over in the Jack Fork Mountains. Stump holler village name of Clifton. He 'uz passed out under a wagon fulla contraband tarantula juice. When I finally got 'im awake and talking, claimed as how he'd been visitin' with a limber-legged woman lived on a farm down that way."

Stopped in the lobby and Carl eased up beside us. "Must've had more'n traffickin' in illegal whiskey in mind when you snatched him up," Carl said.

Barnes nodded. "Yep. Sure 'nuff. Just happened as how I 'uz in possession of a legal warrant namin' him, and his more'n worthless brothers, in the ambush murder of a travelin' book peddler name of Marcel Cushman out of Independence, Kansas. Seems the Coltrane boys happened on Mr. Cushman camped on a creek havin' a bit of breakfast over near Council Hill. Beat on the man till his head was nothin' but a sack of jelly, poured coal oil all over 'im, then set the poor bastard ablaze."

Felt Nate at my elbow when he said, "Jesus. Hadn't even heard about that killing."

Barnes led the way up the staircase to the second floor. With one hand sliding along the railing he said, "Oh, the Coltrane boys got more'n one dodger out on them for murder. Didn't surprise me a bit when Wilton told me 'bout that poor, unfortunate Cassidy family. Hated to hear it, though. 'Specially the part 'bout the youngster. Shockin', but not all that surprising."

Stopped them all just outside the U.S. marshal's office door. Gave them all my most serious eyeballing. Bored in on Carl and Nate. Said, "You know why we're here. Heard what Mr. Wilton said about finding Benny's brothers and the missing girl. We've got to get as much out of this polecat as we can."

Carl perked up and grinned. Sounded like a stalking cougar growling when he said, "Don't worry, Tilden, he'll talk to me and Nate. Won't take long, either."

Nate offered up a toothy grin, then the four of us kind of muscled our way into the marshal's outer office like a herd of rogue Texas longhorns. Surly, weasel-faced, newly ordained clerk, sitting at a desk just inside the door, stopped beating on one of those mechanical writing machines long enough to get all bug-eyed behind a set of pince-nez spectacles that looked like the bottoms of sarsaparilla bottles.

Prissy-looking dude seemed a bit more than flustered, when he shuffled, stacked, restacked, and then whanged a thick pile of papers against the green pad covering his symbol of authority. Brass plate, mounted across a wedge-shaped piece of walnut, designated him as Mr. Harvey Crumb. Carlton would later opine that Crumb's nameplate should have included the title of "His Eminence," or something along those lines.

Snatched his sissified glasses off and impatiently tapped them against the back of his hand. "And exactly what can I do for you gentlemen today," Harvey Crumb snapped. Then, His Grand Pooh-Bah-ness glared at each of us individually, as though examining a group of outhouse cockroaches he just might swat with his weighty stack of important-looking documents.

Barnes started to growl at the pencil pusher, but I quickly placed a quieting hand on his thick-muscled arm, then said, "Mr. Crumb, we are here at the instructions and behest of Judge Parker's chief bailiff. According to George Wilton, you should have a man waiting for us to question in Marshal Dell's holding cell. Would be most appreciative if you could provide us with a key to the cell and escort us inside. If that wouldn't be too much trouble for you."

Crumb slapped the sheaf of papers onto his desk, snatched a drawer open, and jerked out a large brass ring that sported a number of different-sized keys. He evil-eyed all of us again. Might as well have shouted that we'd inconvenienced the hell out of him. Officious goober said, "The jailers just brought your man up from the central lockup downstairs. He smells like a dead skunk dipped in a tub of week-old horse urine. Want you to know I had no warning of this meeting prior to his arrival and am not at all happy about the inconvenience. Plan to take this up with Marshal Dell when he returns, by Godfrey."

Then, the prissy scamp hopped up like his narrow butt was on fire. He pranced over to the door to the marshal's private office and flung it open. Stepped to one side and majestically waved us in.

Interior of the U.S. marshal's official, personal headquarters proved quite spacious. As most of my assignments came directly from George Wilton or Judge Parker, I rarely had any reason to visit with Marshal Dell. Was always surprised at the enormity of his private workspace and, except for the two glaringly out-of-place cells against the easternmost wall, its impressive sumptuousness.

The single room encompassed an oblong space that ran along a sizable portion of the entire front wall of the courthouse. Perhaps twelve by twenty feet, the room was furnished in dark, heavy furniture and thick, colorful, Persian carpets. A highly polished mahogany conference table, fully capable of seating eight or ten people, sat but a few feet outside the heavily barred, abbreviated lockup against the wall to our right. A set of thick curtains, used to hide the tiny prison when it was not in use, and that appeared to match the carpet, had been pushed to one side thereby exposing the object of our interest.

Red-faced, Crumb marched to the only occupied chamber of the pair, slammed a key into the ironbound slot, and jerked the door open. "Get up," he yelped. "You have important visitors."

A man, of perhaps twenty years, rolled off his straw-filled

cot with his back to us. He stretched like a lazy cat, turned, and flashed us a huge, welcoming smile. "Why, hello, boys. So glad y'all could come by."

He took a couple of steps, then reached up and hooked his fingers over the open jail cell door's iron frame. Man absolutely oozed an aura of contemptible confidence. "Anybody bring a bottle with 'em," he grunted. "Ain't had a got damned thing to drink since this big oaf snatched me up and dragged me back to civilization. Gettin' mighty by-God dry," he said and grinned again.

Barnes Reed reached out, grabbed Benny Coltrane by the shirtfront, snatched him off his feet, then dragged him to the conference table. Lifted the man up like a corn-shuck doll and stuffed him into an empty chair. Got right up in the accused killer's face and snarled, "This here's Deputy U.S. Marshal Hayden Tilden, Coltrane. He's got some questions for you. Best pay attention."

Benny swept the three of us with a wide, insincere, self-important smile, then said, "Why, I live to serve, Deputy Marshal Reed. Hell, you know that. Us Coltrane boys are always ready to offer aid to any of the bold men who wear a badge for Hangin' Judge Isaac Parker. Should help the law all you can. That's what my dear, departed ole pappy used to say."

Barnes shook his head in disgust. Barely able to control his temper, he glared at Coltrane like he wanted to rip the man's empty head off and stuff it down his blood-gushing neck. Still fuming like a burning bank building, Barnes backed away and took a position leaned up against the edge of Marshal Dell's fancy, mahogany desk. Would've sworn I could see red under the dusky skin covering his face and hands. Man stared steely daggers into ole Benny's back.

As Carl, Nate, and I surrounded the bigheaded bandit and possible child murderer, I said, "You and your brothers have been right busy, haven't you, Benny?"

Coltrane studied his twiddling thumbs for a second, arched an eyebrow, glanced up, and flashed that wide, crooked, sneering grin again. "Well, must admit I do come from a long line of hardworking, industrious folks, and that's a pure fact.

Coltrane family's always prospered, no matter the economic condition of our surroundings. Yessir, we're a hardworkin' buncha model citizens."

As though completely unconcerned with the proceedings, Carl pulled a folding knife from his pants pocket. Started digging at his fingernails with the tip of the biggest blade. Didn't bother to look at Coltrane, when he came near whispering, "Hear tell as how you *hardworking, industrious* Coltrane boys went and kilt a drummer name of Cushman. God-fearin', upstandin' citizen of Kansas. Never done a soul any harm. That right, Benny, my boy?"

Coltrane's haughty smile bled away and was quickly replaced with a teeth-baring sneer. "Yammerin' at the wrong man, *deppidy*. Might as well be talkin' to this here table, 'cause I don't know nothin' 'bout no dead book peddlers."

Big, toothy grin popped out on Nate Swords's face. Knew exactly what he was about to say. My friend leaned back and slapped the protruding grip on one of his pistols. Kinda chuckled, then said, "Nobody mentioned a single thing 'bout the man bein' a book peddler, you loose-mouthed son of a bitch. Just how'n the blue-eyed hell did you know the dead feller made his living selling books?"

Coltrane's eyebrows pinched together, as he squirmed in his seat. Then, swear 'fore Jesus, he rammed a finger up his nose to the second knuckle. Picked around inside like he was mining for gold somewhere up near the top of his skull. Self-importantly examined his discovery for a second. Grinned when he flicked the snotty booger Carl's direction. My red-faced friend hopped aside.

No doubt in my mind that things were about to take a decidedly weird detour, when Carl shot a glare at Coltrane that could've easily blistered paint off a Pennsylvania barn.

"Seems I did hear somethin' about that particular killin'. Can't remember exactly what, though," Coltrane offered. He flipped the same finger in the general direction of Barnes. "Hell, big son of a bitch yonder's already run me through the mill over that drummer once. Don't know nothin'. Cain't tell you ignorant sons a bitches what I don't know, now can I?"

"Doesn't matter," Carl growled. "We'll let Judge Parker, and a jury of your peers, decide your fate over that one. But, we are interested in what you can tell us about the Cassidy girl."

Damned near imperceptible, but Benny's shoulders slumped a mite. He twisted lower into the chair, as though trying to corkscrew himself away from a perceived threat. Went to scratching and squirming like the kid who'd been caught doing something that he shouldn't have been doing.

Scratched his chin as though in deep, concentrated thought. "Cassidy girl?" Benny said. "You boys 'er wastin' all our time, by God. Don't have no idea what you're talkin' 'bout, *deppidy*."

Take it from me when I tell you, the man had a way of spitting the word *deputy* out like he was trying to knock a yellow jacket out of the air with a gob of spitty phlegm the size of a shotgun shell.

Nate threw his head back and let out a derisive chuckle. Said, "You just don't know anything about anything, do you? But I'd bet you're fully aware that you're workin' on makin' all us lawmen believe, beyond any doubt, that you'd have to go back to school and study up to be a half-witted idiot."

Our prisoner humped up and went to yammering at Nate like an angry tomcat. Snapped, "Truth be known, *deppidy*, Benny Coltrane don't personally give a royal pile of runny shit what you do-right sons a bitches think about a single by-God thing."

Quicker than field corn going through a fat goose, Carl's hand flicked out. Like a striking rattlesnake, he smacked Coltrane across the lips so hard, just seeing the lick made my teeth hurt. Blow was what Carl would have laughingly referred to as a "love tap." But the resounding smack for damned sure got ole Benny's attention.

To say Coltrane was a bit surprised would've been the understatement of the decade. Looked to me like our question-and-answer session was well on the way to getting about as serious as a brain killer of a stroke.

7

"... BE PISSIN' BLOOD FOR A MONTH WHEN WE GET DONE."

BENNY COLTRANE SLUMPED deeper into the Moroccan leather of his chair and rubbed the fresh weal that glowed on his cheek. He followed that bit of business up with a somewhat less-than-enthusiastic glance of feigned defiance around the room. In spite of his seeming insolence, I detected a definite, although well-concealed, crack in his disrespectful attitude.

"Where's the girl, Benny?" Carl said, then flashed a friendly grin.

Coltrane reared back in the chair, as far from Carl as he could get, then yelped, "Got no right to go a-hittin' on me like that, goddammit. Jus', by God, cain't be treatin' a feller like that."

One-handed, Carlton snapped the barlow closed, dropped it back into his pants pocket, then leaned over in Benny's face. Hissed, "You don't tell us somethin' 'bout the location of Miss Daisy Cassidy that's useful, and mighty damned quick, I'm gonna beat the unmerciful dog crap outta you, ole son. Get through with your sorry, back-shootin' ass won't be enough of you left to run through my granny's flour sifter."

White-knuckled, Coltrane clasped both padded arms of the chair with talonlike fingers. Shot a hot-eyed, inquiring glance my direction. "You gonna let this vicious, redheaded son of a bitch beat on me like he says, Mr. Tilden? Hell, I done heard as how you're a dangerous man in a gunfight, but a fair one once a man's caught. Never suspected a famed lawdog like you for such barbaric behavior."

In the manner of a starving wildcat, Nate took Carl's lead. Jumped at Coltrane, pushed Carl aside, and seized the slippery snake by the collar and shook him. "Sweet Jesus, where'd you learn a three-dollar word like *barbaric*, Benny? *Barbaric* for the love of Jesus. I personally wouldn't have bet a single, thin, Yankee dime on whether you'd ever even heard such a word. Sure as hell wouldn't have ever been made to believe that half a haircut like you would know what it meant."

Prisoner slapped at Nate's hand, then twisted out of his grasp. "Yer all crazier'n a pack of shithouse rats," he yelped. "Ain't never had no lawmen go'n treat me like this, by God."

"Like what?" a grinning Barnes Reed called out from behind Benny. "Ain't got a mark on you yet, you evil little sack of rat crap. But there's the very real possibility that when we let you outta here today, you could very well hobble back to the general-population cells, down in the basement, in a lot worse condition than you came out."

Stricken by the sudden, and very physical, turn of events, a once self-assured, overly confident Benny Coltrane twirled in the chair so he could see Barnes. Instant rash of beaded sweat poured off his forehead, when he whined, "What in the hell's that mean, Reed? That a threat? You threatenin' me with some kinda beating just short of death-dealin' violence? Might have to complain to the . . ."

"Complain? Complain to who, you ignert bag of horse dung," Carl yelped. Then, he grabbed the arms of the chair and jerked the now-quaking Benny Coltrane back our direction. "What my friend Deputy Reed is implyin' is that we just might be forced to each take a volume of them law books outta that shelf yonder, open 'er up, and beat you silly with it. Paper won't leave a mark on you. But you'll be limpin' like a peg-legged Civil War veteran and pissin' blood for a month when we get done."

Gaze darting around the room, Coltrane had the look of a cornered rat when he said, "You wouldn't do that. Ain't no way you'd do that."

Carlton smiled. "Tilden won't. Reed might not. But me'n Swords will. And trust me, ole son, you'll tell us every secret thing you've ever tried to hide from anybody. Hell, you'll even admit to the time you first peered down the cotton pantalets of little Mary Damp Britches, and commented on how what you saw looked like she'd been hit with a hatchet."

Big vein in Benny's neck went to throbbing so hard I could see it. His worried, restless gaze rubbered around the stuffy room from one of our faces to the other. In spite of looking pitiful enough to make a thousand-year-old angel weep, he couldn't find a bit of sympathy anywhere.

Sorry skunk went to scratching and squirming again. Then he said, "Well, uh. Well, uh, uh. Shit almighty, what was the question? Done forgot what you bastards asked me 'fore you went and started beatin' on me."

Carl shook his head and grinned. Said, "You ain't even begun to have anyone *beat* on you yet, you stupid bastard. Think someone mighta slapped you a mite, but so far that's been the limit of it. Screw with me and I'll jerk your arm off and hammer you into the floor with the bloody end of it."

Fingers wrapped so tightly around the chair's arms he appeared on the verge of shredding them into a pile of sweat-soaked leather, Benny bent over at the waist and yelped, "Mighta slapped me? That what you just said? Shit almighty, you damn near knocked all my teeth loose, that's what you done, by God. Beat me to death with my own arm? Mean-assed son of a bitch."

Carl's open hand shot forward again. The open-fisted crack, crossways of Benny's opposite cheek, sounded like a pistol going off in the closed room. Red welt that bore an unsurprising resemblance to a man's fingers and palm immediately popped up on the flabbergasted gunny's face.

Coltrane sucked in an astonished breath, then hocked a glob of red-flecked spittle onto the floor. Wiped his blood-seeping mouth on a dirty sleeve. "Done gone and busted my lip, you son of a . . ."

With no warning, Carl delivered another mind-boggling, open-palmed rap that caught Coltrane across the entirety of his forehead. Benny's empty noggin snapped backward like the popper on the end of a bullwhacker's favorite whip. Would've sworn I heard bones in the man's neck crack. Had he rolled onto the floor with a fistful of his neck bones reduced to powder and a snapped spinal column, scene wouldn't have surprised me one bit.

Dazed, the back-shooting slug's eyes rolled around in their sockets. For a second I thought he really might fall out of the chair. But in that single instant, I witnessed all the swaggering bluster and outlaw bravado drain from his face. Happened quicker than a hot iron can scorch a Baptist lady's favorite Sunday-go-to-meeting dress.

Got to say as how I never liked watching a man break. Even one of such reputed low-life orneriness as Benny Coltrane. Hard to work up much sympathy for the kind of murderous scum who'll slaughter women and children, but we needed what the stink-spraying polecat could tell us. And we needed it as quick as it could be obtained.

Felt then, and still feel to this very instant, that if slapping the dog stuffings out of skunk like Benny Coltrane could circumvent another heartless murder, then so be it. All you highfalutin pansies, pantywaists, and bleeding hearts who live your lives in a chicken coop and that don't agree with that blunt assessment had best hope no one ever murders your entire family—two of 'em with a double-bit ax.

When his head finally stopped wobbling on its long, thin, bony stalk, barely heard it when Coltrane mumbled, "All right, all right. What is it you mean-assed, badge-wearin' bastards want to know? Just ask. Swear 'fore Jesus, tell you whatever I can. Won't hold nothin' back. Got my word on it."

Grinning, Carl and Nate backed off a step or two, glanced over at me, then torqued their heads to one side like curious dogs. I took the obvious hint and said, "Where are your less than worthless brothers, Benny?"

Man looked up at me like he wanted to crawl off and die, but said, "Far as I know they're still down in Texas, Marshal Tilden." He shot Carlton a quick glance and added, "And that's the God's truth, so far as I know it. Swear on my mother's grave."

"Texas?"

"Yeah. Said they 'uz goin' to Fort Worth. Gonna spend some time in Hell's Half Acre 'fore they come back this direction. You know how it is. My brothers are the kind of fellers what like to drink, gamble, and whore around till they just wear themselves slap out. Six months from now they'll do it all over again. 'S all I know."

Leaned a bit closer. Tried to sound comforting when I said, "Where's the girl, Benny? Where's Daisy Cassidy?"

Coltrane did a corner of the eye check to make sure Carl wasn't about to slap the bejabbers out of him again. Then, snapped another worried gaze directly into mine. Man suddenly went to shaking as if suffering from malaria. After some effort, he regained control of himself and said, "Please don't let that little redheaded son of a bitch hit me again. Okay?"

"Have my word on it. Marshal Cecil won't hit you again."

Not sure he believed me, because he kept eyeballing Carl before saying anything. "Honest to God, my word of honor, I couldn't say, Marshal Tilden. Swear, I'm tellin' you the God's truth. Swear it. Just couldn't say. Don't have no ideas on the subject of Daisy Cassidy's whereabouts."

Nate pulled the makin's and started rolling a smoke. Said, "Way we heard the bloody tale, them brothers of yours took Miss Cassidy down to Hell's Half Acre and whored her out to anyone with enough money to pay for an evening's carnal entertainment. That true?"

Coltrane's gaze swiveled around the room, as though his head had somehow become detached from his neck. "Now that ain't true, by God. Jus' ain't true. Ain't nobody gonna make Daisy Cassidy do nothing she don't want to do. Gal looks like that 'un has a mind of her own. Does as she damn well pleases."

Three of us took a surprised half step backward at the exact same moment. Couldn't believe what we'd just heard. Benny Coltrane had unwittingly placed himself in Daisy Cassidy's company, at some point. Think we were all amazed at his astonishing inability to keep the information to himself. Tight mouthed up till that point, he'd inadvertently given away a piece of what might prove vital information.

I moved in real close to the man and placed a reassuring hand on his arm. "How do you know what Daisy Cassidy would or wouldn't do, Benny? Sounds to me like you two might've known each other a bit better than any of us realized."

Mask of twisted panic shot across Coltrane's unshaven face. "No. No. You musta misunderstood. Not me. 'S my brother. Jesse. The good-lookin' one. 'S how I know about Daisy. Honest. That's the God's truth. Hell, any gal as looks like Daisy ain't gonna have nothin' to do with a feller like me. But Jesse, now there's a different story altogether. He's always been able to keep company with them good-lookers, you know."

Carl made a springing leap toward Benny, kicked hell out of one the chair legs. Drew his hand back again, as though he was about to slap poor Benny's eyeballs right out of his head. "Quit mealy mouthin' around, you walkin' bag of manure. Get to it, or swear to bleedin' Jesus, I'm gonna knock you into next month."

Arms and hands covering his face, Benny dodged and weaved in the chair like a sitting boxer in the fight of his life. Once he realized the blow wouldn't fall, he peeked from between trembling fingers and said, "Went to the Cassidy place after we hit the Elk Horn Bank in Winslow."

Nate shook his head. "Why? Seems like a stupid move to slow your getaway after robbin' a bank. Hell, the Cassidy farm's just a bit more'n five miles from the scene of the robbery."

Benny's head bobbed up and down, as though he couldn't agree more. "Hell, I know that," he said. "But Jesse couldn't get within ten miles of that gal's scent without sneakin' by her daddy's farm. Tole us he wanted to stop by and pick the girl up for the trip to Texas."

Tapped him on the arm again to draw his attention my way. "You're telling us Jesse planned to take the girl with him to Fort Worth? That what you're saying?"

"Yeah. Yeah. But see, when we got to the farm her ole man said as how she warn't there. Not at home. Swear on my mother's sainted head. Soon's I heard that, I left Jesse and Leroy arguing with ole man Cassidy. Last I seen any of 'em, they 'uz all standin' in Cassidy's sorghum field yellin' at each other. Hell, I already had me a gal. Lives a few miles from Clifton. If'n I hadn't stopped for a drink with that buncha travelin' coyote spit peddlers, Marshal Reed never woulda cotched me the way he went and done."

"'S not what you told Marshal Reed," Carlton said. "Did some loose-mouthed bragging about your part in a triple murder."

Benny's face and neck turned red all the way up to his hair line. "Didn't know 'bout them killins till Marshal Reed confronted me with 'em. Just runnin' off at the mouth when I said I took part. Honest to God. Wasn't there when them folks got kilt. Swear it. Didn't even know they 'uz dead till Reed asked 'bout 'em. Had already left the scene. Didn't have nothin' to do with none of it."

"Truth is, we don't care, Benny," I said. "Just one more question for Judge Parker and the court to settle. But we do care about the girl. You should want us to find her. Gal ought to be able to confirm that you didn't take part in the killings."

Coltrane's bewilderment appeared to deepen. Drop of sweat the size of a nickel dripped from his nose.

Nate blew a stream of cigarette smoke at Benny, then asked, "Just how'n the hell did a dry-gulchin' brigand like Jesse meet a farm girl like Daisy Cassidy to begin with?"

Coltrane shook his head and looked miserable. "Not sure."

"That's just more bullshit, Benny," Carl growled. "Best come up with a better answer'n that one."

"Tellin' the truth, you mean-assed son of a bitch."

Carl made a menacing move Benny's direction, but I waved him off.

From behind lifted arms, Benny said, "God's truth. Just not sure. Maybe he met her in one of the mercantile stores in Winslow. He never said as how they'd met one way or the other. Hell, the man could walk away from a cold camp in the middle of Palo Duro Canyon at the darkest hour of the night and come back two hours later with a woman."

"Well, now, that's quite a skill to have," Nate said around the cigarette dangling from his lips.

Benny grinned as though happy that someone appeared to believe him. "'S the God's truth. Always had women around him, no matter what. Met Daisy 'bout a year ago, I guess. From then on, ever'time we went through Winslow, he'd make a point to creep by her daddy's farm. Cassidy gal was different from any a them others he usually hung around with."

Thumbs hooked over his pistol belt, Barnes Reed moved closer to the interrogation again. "How so?"

"Hell, I don't know. Gal just had the power to bollix him all up. Mention her name, Jesse just seemed to get so confused he didn't know whether to smile, spit, or swaller. Me'n Leroy made fun of him over it. Hell, Jesse'd force us to ride a hundred miles outta our way so he could tiptoe up to Daisy's bedroom winder at night. Spend a little time rolling 'tween her sheets."

"Jesse was gonna take her on the run with him?" I said. "That's your story?"

"Honest, Marshal Tilden, it's all I know. All I can tell you. We robbed the bank, hadn't got a mile outta Winslow when Jesse informed me'n Leroy that he was gonna stop at the Cassidy place for Daisy. Got there and the girl's old man claimed she warn't there. That's when I left."

"So, you were gone by the time the killin' started?" Barnes said.

Coltrane wagged his head back and forth like a tired dog. "Swear 'fore Jesus, gents, don't know nothin' 'bout them poor folks gettin' dead. Wouldn't surprise me if Jesse kilt the girl's pap, but I have a real problem believing he had anything to do with the woman and kids. Just ain't like Jesse a'tall. Swear on my mother's grave. Story just don't sound like Jesse."

"How about Leroy?" Carl said.

Coltrane looked confused. Rubbed his chin with the back of one hand. Scratched his head. Then, gradually, the confusion appeared to turn into misery. "Suppose he mighta done 'em. Leroy's not all there, you know. Got a bent rod in his thinker mechanism. Hell, he's the one what shot that drummer, then beat on him with the butt of a rifle till his head was nothin' but a wad of goo."

After a moment of uncomfortable silence fell over the room, I said, "Well, think we've got all we need." Glanced over at Barnes. "Might as well put him back in the cell, Marshal Reed."

Barnes grabbed Benny by the arm and lifted him out of the chair. Heard the cell door clang closed behind me as I headed for the hallway behind Carl and Nate.

Almost out of the office when Benny Coltrane called out, "Marshal Tilden. Marshal Tilden. Could I speak with you in private for a few seconds?"

Barnes pushed past me, as I turned back into Marshal Dell's private fiefdom and made my way to the lockup.

Fingers grasping the cell door bars, Benny peered into my eyes and said, "Swear it warn't me what kilt that drummer, Marshal Tilden. Three of us was just riding along and came up on him camped not far off the road. Leroy snatched his pistol out and blasted hell outta the man 'fore either of us could stop 'im. He's like that, you know. Then he beat the poor son of a bitch to pieces after shootin' 'im. Made me sick."

"Gonna be a hard sell in court, Benny. If nothing else, you were there when it happened, and never bothered to tell anyone about it till now."

Stared at his feet while he toed at the floor. Gripped and

regripped the cell door bars. "Yeah. Admit it don't look good. Worst of all though, know I went and shot off my braggin' mouth when I should've kept shut. But, honest to God, didn't have nothin' to do with them Cassidy murders neither. First I heard them folks was dead was when Marshal Reed started questionin' me 'bout 'em."

"Terrible mistake on your part, that's for certain."

"Truth is Marshal Tilden, I ain't never kilt nobody. Nobody. Just don't have the stomach for it. Not like Jesse and Leroy. Look, gotta admit, I've tried to help you as best I could. Told you everything I know. Be right grateful if you could put in a good word for me with Judge Parker."

Nodded, then said, "Not sure it'll help much, but I'll do what I can."

"Do appreciate it, sir. Sure wouldn't want to hang for three or four killings I didn't commit, you know."

"Well, Benny, might've been to your advantage if you had got away from your brothers. Wouldn't be in the fix you find yourself in right now."

"Yeah. Yeah. You're right. But, there's nothing as powerful as blood, Marshal Tilden. Hard to get away from blood. Nothing like it to bind you to other people."

Twirled on my heel, had the doorknob to the office in my hand when I heard Benny say, "Best take care around Leroy. Man's dangerous in the extreme. He'll kill a feller in a heartbeat. Laugh while he's killin' a man who's carrin' a reputation like yours."

8

"... This Here's a Robbery. Best Go To Gettin' Your Money Out ..."

NEVER HAVE BEEN one of those folks who subscribed to the idiotic notion that "everything kind of happens for a reason." Near as I've been able to tell—good, bad, or indifferent—life just comes to pass. Seems to me as though day-to-day events often have a tendency to simply lie in wait for our unknowing, blind arrival, ready to pounce on us like wild, stalking animals.

At times it's almost as if God himself hides in an alleyway like any common highwayman, ax handle in hand, waiting for us to come along so he can jump out and knock the bejabbers out of us. Nothing we can do about any of it, except try like blue-eyed hell to survive whatever He throws our direction. Am convinced that what happened on the way to Fort Worth is illustrative of that philosophical conviction.

Spent the rest of the day, after we'd had our little heart-to-heart with Benny Coltrane, getting ourselves packed, primed, and ready for the trip to Texas. Kissed Elizabeth good-bye early the next morning. Could tell the girl was none too happy about me leaving on another raid south before she had adjudged my recovery as complete and worthy of her approval. But, as had been true in many a case in the past, she accepted the inevitable, albeit with a forced smile and creased forehead. Held me close and whispered undying love into my ear before we parted. Was a difficult leave-taking and weighed heavily on my thoughts and heart for days afterward.

Couldn't have picked a better morning to begin our journey. Sun came up behind cotton boll clouds like a polished, solid-gold coin. Met Carlton and Nate down by the river not far from the courthouse. Ferried our animals across, then took a leisurely ride over to the Katy line's depot in Checotah.

Carl didn't complain, but I could tell that his sore rump still bothered him a mite more than he would have liked. Being as how all three of us nursed wounds of various sorts, the man wouldn't have grumbled about his situation no matter how irritating or miserable his circumstance.

Arrived in Checotah little before noon that day. Thick bank of greenish-black clouds had come in from the west, by then. Loaded our animals and gear onto a freight car attached to the M.K. & T.'s Flyer, headed for Fort Worth.

Only other passengers I took note of when we boarded were a couple of young Indian fellers dressed in suit coats, white shirts, and flat-brimmed black hats. They had seats on either side of the center aisle near the day coach's back door. Two or three white chaps, who looked like drummers of some sort, sat scattered about here and there.

An Indian girl who appeared to be traveling alone didn't look up when we passed. Couldn't see anything but the back of her head as I walked by. There was also an elderly gentleman, who had an enormous, bright orange pumpkin on the seat between him and his traveling companion—a round-faced, big-eyed boy of about ten years. They occupied seats a little over midway down the aisle toward the rear of the coach.

Carl and I took vacant spots not far from the old man and boy. Sat side by side. Carl brought that gold-fringed silk pillow for his still-aching behind. Couldn't say as I blamed him much. Always felt those damned coach benches back then had been specifically designed by Satan's most malevolent, red-eyed imps especially to torment the unwary traveler. Being as how we'd just spent half a day in the saddle, those harder-than-frozen-turtle-shell seats didn't help my sore-tailed amigo's tender condition at all. Grimaced as he settled into his fluffed-up nest, but didn't say anything.

Seats in the Katy line's passenger cars back then were arranged in pairs, facing each other. So, Nate took the spot across from us next to the sizable pile of our stacked goods. Mountain of traveling necessities consisted of saddlebags, rain slickers, shotguns, rifles, ammunition, and foodstuffs. 'Course, there might've been a bottle, or two, of bonded-in-the-barn jig juice in there, somewhere, as well.

Our collective skinny behinds had barely hit those uncomfortable, badly upholstered, torturous, coach benches when the M.K. & T.'s massive, thirty-five-ton, eight-wheeled Baldwin Mogul locomotive vented a torrential cloud of white steam that wafted past our window. Great iron beast thundered to life, shook heaven and earth, and gradually began creeping away from the Checotah depot.

Passenger coach, four other cars carrying freight, and the caboose, snapped against their couplings in a series of thumping, metallic cracks. Whole shebang trailed along like individual links in a slow-moving, snakelike chain being dragged south by a rumbling, monstrous, man-made demon that belched endless plumes of roiling black smoke from its gigantic stack.

For reasons I never understood, trains, moving or not, always had a decidedly narcotic effect on Carlton J. Cecil. Soon as the man took a seat and propped his head against the window, he invariably fell into a deep, childlike sleep. No point trying to carry on a conversation with him five minutes after leaving any depot in the continental United States.

Given a decided lack of conscious company, I was about to prop my feet on our pile of goods and take a nap myself. Glanced over and noticed that Nate's misty-eyed gaze was locked on something over my shoulder. Swear 'fore Jesus, the man had that *instantaneously infatuated* look plastered on his face, typical of someone who's just seen a beautiful woman and can't take his eyes off her. Twisted around at the waist in an effort to get a gander at what had so galvanized his undivided, slack-jawed attention. Lord God, but I didn't have to look far.

In the seat behind us, that Indian gal we'd walked past turned out to be one of the most beautiful people I'd ever laid eyes on. Enormous, soft brown eyes gifted with an open, friendly gaze that came from a flawless, tawny, full-lipped face. Her stunning countenance was framed by shimmering, ebon-colored hair that cascaded onto girlish shoulders and ran down her back in a river of gleaming black.

She sported fancy ear-drop decorations comprised of a trio of multicolored, dangling discs that matched an elaborate, woven, or perhaps crocheted, necklace of red, white, yellow, and dark blue. Broad as a man's hand, her intricate choker served to enhance a flowing turquoise dress trimmed in brilliant white embroidered stitching. A belt, that matched the necklace with precise exactness, encircled a waist so slight a grown man could have easily encircled it with his hands.

Appearing unspoiled by a world she likely knew little of, the fantastically beautiful girl sat alone, slim-fingered hands primly crossed in her lap. A mysterious and enigmatic smile danced across youthful, naturally ruby-colored lips. The entire glorious package easily proved more than enough to command the attention of any male not headed for direct and immediate burial.

Glanced back at Nate. Grinned and said, "She's a beauty, all right. Perhaps the most beautiful thing I've seen since the day I met Elizabeth when I first arrived in Fort Smith. Somewhat surprising, though, that she appears to be traveling alone. Would've thought an Injun gal of such rare beauty would be accompanied by a chaperon of some sort—friend or relative. Someone to protect and see after her well-being, you know." And then, more to myself more than anyone else, added, "Given the state of outlawry 'round these parts, no girl as looks like that should be traveling the Nations all by her lonesome."

Swords, who looked like he'd just homesteaded a big, puffy, white cloud, flushed, squirmed in his seat, picked at lint on his pants, then went to eyeballing his feet. "Yeah. She's right pretty, and that's a pure fact. Can't say as how I've ever seen anything to match her. Got any idea what tribe she's from, Hayden? Can you determine anything from her outfit?"

"Choctaw, near as I can tell. But don't take my word on it. Not much of an expert on the subject, to be absolutely truthful." Jerked a thumb Carl's direction. "Our resident authority and trail mate's asleep. Probably won't wake up till the train stops moving. And maybe not even then."

Swords shot another fleeting, nervous glance at the girl, fidgeted, then went to staring at his toes again. "She sure is somethin', Tilden. Sure is somethin'. Don't think I've ever seen anything quite like her."

"Gal's done got you repeating yourself, Nate." Leaned over and whispered, "Why don't you stroll on over? See if you can engage that pretty little thing in a bit of friendly conversation. No parents to cramp your style as I can see. Bet she'll enjoy the company of a handsome young feller like you."

Nate appeared surprised and slightly embarrased by my suggestion. "Think she'd talk to me?"

"Well, you sure as the dickens won't find out sitting here with a couple of old married farts like me and Carl. Got a long trip ahead of us, son. Nigh on ten hours, or so. If I were you, and had any interest at all in that sweet young thing, I'd be back there in a hummingbird's heartbeat. Hell of a lot better than sitting back here telling lies about how you're gonna grill up a batch of raccoons for me."

He grinned, rifled a narrowed gaze around me again. Got a sudden and resolute look about him. Pulled at the brim of his hat, then stood. "Wish me luck," he said and stepped into the aisle.

Heard them exchanging pleasantries a few seconds later. Couldn't tell exactly what was said, though. Just know he didn't come back, and after a couple of minutes, I snuck a glance to see that he'd taken a seat with his back to me, and that the beautiful girl was smiling.

Must've dozed off myself. Woke to find that we were no longer moving. Figured we couldn't have gone all that far. Peered out the window. Looked as though the train had pulled onto the Nickel Creek siding a bit south of McAlester. Reckoned as how a northbound would come flying past just about anytime. Stood, stretched my back a bit, then dropped into the seat Nate had vacated.

Looked up and noticed that the Choctaw girl's smile had turned into flirtatious laughter. Felt pretty sure if she had batted those eyes at me the way she batted them at Nate, would've had the exact same effect that it appeared to be having on him.

Pushed back into the seat, went to pull my hat down over my eyes. Up front, train car door popped open and slammed hard against the wall. Couple of young Indian types, who looked like the twins of those sitting at the back of the coach a few seats behind me and Carlton, entered with a cocked pistol in each hand.

Didn't really register at the time, but the leader of those gunnies had a scarlet-colored sash tied around his skinny waist. Should've recognized Buford Cougar as soon as he stepped through the door, but didn't.

Looking back on that day's surprising and deadly events, from the vantage point of full knowledge, still can't, to this minute, believe I'd grown so unawares and dull witted in the short time Carlton, Nate, and I'd spent sitting on my veranda playing checkers and nursing our individual hurts. But hell, that's exactly what you can expect from inactivity and enforced relaxation.

Saw Nate swing his attention the grinning gunmen's direction. Watched, from the corner of my eye, as he stiffened and pushed himself hard against the seat back. Way I had it figured, Nate saw the exact same things I did and at about the same instant. Behind the brace of cocked pistols those Indian fellers carried stood men whose eyes were flat, dead, emotionless, and downright frightening.

With as little in the way of movement as I could pull off, kicked the bejabbers out of Carl's closest foot. His eyes popped open like a set of paper window shades in a parlor house bedroom.

"Wha . . . what, what the hell's goin' on?" he growled. "Why'd you go a-kickin' on me like that, Tilden? Dreamin' 'bout the first time I seen Judith. Remember. She 'uz nekkid, bathin' herself in . . ."

Shushed him into silence about the time the boys at the back of the car, who'd started out riding with us, hopped up with pistols in their hands, too. At almost the exact same instant, one of the pair up front, feller wearing the red sash called out, loud enough to be heard from one end of the car to the other, "All you white devils shoulda done figured it out by now. This here's a robbery. Best go to gettin' your money out and handin' it over." Boy had a kind of strange, spine-chilling smile on his face when he made his announcement. That's when it finally came to me who he was.

Carlton socked his hat down, then blinked a couple of times to clear his head. Even though all he could see was the pair of gunnies behind me, he took in the whole state of affairs in a matter of a few eye-blinking seconds, then whispered, "Well, this here situation goes way beyond stupid, Tilden. These silly bastards don't have any idea what they've gotten themselves into."

"Easy," I hissed. "Don't have the slightest doubt we can take 'em, Carl. But let's just be careful how we go about it. Don't want any of the other passengers to get hurt, if we can keep such a sorry instance from happening."

Threw a quick glance at Nate. Man had leaned toward the panic-stricken girl. Held one of her hands in his. Figured as how he already had the fingers of his free hand wrapped around the walnut grip of the Colt lying across his belly. Crouched and tense as a freshly tightened banjo string, he appeared more than ready for a blistering fight. But the handsome young woman's presence had placed him in a rather dangerous and precarious position, one that made me uncomfortable for the safety of both of them.

From the corner of my mouth, I whispered, "Gonna stand and try to toddle across the aisle, Carl. See if I can draw their attention my way, maybe slow 'em down a mite. Stay focused. When I make my move, you take the two in back. Do not hesitate. I'll go for the leader and his idiot partner."

Carl flashed a death-dealing grin. Hissed, "Them two snaky bastards in back're already dead where they stand. Just don't know it yet."

Brought my hands up as though surrendering to the circumstances. Stood, then edged sidewise into the aisle. Thought for sure everything was going right well, till the feller with the sash fired a shot into the seat back right in front of me. Big gob of dust, rendered wood splinters, leather seat covering, and horsehair padding flew into the air, then rained down on everything within three feet of where I drew to a quick, unflinching stop.

Thunderous, ear splitter of a pistol shot inside the confines of that coach came nigh on to being deafening. Totally unnecessary bit of gun work scared the bejabberous hell out of that poor girl. She let out a stunned screech that sounded like a shoat caught under a wooden gate. The mind-numbing thought suddenly flashed across my mind that the crazy bastards who'd just stormed into our midst might well kill us all.

9

"Gonna Have To Get in Line fer Some a That Gal, Buster."

TRUTH BE TOLD, there's just nothing like getting shot at, from incredibly close range, to bring a man's jumbled, fast-moving thoughts into absolutely clear focus. Your senses instantaneously sharpen to the point where your entire body turns into nothing more than a set of oversensitive, raw nerve ends that ache for immediate release. The air, all around you, becomes crystalline, as clear as a tub of fresh-fallen rainwater. Atmosphere crackles with electricity, as though triple-tined pitchfork lightning just fell somewhere nearby. You can hear sounds normally reserved for dogs and certain breeds of south Texas fruit bat. Itching fingertips tingle for the feel of iron, heat, and gunpowder. Prospect of sudden death becomes so real, so tangible, you can taste the imminent arrival of spilled blood at the back of your throat.

Only hesitated for maybe half a second after that first pistol shot. Then, just continued my move away from Carl, until I could stand between the seats across the aisle.

In a flat, near lifeless tone, the sash-wearing bandit waved his still-smoking pistol at me. Almost jokingly, he said, "Tell you what, mister, you just go on ahead and take one more step. Guarantee it'll be your last one amongst the living. Once we're gone, your friend there'll be buryin' you outside next to the tracks."

Palms turned up, empty hands still reaching for heaven, I smiled. "Oh, I believe you, Coog, every word. Wouldn't trifle with a man of your iniquitous reputation."

Bandit rocked back on his heels, flashed me a big toothy grin. "Well, well, well. Ain't this somethin'. 'Pears as how you've heard of me. That right, mister?"

Always fascinated me that a universal trait of many bad men seemed to be the necessity to be "known." "Oh, yeah," I said. "Heard plenty about the Buford Cougar gang. Most of it from newspaper articles over the past month or so. Figure as how just about everybody in Fort Smith and the entire Nations has heard of you boys by now."

Buford Cougar's smile grew till it almost took over his entire face. He torqued his head to one side. Cast a quick, knowing glance at the man next to him, then refocused on me again. "Here that, Buster. We're famous. This here pilgrim's done heard 'bout the Buford Cougar gang. Bet he even knows the names of all you other boys as well. Prolly read about us in that *Fort Smith Elevator* story 'peared in last week's issue, I'd wager."

Nodded and tried to sound friendly, when I said, "Did indeed. Yes, sir, that's the pure fact of the matter. Scarifying article mentioned as how you fellers appeared to have sprung up out of nowhere like mushrooms after a heavy dew, or maybe the ghosts of walking death. Why, as I understand it, in a matter of weeks you've paved the way to the most violent crime spree since Judge Parker took his seat in the Western District Court of Arkansas. Made quite a reputation for you and your friends a very short time."

Sounded good bit more than a mite smug when the guy standing beside Cougar, one he'd called Buster, giggled, shot Cougar a knowing, sneering glance, then said, "Well, now, should be pretty plain as how we do work harder'n most, when it comes to our chosen profession of rapin', robbin', and killin'.'"

Had them puffed up with their own self-importance. Decided to keep it up. "You boys started off over in the Sans Bois Mountains near the little town of Jasper, as I recall. Brutally assaulted a widder lady name of Harris. Story goes as how you boys caught her moving some furniture between one home and another. Shot her twelve-year-old son to death right in front of her, when he tried to protect his mother. Then took turns going at the poor woman. Story goes, she could barely walk when you finally got done. Impressive beginning."

Buster, threw his head back, cackled like a madman, then said, "Ass-aulted. Good word fer what we done, all right. Boy hidie, 'at ole gal 'uz a sure 'nuff a fun time, tell you fer true, mister."

"That a fact?"

"Hell, yeah. By God, she fought like a wildcat. I 'uz fourth in line, but it 'uz still some of the best stuff I done ever had. Wish she 'uz here right now. Take fourth place just so I could do her again, by God."

Had to grit my teeth, but went on trying to lull them into doing something stupid, or losing their concentration, if for only a fraction of a second. "Reports from witnesses are that two days later you boys broke in on a farmer from over near Bee Hive Creek. Forced his wife to cook a big meal for you. Heard five of you ate three dozen eggs, whole slab of bacon, and twenty biscuits. Drank a gallon of milk."

Buster smiled. "Yep. 'S true all right. Yep."

"Then, each and every one of you took turns assaulting the kindhearted woman what cooked all that stuff for you. Made her agitated husband watch the entire dance. Then, just for the hell of it, you went and killed the dickens out of him. Story I read said as how one of you hit that poor man in the head with a hatchet."

Didn't bother to turn around and look when one of the guys behind me chuckled, then said, "That'd be me, by God. Splattered his worthless brains all over hell and yonder. Made that goddamned slut a his mop all them brains up 'fore we

left. But that was after we all went and took another run at
'er." Men were so full of themselves they just couldn't pass
up the chance to brag.

Heard a muffled, groaning grunt come from Carlton's direction. Knew beyond any shadow of doubt that if I didn't get
a clumsy rise out of them boys soon he'd take the situation
into his own hands. "Day or two later, you met a feller over
near Chokecherry Hill. Stole his horse, fifty dollars, and a
gold watch."

Buster sounded right smug, near high and mighty, when
he said, "Yeah, but we didn't kill 'im."

Nodded my agreement, but added, "Well, that's true
enough, Buster. But, way I heard the story, you boys stood
around and debated for almost two hours about whether or
not you *should* kill 'im. Even took a vote on the question.
Leastways according to the *Fort Smith Elevator*'s detailed
chronicle of all your dastardly deeds."

Different voice behind me called out, "Yeah. Come up
three to two in favor of lettin' him live a bit longer. Personally, I wanted to kill 'im right then and there. Wouldn't be
talking 'bout the son of a bitch now if'n we'd a done what I
wanted."

Cougar shot a wicked glance over my shoulder and yelped,
"Well, you're an idiot, Bartholomew."

Bartholomew didn't take well to being called an idiot.
Voice from the back of the car came up in volume and tone
by several notches, when he called out, "Might be the self-
professed leader of this gang, Buford, but you ain't the Lord
God Almighty, by God."

Sounded to me like cracks had begun to form in their
armor. Figured to keep them going when I said, "Not long
after that, you boys murdered hell out of a stock trader down
on the Muddy Boggy. Gent named Callaghan, as I recall."

Cougar's right-hand man went to laughing again. Ole
Buster brought one foot up, then stomped back down. "Wearing that rich bastard's boots. Hand tooled in Fort Worth by-
God Texas. These here shit kickers musta cost that dumb son
of a bitch three hundred dollars, if'n they cost him a red cent.

'Course, he ain't got much use fer 'em now. Given as how I blew all the brains out'n his stupid head."

Held the most obvious back till last, when I said, "And, so far, you've robbed half a dozen of the Katy line's trains. Got a sizable sum of money posted on your heads as a consequence."

Buford Cougar waved his crew into silence. "Actually this 'un here is our ninth. Near as we've been able to tell, damned railroaders are so stupid they can't even keep track of who's robbin' 'em or how many times we do it."

Not to be left out, Carlton snarled, "Oh, I'm sure M.K. and T. management will know all about what you boys did here today."

Cougar looked so proud he could've licked himself all over. "Good. Damned good. See, we're a bad bunch, mister. Time we're finished, this here gang of mine's gonna be the most famous crew of robbers and killers ever done come outta the Nations. Have our names in newspapers all over the country. Even places like San Fran-by-God-cisco. Not just that pissant rag in Fort Smith."

"Seems to me you boys are studying for a hanging, Cougar. Sure that's what you want?" I said.

"Hell, yes. Wasn't nothin' till we started robbin' and killin' folks. Now, names of Buford Cougar, Buster Lucky, Bartholomew January, Samuel Boston, and Edgar Sampson gonna be spoken in whispers by scared kids and terrified parents. We're gonna be feared and respected from the Verdigris River in the north, all the way to the Red in the south. But right now, we've got a train to rob."

Cougar's helpmate flashed a snaggle-toothed, twisted grin, shoved one pistol behind a broad, silver-buckled, leather belt, then strolled up beside the Indian girl. He slipped several fingers into her hair. Held it up as though looking at a vein of hand-spun, Black Hills gold. Glanced back at his boss. "Why don't we do fer this here gal first, Buford. Damn, but she's a looker. Won't even mind goin' fourth agin fer a piece a this stuff. Hell, I'll even go fifth. Dip my wick in her fine-lookin' gloriosity any ole time, any ole way."

Barely heard him when Nate growled, "Touch her again, you ugly stack of walking horse manure, and it'll be the last thing you ever do."

Buster's pistol barrel caught Nate a glancing blow across the cheek. Rocked my friend's head sideways. His hat flipped into the aisle. Hit the floor and twirled around like a kid's top. Surprised me the blow didn't knock him cockeyed and unconscious.

Buster grabbed the girl by the arm, then glared at Nate. "Maybe I'll let you watch while I do 'er, you smart-mouthed son of a bitch. Cheerin' audiences don't bother me none. Hell, more the merrier's what I always says."

"Let it go, Buster," Cougar yelled. "We've got way more important fish to fry right now."

Nate's cheek leaked blood when he snatched the girl back into her seat, then came up with an open-palmed, roundhouse right that damn near knocked Buster Lucky's eyes clean out of his head. Stunned gunman spun around, ricocheted off a couple of empty seats, then bounced against the front wall of the car.

Crazy son of a bitch regained his footing, stormed back over to the girl, and grabbed her by the arm again. "I want some of this woman, Coog," Buster yelped. Then, he leaned over Nate. Shoved the muzzle of his pistol barrel into Nate's ear. "And when I'm finished with her, wanna kill the hell outta this here bastard."

One of the bandits behind me took considerable pressure off Nate when he called out, "Gonna have to get in line fer some a that gal, Buster. Figure all a us'll have a bit 'fore you get any. 'Sides, if'n I 'uz her, or any other woman for that matter, wouldn't want you gettin' anywheres close to me with that ugly little thang of yours."

Buster Lucky cast a wild-eyed glare toward his cohorts at the back of the car. Thin, cruel lips twitched and slobbers dripped from his quaking chin when he said, "Maybe I won't be the last 'un this time, Sam. Just maybe not this time, by God. I found 'er. Pretty good chance I'll be first today. Maybe I'll kill everbody here, do as I goddamned well please. Sendin' all you bastards to Jesus ain't no problem fer a man as bad as me."

Tension level shot through the roof. Knew I had to do something before the killing got started. Anything. And damned quick.

10

"No Way You Could Have Foreseen Something Like This."

OF A SUDDEN everything got numbingly quiet. Seemed as though I could hear the hair in my ears growing. No doubt in my mind, none at all. Bony-fingered Death had stepped onto the M.K. & T. Flyer's day coach. Old soul stealer had his blood-smeared sickle sharpened up and ready for use.

Buford Cougar appeared amused by Buster Lucky's discomfort, threats, and the whole tension-filled situation in general. Smiled like an asylum-dwelling loon when he said, "No time for women today, boys. Even for one as good-lookin' as this 'un. Need money a helluva lot more'n we need a female, willing or otherwise. Get our hands on enough money, we can buy all the women we want. Find a willing one anywhere in the Nations we wanna stop long enough to look."

Nate twisted around in his seat. Threw me a pained, wordless glance. Man might as well have screamed, "What the hell we gonna do, Tilden? Gotta stop this madness before it turns on the girl."

'Bout then, a northbound M.K. & T. freight clattered past on the main track not ten feet away from our spot on the siding. Unthinking, Cougar and his toady recklessly took a quick look out the window at the passing train at almost the exact same instant. Their carelessness proved exactly the opportunity I'd waited for.

Had my belly gun out and up before either one of them even knew what hit him. Crushing first shot caught Cougar in the throat, just above the notch in his breastbone. Bullet bored through his voice box, blew it to smithereens. Sawed its way through muscle and sinew, then exited in a clump of gore that spattered the wall at his back like a bucket of leavings from a slaughtered steer. He gagged, stumbled, dropped one pistol, then went to grabbing at the geyser of blood that spurted from the thumb-sized hole in his neck.

Quicker than double-geared lightning, Nate slipped his weapon and hammered Cougar back against the coach's door with twin blasts that caught the murderous outlaw dead center. Pair of two-hundred-fifty-five-grain slugs crushed the gang leader's breastbone as surely as if a draft horse had knocked the man down on a cobblestoned street, stepped on him, then pulled a beer wagon over his still-flopping corpse.

Half a heartbeat after Nate fired, my second blue whistler smacked Buster Lucky in the left ear. Happened before he even had a chance to turn away from watching the M.K. & T. rattler fly by outside. Pea-brained idiot still grinned at all the smoke and noise when a good portion of his rat-sized brain and a scarlet cloud of blood as big as my doubled-up fist decorated all the seats and windows around him.

Evil bastard didn't even twitch when he went to the aisle's wooden floor like a sack of rusted horseshoe nails. Figured him for deader than a pile of well-aged buzzard feed. Made no difference to Nate Swords. Boy stood, took aim, and put three more in ole Buster's sorry hide.

Though injured to the point of being little more than a dead man walking, Buford Cougar managed, somehow, to keep himself erect. He stumbled backward and thumbed off at least three wild, aimless shots before he sagged against the passenger car's front door, then slid to the floor in a blood-soaked heap. Rolled onto his stomach and made more choking, gurgling, frothy sounds, until he finally bled out and passed on to his ultimate reward.

While I was preoccupied with the back-shooting killers up front, Carlton jerked both his pistols and sent a blistering, double-handed wave of hot lead at the pair behind me. Couldn't take the time to count, but between what he put in the air, and what Cougar's other two underlings managed to get off as they fell dying, must've amounted to near a dozen shots. When the blasting came to an end, my ears rang like Mexican cathedral bells. Back of my throat ached with the coppery taste of too much blood and quick death.

To this day, swear I don't think any of Buford Cougar's boys could shoot for spit. If a single one of that bunch could have, on purpose, hit his own ass with a set of moose antlers and ten free jabs, I'd of been rudely surprised. Still and all, it bordered on a godsent miracle none of them had managed to hit me, given as how I was the only person, other than the train robbers, who was standing. Made a hell of an easy target, but didn't get a single scratch. Unfortunately, that beautiful Indian gal wasn't near so lucky.

By the time everything finally quieted down, so much spent powder still hung in the air a body couldn't see worth a damn. Didn't realize we even had a problem. At first, thought for sure the whole violent dance had shaken out just as fine as frog hair, and that everyone, except members of the vicious Cougar gang, had survived in fine shape.

Then, through the gradually thinning cloud of roiling, grayish-black gun smoke, spotted some of the other passengers as they began to nerve up and move about. Everyone who could walk hit his feet and headed for the nearest door. Sounded like a herd of stampeded cattle as they bolted for safety.

Amidst all the yelling and door slamming, heard Nate Swords moan, then say, "Oh, sweet merciful Jesus. No. Not this. Please. Not this."

Holstered my pistol. Over one shoulder called out, "Carl,

mine are either down or dead. Check on those two in back. Make sure they're incapacitated or finished as well." Didn't wait for an answer. Knew he'd do what I said.

Made my way into the aisle and found Nate down on both knees like a man beseeching God for eternal forgiveness at a traveling prayer meeting. Had his hat clutched against his chest with one hand. Kept running the fingers of the other hand through sweat-drenched hair. Groaned like he was badly wounded or dying. Thought sure he'd taken a bullet someplace important.

Was so concerned, I laid a hand on his shoulder. "Show me where you're hit, Nate."

He didn't look at me, just shook his head. Thought the man would weep when he mumbled, "Ain't me, Tilden. It ain't me that's been shot." He moved to one side and slid into a kind of awkward, half-sitting, half-squatting position up against the end of one of the day coach's seats. Left plenty of room for a look at the horror his crouching figure had hidden.

On the floor, between the seats he and the girl occupied but a few seconds earlier, twisted, as though somehow broken at the waist, that stunningly attractive Indian child lay motionless, misshapen, doll-like. Glazed and unblinking, her doe's eyes stared, without seeing, at the train car's bullet-riddled ceiling. A single tear traced a delicate, sparkling line from one fawnlike orb to a damp, red-besmeared ear. Drenched in fresh blood, the entire front of her glorious turquoise-and-white dress clung to a lifeless body as though plastered there like a layer of gore-drenched newspaper.

Scrambled down. Rolled the child flat onto her back. Placed a shaky finger under an already cold jaw. No pulse at all. Nothing. Spark of life had been rudely snuffed out. Lifted the girl up and took a quick look at her back. Bullet appeared to have hit her at a slight downward angle. Most likely fired by Buford Cougar, at a range of no more than ten feet, the .45-caliber pistol slug had punched thorough the flimsy seat back, bored a deadly path through her childlike body, crushed bone, sliced through muscle and nerves, then exited by way of a considerable, gaping hole in an unmoving chest.

Gently laid her back down. Closed those beautiful brown eyes with my fingertips, then glanced over at Nate. What I saw on that boy's face came nigh on to breaking my heart. If all the tortured souls of those condemned to the lowest levels of Satan's playground could have walked down that rail car's center aisle, not a single face of those tormented beings would have matched the pain etched across that boy's sad countenance.

Seemingly bereft of hope, he beat at one leg with his hat. Turned away from me and stared at the floor. "Just can't believe it, Tilden. Simply beyond all understanding. Few minutes ago she was beautiful, vibrant, sittin' here talking with me. Few seconds ago she looked into my eyes as though pleading for me to take care of her. And I told her I would. Said I'd protect her from any harm."

Rested a reassuring hand on the boy's shoulder just as Carl eased up beside the two of us. Know for a fact that it didn't help much, but I said, "What happened here today's not your fault. Did all a man could be expected to do, Nate. No way to avoid this one. Given the Cougar gang's reputation, if we had let this lunacy go any farther, she might well have suffered at the hands of these bastards in ways none of us can even begin to imagine. If Buster Lucky'd had his way, well, I personally don't even want to think about it."

Nate squeezed out a single enormous tear. Wiped it away with the back of one bloody hand. Said, "Her name was Little Cloud. Rachael Little Cloud. Soon's she told me that I thought, my, oh, my, her name's as beautiful as she is. And now, God Almighty, sweet God Almighty."

Carl tapped me on the shoulder with his still-smoking pistol barrel. "Boy's bleedin', Hayden. Look."

Reached down and pulled at Nate's vest. Words just kind of slipped out. Couldn't stop 'em. "Good God," I said. "Thought you told me you weren't hit. How bad are you hurt, son?"

Swords pushed up, propped himself against the seat at his back. We both plucked at a blood-soaked shirttail. He pulled the garment aside and fingered a dark, deep, ugly gash across the ribs on his right side.

"Bullet that killed Little Cloud must've scorched me a mite. Sweet Jesus, Tilden, swear I didn't even feel it." He ran a finger that shook along the dripping, angled slit that sliced across the bones of his rib cage. "Still don't feel it. Nothin' but a scratch, though. Been hurt worse more times than I can remember."

Must admit as how the rest of that afternoon is still something of a hazy blur in my cankered memory. Tend to bring those events to mind in bits and pieces. Do recollect that the train hadn't been back on the main track again and rolling for very long when it slowed, pulled over, and made its regular stop in Atoka.

'Course the conductor, wiry scamp named Henry Bankhead, hopped off and went to running up and down the depot platform screaming at the top of his lungs about robbers, killers, death, and mayhem. Red-faced and nigh on apoplectic, he dragged the stunned station master over just as we were laying Little Cloud atop a baggage cart we found sitting just a few feet outside the depot's busy waiting room.

Dancing like a frog in a hot skillet, Bankhead hopped from foot to foot and said, "This here is Amos Studdard, station master, telegraph operator, and chief agent here at Atoka, Marshal Tilden."

Nate, Carl, and I removed our hats and backed away from Little Cloud's limp body.

Studdard stumbled as he came up beside the girl's pitiful corpse. Snatched his leather visor off. Went to trembling all over like a man in the throes of some horrible affliction. Then, swear 'fore Jesus, he covered his face with both hands and wept like a baby. Conductor kept patting his friend on the shoulder, but Studdard appeared past consoling. Took near five minutes for the poor feller to get control of himself again.

Twisted his visor between trembling fingers, cast a swollen-eyed gaze at me, and said, "This girl, Rachael Little Cloud, was a Choctaw princess, Marshal. Most beautiful Indian gal as I've ever seen. Beloved by all her people. Her father's Chief Jacob Black Horse."

Tried to explain what had transpired, but I don't think, to this very day, Studdard heard much, if any, of what I said. He kept staring down at Little Cloud, mumbling to himself, moaning and twisting at that visor.

Soon as I finished up with the sad tale of Little Cloud's unfortunate demise, a blank-faced Amos Studdard flicked a slack-jawed stare from the dead girl's face to me and said, "Love of God, she's just turned eighteen. Sweet. Smart. Beautiful. Really independent for a Choctaw girl, though. Her family didn't want her traveling alone, you know. But she had close friends up in Vinita. I made personal assurances to Black Horse and her mother that the trip would be easy as pie, and she'd be fine."

Barely heard him when Carl offered, "No way you could have foreseen something like this."

Studdard grimaced like someone invisible had slapped him across the face. "Damn well gave my personal guarantee of the girl's safety. Sweet Jesus, I told those folks she'd be as safe as a newborn babe while traveling on one of our trains. Assured those wonderful people they had nothing to concern themselves about. No need for a chaperon. God Almighty, what am I gonna tell 'em now?"

Distressed station agent eventually did buck up and take charge of the situation. As if by magic, he suddenly grew steel in his spine. Started giving directions and orders like a battlefield general. Arranged for Nate to get patched up. Even assumed the responsibility of taking care of Little Cloud's body for us. Mighty sad bunch that carried the poor girl's shattered corpse inside the depot that day.

We cleaned the child up, as best we could. Wrapped her in a spotless sheet. Not sure to this very moment where that sheet came from. Laid her out atop the mahogany desk in Studdard's office. Somebody placed a bunch of the most beautiful yellow flowers I'd ever seen on her chest. Flowers just seemed to appear out of nowhere.

Remember Nate stood next to the body, holding his hat in his hands. Devastated man couldn't do much but shake his head. But I did hear him when he said, "My, oh, my, but she was a beauty, Tilden. Sweet natured, too. Told me about her family. Smart as whip. Fine company. Wish we could've had more time together. Hell, wish we'd . . . Oh, well, Lord God, but I do wish it."

Being as how Nate's mind was somewhere else, me and Carl made all the arrangements for Buford Cougar and his bunch of lethal varmints. Number of the Choctaw Light Horse showed up within a matter of minutes of the train coming to a stop. They were most cooperative in helping us out.

Discovered that the three men who'd died with Cougar were for certain sure none other than Buster Lucky, Bartholomew January, and Samuel Boston. Given their recent outlaw history, considerable rewards existed for those boys. Time we totaled it all up, amounted to almost six thousand dollars. Get to killing, robbing, and raping people, the value of even the most worthless among us tends to go up.

Conductor Bankhead stepped forward and offered as how, during the attempted robbery, he'd seen a feller standing near the caboose holding the reins on five horses. I figured Edgar Sampson must've bolted soon as the serious shooting started. Given the passage of a few days, Carl and I both felt sure he would disappear into the unassigned territories never to be seen again.

Sent a short telegram to Mr. Wilton. Explained that we'd been unavoidably delayed. Said we'd lay over till the girl's family came in to claim her body—which Amos Studdard made arrangement to have placed in a local ice house.

Nate wanted to stick around Atoka and attend whatever went for a final service for Little Cloud. But after a day and a half of idle time in that train depot, with nothing to do but wear out a checkerboard, walk the floor, or play cards, Carlton was about ready to bite the head off a hammer. Unfortunately, Little Cloud's kin never showed. Studdard pulled me aside and ventured the guess that the girl was unexpected, and that her family might take as much as a week to locate. Took some serious talking, but we finally persuaded Nate that we needed to be on our way—get on down to Fort Worth.

Have not the slightest clue how he managed the feat, but before we got headed out again Amos Studdard put every M.K. & T. employee in Atoka to work cleaning up the mess in that shot-to-pieces passenger car. Arranged to have it parked on a siding and had everything except a bullet hole here and there repaired in right short order. Got it added onto a southbound rattler a little after noon a day and a half after we first arrived.

Engineer laid the spur to that big ole Baldwin locomotive and by the time we reached Denison, felt as though we'd left most of the unexpected sorrow we'd encountered behind. Don't think Nate said half a dozen words till after we crossed over the Red River.

Even back in them days, I never was much of one for omens and such. But our fateful trip south had started out about as badly as it could have, and as we passed over the Red River I had a malevolent, prickling sensation run up and down the back of my neck. At the time, felt that watching a beautiful young woman with her whole life ahead of her die in a friend's arms might've had something to do with it. Not sure, and truth be told, it didn't really matter. Was just that those events set me to wondering just how much worse things might get before we made it back home. By then I'd decided it was time that Nate Swords knew everything there was to know about the Brotherhood of Blood.

11

". . . Fired Both Barrels Into the Back of Jimbo's Head."

TRAIN CLATTERED ALONG between Denison and Denton. Soothing rhythm and vibration of the tracks surged up through the floor and set a man's head to lolling back and forth. Rolling, hilly, tree-poor countryside of stunted bushes and dry grass slid by my window. Wedge-shaped, greenish-black thundercloud had crawled over the horizon in the west, and was rapidly turning daylight into near dark. That ugly, churning, morass of water-logged clouds further dampened our already depressed spirits and appeared on a course to blow directly over the top of us. Coming storm dropped glittering, pointed spikes of pitchfork lightning in every direction followed by distant, rumbling, earth-thumping thunder. Spotted terrified animals darting, here and there, out front of the rapidly approaching tempest.

Elbowed Carl back into wakefulness, then said, "Well, you've been pushing me to do this for a spell now. Think it's time we told Nate 'bout the Brotherhood."

He yawned, stretched, then flashed me a pleased grin. "'S good by me."

Jerked a thumb toward the back of the car. "Got up about ten minutes ago. Think he strolled out onto the platform. Might be having himself a smoke. Or maybe he just wanted to be alone. Why don't you go round him up? We'll sit the boy down and tell him the whole tale."

Carl came erect like an unfolding carpenter's rule. Slapped his hat on and said, "Good idea. Maybe what we've got to tell him will take his mind off Little Cloud for a few minutes." He wobbled to the rear door of the day coach and, in less than a minute, he and Nate swayed back to our set of gear-laden seats. Overdose of supreme woe showed on our morose young friend's face like a set of deep, self-imposed scars.

He flopped down in the seat across from me and socked his hat onto one knee. "What is it? Whatta you want, Hayden?"

Shot Carl a quick glance. He shook his head and shrugged, as if to say, "Swear 'fore Jesus I didn't say nothin', Tilden. Not a single enlightening word."

Fingers knitted in my lap, I leaned Nate's direction and said, "Sure you recall the terrible circumstances surrounding my and Carlton's decision to take you into our group."

Nate gifted me with an unenthusiastic tilt of the head. "Brought me on board when Selby Hillhouse murdered your friend, Billy Bird. The resulting search for Maynard Dawson, Charlie Storms, and Cotton Rix was my first trip to Fort Worth and Hell's Half Acre. Still believe that jaunt was the serious beginning of my real, genuine education as a deputy U.S. marshal. Everything up till then didn't amount to a hill of beans. Hadn't been for you boys, I'd most likely still be spending the majority of my time chasing horse thieves and whiskey runners."

Slid onto the edge of my seat. "Thing you don't know, mainly because Carl and I've had a bit of difficulty dealing with the death of our good friend Marshal Bird, is that the three of us made up a very select and special group of men. A trio of law bringers like none other in the whole of Judge Parker's cadre of deputy marshals."

The spark of growing interest began to show in Nate's eyes. As he pushed up in his seat, I shot a glance out the window over his shoulder and saw a knifelike blade of heavenly fire fall from thick, soot-black clouds five miles away. Rumble of thunder took several seconds to get to us. Window rattled when the wavelike bump of dense air finally hit.

Elbows resting on his knees, Nate edged closer to me. Leather complained when he rearranged his pistol belt. "You know there've always been rumors about you boys, Tilden. Persistent, dark, strange rumors."

"What kind of rumors?"

"Oh, nothing definitive. Little more'n old ladies' gossip, I always felt. All 'bout how you fellers rarely bring anyone back alive when you go out on a manhunt. Figured if such tales amounted to anything at all you'd let me in on the secret, when you got good and ready." Then, as if fearing he might have overstepped his bounds an inch or two, he added, "That is what we're talkin' 'bout here, isn't it?"

Conversation fell into whispers when I said, "Before this goes any farther, Nate, I must insist that you swear on your honor that what we're about say to you will never be repeated. And I do mean never. Even if you decide against inclusion, you must swear that you'll not reveal what you hear from the two of us today. You've got to agree with this most important condition before we can continue and talk about anything else."

"Okay. Sure. I'll . . ."

"No. Don't comply so quickly, so easily. This is, perhaps, the most serious matter to confront you in your entire life. I think that you, at the very least, should give it a few seconds' thought. Because once you've heard what Carl and I are about to say, your life will never be the same again. You will be forever changed, and that's not stretching this business in the least."

A nervous grin etched its way onto Nate's twitching lips. "Well, damn, that sounds right ominous."

Carl perked up and added, "He's not kidding, Nate. This is grave business. Story you'll hear, and the life-changing proposition we'll ask you to consider, could prove the most significant event in your life up till this very instant."

Fleeting look of momentary confusion flickered across Swords's pinched brow. He pawed at the stubble on his chin, then stared at the day coach's ceiling for near a minute. Wagged his head, like an old dog looking for someone to scratch the back of his neck, then said, "It sounds most intriguing, to say the least, Tilden. Can't wait to hear what you boys have got to tell me. So, why don't you go on ahead and spit it out."

Shook my head. "Not until you raise your hand and swear before God, Carlton J. Cecil, and me, that what you're about to be told won't go any farther than the seat where you sit."

Behind a sheepish grin, Nate raised his right hand. "I swear 'fore Almighty God, I won't mention anything we talk about today to a living soul." As his hand dropped back into his lap, he added, "That good enough. Work for you?"

Glanced over at Carl for his approval, then said, "Several years ago I arrived at a confidential agreement with Judge Parker himself. I became what you might call the secret instrument of justice's righteous fury when all else fails. In essence, Deputy Marshal Hayden Tilden acts as the final arbiter of life and death for those malevolent souls considered beyond the reach of the law, as we know it. For those men who feel they have no limits to their behavior, I am the limit. My commissions in this area are delivered to me by way of the judge's chief bailiff, Mr. Wilton. He acts as a necessary buffer between me and the judge."

Let my somewhat confounding pronouncement sit on him a few seconds before adding, "After a number of bloody and difficult undertakings in this area, I came to realize that, given the depraved depth of lawlessness in the Nations, the assigned tasks often required the attention of more than one man. As a consequence, unbeknownst to Judge Parker, or Mr. Wilton, I enlisted Carlton to assist me in my efforts. Eventually, after due consideration, we took Billy Bird in as well. Sworn to the deepest of secrecy, we began calling our small, elite circle the Brotherhood of Blood."

Nate's head snapped back. "And you're saying that you want me to become a part of this *Brotherhood*?"

"Yes."

"Well, while I think I understand what you just told me, what, exactly, would membership in the Brotherhood entail?"

Motioned for Carl to take up the conversation. Figured the details of our agreement would sound better coming from him. He sat up in his seat and glanced around the coach as if to make sure no one was listening in, then said, "Anytime Hayden receives one of these *special* projects, Wilton gives him the discretion to pick whoever he wants to help out."

Nate tapped the brim of his hat with a nervous finger. "Goes a long way to explaining why you three spent so much time together. And why whispered rumors have always persisted that Tilden didn't necessarily have to bring 'em back when he went out after 'em."

"Yes, and no one appears to have cared, one way or the other, that in all the cases in the past, Billy and I were the ones Hayden picked to accompany him on his searches."

"Never gave it any thought myself."

"Good. Now, here's the piece that might prove the most important part of what we want you to know. Out of his own pocket, Hayden will pay you and me an additional amount equivalent to the rate we earn for our services as deputy U.S. marshals. And he will personally see to it that we all share equally in any rewards and postings on wanted men, whether we deliver them dead or alive. In this deal, there's none of that ole crap about, well, you killed 'em, you don't get a dime from the government, and buryin' 'em is your expense and responsibility."

At that point I felt it necessary to interrupt. Waved Carl into silence and said, "See, Nate, in most cases we don't usually go out to bring anyone back. In every instance, thus far, the crimes of the accused were believed to be so far beyond the pale that we were sent to dispatch them. Feeling has always prevailed that once our job is done there must be no chance for time and a smart lawyer to put the most evil among us back into the midst of an unwary public."

Nate scratched his head. "But that's not the case on this

run, is it? Did I misunderstand, or haven't we been sent out to bring the Cassidy girl back to Fort Smith?"

From the corner of his mouth, Carl hissed, "That's true enough. But should we run Jesse and Leroy Coltrane to ground, while searching for Daisy Cassidy, they won't be dragged back for a trial by their peers and the kind attentions of hangman George Maledon."

Could see the cogs and wheels in Nate's well-honed thinker mechanism whirling. He bent forward, both elbows on his knees, and stared at the toes of his boots. Scratched his head again. Then, after some more thought, he sat back into his seat and pinned me to my spot with a narrow-eyed gaze.

"Tell you what, Tilden. This is just the kind of job I'd hoped for when I first took up the badge. Deep down I've always believed that unvarnished vengeance was the way to go. Wanted someone to turn me loose. Slip my leash. But it didn't take long for me to realize that once we'd caught the sorry bastards and brought 'em back for trial, they just might well get turned out for us to have to go out and catch again."

Great wave of relief swept over me. "So, can we take it that Nate Swords is the newest member of the Brotherhood of Blood?"

"Damn right you can. I'm your man, Tilden. While I'm sure there are others who'd run from such a proposition like their hair was on fire, I ain't one of 'em. Place my hand on the family Bible and swear my faith in this project, if you'd like. Want to know why?"

Carl let out a happy snort. Slapped Swords on the leg. "Well, even if Tilden don't want to hear your story, I sure as hell do."

"Every man has his own reasons for taking on such difficult responsibilities, Nate. I'm sure you have yours. There's no real need, or requirement, for you to explain yourself—unless you just feel compelled to do so."

A subtle hardness formed at the corners of our newest member's eyes. "First real killer I had to go out after was a skunk named Big Bob Stackhouse."

Carlton grunted and twisted in his seat as though someone

had hit him in the side. "I remember that son of a bitch. He murdered Deputy Marshal Jimbo Jones."

Swords nodded. Snatched his hat up and began picking at the horsehair band. "Two of 'em met up and set to playin' cards in a disreputable joint up in McAlester. Evening went along fine enough until Jimbo accused Big Bob of markin' the deck. Guess Bob must've known for damned sure he was overmatched in the lead-slinging game, so he hopped up and headed for the joint's door."

"Came back a few minutes later with a ten-gauge Greener, as I recall," Carlton said.

Nate gritted his teeth. "Sneaky bastard didn't even bother to go back inside. Jimbo was shuffling the deck for the next hand. Had no idea what was about to happen. Ole Bob leaned over the batwings and fired both barrels into the back of Jimbo's head. Killed Jimbo and two others sitting at the table. When the smoke finally cleared, wasn't anything left of poor Jimbo's noggin but the neck bone. Heard tell as how the man's brains decorated everything and everybody within ten feet—including the two other dead fellers."

"Well, fellers in attendance of that cowardly deed testified for the grand jury that it was the most brutally bloody act they'd ever witnessed," I said.

Swords thumped at specks of dust on his hat brim. "Yep. Well, I caught up with that man-killin' son of a bitch in a cane break down on White Grass Creek, 'bout two miles north of the Red River. After I shot him twice, dragged Big Bob's sorry ass back to Fort Smith, and threw him in jail. Jury convicted the back-shootin' skunk. Damned if he didn't bypass Judge Parker and have his crooked lawyers file an appeal with the president. Got a new trial, and I'll just be kiss my own ass if those bastards on the jury didn't set him loose again. And they did it all after he'd already been convicted once and sentenced to hang."

Carlton crossed a booted foot onto his knee and set to spinning the rowel of one spur. "Went out and committed an act most considered worse than blowin' Jimbo's head off, didn't he? Killed somebody else, as I recollect."

Swords stared out the day car window at the lightning and coming rain. "Ole Bob celebrated his freedom by gettin' good and drunk over in Pocasset. Raged up and down their main thoroughfare firing off his pistol. Number of people tried to stop him. But before they could chase him down, he ran his horse over a child that had the misfortune to stumble into his drunken path. Kid's dress got tangled up around one of his animal's feet. Way I heard it, when they finally got Bob's horse off that ill-fated little girl, she didn't have an unbroken bone in her body."

"Yeah," Carl said, "but them Pocasset folks didn't bother to send for a deputy U.S. marshal, or any of the Light Horse Police. If memory serves, they snatched Big Bob off his mount and strung his sorry ass to the nearest cottonwood tree."

Angry grin bled onto Nate's lips. "Yep. And that's why I'm more than pleased to accept your invitation to be a part of the Brotherhood of Blood. If Bob Stackhouse had swung from Maledon's Gates of Hell gallows the way he should've in the first place, that child he stomped to death would still be alive. Figure if killin' one of the sons a bitches we go out after saves another child's life, it'll sure as hell be worth it."

Conversation faded and eventually died off after that. Train wheeled along into the deepening darkness of the gathering storm. Sensation felt similar to going down a well. But it didn't really matter, 'cause now Nate had climbed on board and knew the whole story.

Felt better than I had since the day Billy Bird died. Even relaxed to the point where I nodded off. But every once in a while that train would jerk me back to semi-wakefulness. Sensation of pimpled flesh and wary expectation would surge up my neck again. Tried my best to push it away, but something dark, unexplainable, unknowable kept gnawing at me. Tried to put a finger on the problem, but never could. Just knew that something didn't feel right. Something didn't fit. And that Carl, Nate, and I might well be headed for a dangerous surprise.

12

". . . GOT THAT NARROW-EYED, LAWDOG LOOK . . ."

DARK, VICIOUS STORM hit Fort Worth like a watery-walled sledgehammer just about the time we pulled up to the passengers' loading platform of the Texas & Pacific depot. Was still late afternoon but might as well have been midnight. Raindrops the size of .45-caliber bullets came down in buckets—big, wide-mouthed buckets. Deluge turned every street I could lay an eye on, from our limited vantage point, into a sloppy, muddy, fast-moving, miniature river.

As we stepped from the day coach's platform, an ever deepening darkness, tinged with oppressive gloom, closed around us like a clenched fist. Quickly retrieved our animals and headed up Houston Street in the midst of the worst downpour I'd seen in years—anywhere, anytime. Rushing water came up to our animals' fetlocks. Hit Sixth Street and headed east to Main. Squall got so violent we stopped at the first wagon yard and stable we spotted. Could smell the dry hay and dirt of Turnbow's Livery and Wagon Rental when we rode up to the wide-open double doors.

Bandy-legged gent, who sported a bedraggled, snow-white beard, one pale, dead eye, and a corncob pipe, greeted us. Stood just inside the barn door, one side of his jaw chomped down on the pipe stem, offered up a snaggle-toothed, lopsided grin and said, "Helluva nasty evenin', ain't she, boys? Best climb on down, put 'em up. No point ridin' around in this stuff. Get yourselves inside out'n this weather 'fore all three of you're wet'rn a trio of drowned rats."

Carl hopped off his mount. Hurried out of the downpour. Handed his reins to the geezer. Went to slapping water off his slicker with his hat. Said, "Damn, this another one of them biblical floods or somethin', friend? Or maybe it's just one of them things you Texans brag about doin' bigger'n three times better'n anyone else ever could. Whichever she might prove out, thought I'd seen it rain a time or two till we got here."

Geezer shuffled-footed and kept grinning. Man had considerable more in the way of gums than teeth. He gathered the reins of all our animals, then let out a sharp, cackling, satisfied chuckle as he led them into three nearby stalls. Finally stopped laughing, then went to talking. Had that quirk of personality that set a person to thinking, pretty quicklike, that unless encouraged to do so, he would never stop of his own accord.

"Aye God, gents, when we git a frog strangler like this 'un a comin' straight outta the west, she can last for days. Three hunnert and sixty days of the year Fort Worth's so dry the catfish in the Trinity River are covered with ticks. Then, outta nowheres, we git one a these here gully whumpers."

Nate unbuttoned his slicker and flapped it back and forth like wings. "Gully whumper, huh? Don't think I've ever hear that 'un before."

"Oh, yeah," the coot said. "I've seen 'em where they gets to goin' like God went and pulled the cork. Matter of hours, one like this 'un here can dump enough water to fill up every puddle, pond, and lake in North Texas. But, hell, she'll prolly be gone by tomorrow morning. Two or three days of sunshine, plenty of wind up from the south, and it'll be drier'n the dust in a dead man's pockets."

Hostler set to stripping everything off Gunpowder, kept a frenzied lip going a mile a minute while he worked. "This 'un reminds me of a clod floater we had back in '72. Was the year our only bridge across the Trinity, one out 'hind the courthouse, went 'n washed away—along with what little there existed of the northwest end of town. 'Course, she weren't muchuva bridge in the first place, or town for that matter. Bridge was just a buncha logs laid atop one another. Town warn't much more'n a collection of badly constructed, clapboard houses here and there. Spent two months wadin' over the river after that. Feller I know what had a flat-bottomed boat made a fortune ferryin' folks back and forth. Some hellacious days, back then."

By the time the codger reached Carlton's bangtail, a sorrel gelding my friend affectionately referred to as Shooter, our host had filled our ears to overflowing with an astonishing amount of Fort Worth history and folklore. Longer I listened, the more I came to believe that the majority of his good-natured harangue might or might not have borne the slightest drop-dead resemblance to anything like the unvarnished truth.

He was about to start on Nate's jughead when I stopped him by saying, "You, by any chance, have a hack for rent that sports some kind of top on it, old-timer? Something that would keep the rain off your riders."

Pulled the pipe from the discolored indentation in the corner of his mouth. Man's tobacco-stained lip appeared to have molded itself around the pipe's stem over a lifetime of smoking. He tapped the end of the stem against one of his two or three remaining yellow-brown teeth. "Yep. Sure 'nuff. Got a good 'un. Most times rent it out for funerals. Transport the loved ones to the grave site what cain't be provided for by local undertakers, you know. Be my pleasure to drive you boys anywhere in town my very own self. Hell, won't even charge you fer the ride, bein' as how you're puttin' yer animals up with me and all."

Carl said, "'S a short trip, old-timer. Just up to Second and Rusk."

"Wish to Jesus you boys would stop callin' me *old-timer*.

Name's Turnbow. Fletcher Turnbow. Mighta noticed my name on the sign over the door when you came up. Know y'all prolly think I'm so old I 'uz around when Hell was frosty and jackrabbits still had horns and could fly. Got a few years on me for sure and true, but I ain't exactly hung up my gee-tar yet. Most folks calls me Fletch. You can, too, if you like."

Behind a widening grin, Nate said, "Fine by us, Fletch. Think you can run us up to . . ."

Turnbow threw Nate's saddle atop a set of stall rails. Over a stooped, bony shoulder he said, "Marshal's office, right? You boys got that narrow-eyed, lawdog look all over you. Seen it soon's you strolled into the light. Get y'all headed that direction quick as I can take care a these animals. With me, the animals always comes first, business after." He jerked a thumb toward the open entryway. "Might as well have a sit over yonder by the door. If'n you want to, that is. Coffee's cookin' on the stove in the corner. Go right on ahead and pour yourselves up a steamin' cup. 'S good coffee. Guaranteed finest kind. Have the beans shipped to me special from New Orleans. Roast 'em myself. Tried Arbuckles, and it's good, but this stuff's a bunch better. People come from all over town just to get a taste of my coffee."

We'd almost dried out when Turnbow wheeled his hack out for us. Carriage was damn near the size of a Concord coach. Sported two enclosed seats for passengers and a completely separate one for the driver. The fancy, oversized cabriolet had a leather roof and drop-down curtains for the windows, along with an abundance of hand-polished silver trim. Fancy fenders over the wheels looked to have just been cleaned and waxed. His over-the-top ride even had a pull-down hood to keep the water off the driver.

Nate looked surprised. Ran a finger along a glistening piece of silver on one door. Glanced up at Turnbow in the driver's seat. "Being a poor boy from the backwoods of Arkansas, don't think I've ever ridden in anything quite so grandiose, Fletch. This here's the kind of ride I'd expect to see the governor of Texas or maybe the president of the United by-God States coming down the street in."

Turnbow's tooth-poor smile grew with the pleasure of hearing such compliments. "Ain't she a daisy? Bought 'er off an undertaker down in Waco what went outta business. Still find it hard to believe that an undertaker could go outta business. Hell, people's always dyin', ain't they? He called this here wagon a family coach. Claimed as how it'd actually seat eight people. Don't know 'bout that though. Most I ever had ride in 'er were six. Even with that load of gear you brought, should have plenty a room. Hop on in. Get y'all on up to the marshal's office in less than ten minutes. You boys'll be drier'n a buncha frogs under a cabbage leaf when we arrive."

While the three of us were familiar with virtually all of Fort Worth, as result of our previous visits, it proved difficult, at best, to recognize much in the way of landmarks due to the deluge. About the only things I could see from the windows of Turnbow's coach were the flickering, reddish-yellow lamplights that fell from the windows of various saloons, restaurants, sporting houses, dance halls, and gambling joints. Could barely make out the dull, muted glow of a streetlamp once in a while. Here and there, I did manage to spot the occasional shadowy figure propped against a porch pillar, or sitting cross-legged on a bench beneath a protective cover of some kind. Barely detectable glow from a hand-rolled tended to give them away.

True to his word, Fletcher Turnbow delivered us right up to Marshal Sam Farmer's front door in record time. We hopped down onto the boardwalk and hustled up under the jail's sheltering veranda. Barely got damp in the process, in spite of a sheet of rainwater that rolled off the roof like someone in Heaven was pouring it out of a boot.

Our talkative driver peeked from beneath his impressive coach's leather hood, smiled, then shot us a dead-eyed wink. "Figure you can make it from here to any of the better hotels and not get too wet. Just keep to the boardwalks, boys. Need anything else, send someone down to the yard. Plenty of easily hirable drunks, layabouts, and never-sweats around. Get to you quick as I can." Then he waved, turned his team, and disappeared just a few feet away behind a curtain of falling water and near impenetrable, inky darkness.

Pushed our way into Marshal Sam Farmer's office. Dropped our gear on the floor inside the door. Across the room, half a dozen of Fort Worth's finest were gathered around a checkerboard in a corner next to the cell block entrance.

Tobacco smoke, so thick a body almost needed a hatchet to cut through it, fogged around us, then went to escaping through the open doorway, till Nate shoved it closed.

Soon as the ironbound door slammed shut, place got quieter than the bottom of a fresh-dug grave. All six of the badge toters in the corner turned at the same time. Not a smiling face in the group. Stared at us like we each had two heads and three noses. Some went to tickling the grips of their pistols. Was a damned uncomfortable situation, to say the least.

13

"... KILT THREE PEOPLE WITH A DOUBLE-BIT AX ..."

SURE AS HELL felt like we stood in the middle of Sam Farmer's office with our faces hanging out for nigh on a minute before anything happened. Tight-lipped, moustachioed gent slumped in a squeaking banker's chair behind the marshal's desk was obviously not Sam Farmer. Thick necked and having the broke nosed look of a bare-knuckled prizefighter, he cast a weary glance our direction. Motioned us closer with a hand that held a slender, half-finished cheroot, decorated with a good two inches of steel-gray ash, between tobacco-stained fingers. Shoved the cigar back into his mouth and clamped a set of fine looking choppers onto it like a sad-faced hound worrying an old bone.

Stopped near the edge of the desk and said, "Evening, officer. Have urgent business with Marshal Sam Farmer."

With an almost imperceptible, tired shake of the head he said, "Ain't here."

"Expect him back anytime soon?"

"Nope. Tell the gospel truth, friend, Marshal Farmer had to

make an o-fficial trip down to Waco. Man's testifyin' for the prosecution in a murder trial. Folks down that way 'er lookin' to hang a couple hard-as-nails murderers. Cain't blame 'em much, them ole boys kilt three people with a double-bit ax and a ball-peen hammer. Sam said he felt compelled to stroll on down and help Waco's good citizens out. Got the distinct impression he believed he owed his assistance to anyone as would rid the world of such vicious skunks."

Carlton grunted, then said, "Damn, that sounds familiar. Lookin' for some evil skunks as might've pulled a similar trick ourselves."

I said, "So, bottom line here is that Sam's gone for a spell."

"Yep. Won't be back for three, maybe four days. Might even take him a week. Left me in charge of that bunch of badge-wearin' never-sweats over yonder in the corner. Just keepin' this crew doin' something useful's harder'n herding a pack of alley cats. Want anything important done, appears you're gonna have to deal with me first, and then do it yourself, gents."

I waved at Nate and Carl, said, "These men are Deputy U.S. Marshals Swords and Cecil out of Judge Parker's court in Fort Smith, Arkansas. My name's . . ."

Before I could finish, or add anything else, the broke-beaked bruiser behind the desk hopped to his feet, jabbed a knotty-fingered, knuckle-scarred hand the size of a camp skillet at me and said, "By God, you'd be Marshal Hayden Tilden, I'd wager. Sam said he'd sent a telegram to the authorities in Fort Smith and expected you right quicklike. But I truly didn't have the slightest inkling, from what he said before headin' out, that you boys would arrive anytime soon. Figurin' on maybe the middle of next week at the earliest. Name's Bob Evans, Marshal Tilden. Can't begin to describe how pleased I am to make your acquaintance."

Shook the man's massive, scarred paw, then he slowly sank back into his creaking seat like a kid's carnival balloon that lost its air.

I said, "My pleasure, Mr. Evans. We've only just arrived

in town. Thought we'd stop by and, as a courtesy, check in with Marshal Farmer, then maybe look in on Miss Daisy Cassidy."

"Well, as I said, Marshal Farmer alerted me to your possible arrival. Must admit I'm just about happier'n a two-tailed puppy you made it back to Fort Worth for a visit. Sam never passes up an opportunity to speak highly of you boys with anyone who'll stand still long enough to listen. Says you're the most thorough and accomplished bunch of lawmen he's ever worked with—bar none."

Carl let out a gruff snort. "Well, that's good to hear, but it took Marshal Farmer a few days to warm up to us during our first raid down this way. However, he did come around mighty quick once the serious killing got started."

Big man cast Carl a knowing look. "Had to deal with some bad 'uns on your last trip. That's for damned sure." Then he glanced over at the checkers players' corner. "Some of you boys get the hell up and let this man and his friends have a seat. They look plumb tuckered out, and y'all buncha lazy-assed wretches have been loafin' around in here ever since the storm hit."

One of the checkers group, tubby boy with a bristle-covered, piggish face, said, "Hell, Bob, it's damned awful out there."

"Yeah, well, wouldn't hurt if some of you got the hell back out on the street and at least had a quick look around. We could have killers and thieves on every corner of Houston Street and we wouldn't have the slightest hint of their rude intentions."

Aura of resentment oozed off three of Marshal Farmer's city policemen, as they wrenched themselves away from the game, dragged their chairs over to us, then stuffed their hats on and headed for the street like a trio of whipped dogs. Bolt of instantaneous lightning and clap of shattering thunder rattled the jail and lit up the street about the time they pulled the thick, plank door closed. For several seconds, entire jailhouse buzzed with a crackling electric charge that made the hair stand up on the back of my neck and caused my ears to itch.

Got myself settled in one of the ladder-backed, cane-bottomed chairs, pitched the prosecutor's court order for Daisy Cassidy's immediate extradition onto Officer Evans's desk. Said, "You have the girl locked up back there in a cell, Bob?"

Exhibiting little interest in their contents, Evans fingered the packet of documents for a second but didn't open them. He chuckled, pushed the leather-bound pouch back at me, then said, "Naw, slept in the office first couple of days she 'uz here. Then Marshal Sam put the gal up in a third-floor room over in the El Paso Hotel soon's he got word the court in Fort Smith would foot her bill. Couldn't have any kind of a woman back there on the cell block, locked in with all the local drunks, thugs, and prospective killers and rapists, now could we? Couldn't have one what looks like Daisy Cassidy back there, and that's for damn certain sure. Be a jump onto the dangerous side just lettin' her stroll through."

Felt Carl squirm in his seat. Sounded a mite on the in-credulous side when he said, "You do have somebody watch-ing her, don't you, Bob?"

Nate snorted, then added, "Bet your men ain't buttin' heads for a chance to stand guard over some teenaged gal outta the Nations."

Tin cup in hand, Evans clambered out of his chair. Hobbled over to a potbellied stove in the front corner of the office near the door. Wobbled a bit like a man who might've suffered a broken back at some point. Took a second to get comfortable once he stopped, then poured himself a dollop of fresh stump juice from the blackened pot atop the sooty heater.

He backed up next to the wall near the stove, took a sip of the steaming, thick liquid, then said, "You'd be way off the mark there, Mr. Swords. I've got men on the verge of pulling knives on each other just for the chance to get a ten-second look at that Cassidy gal. Well on the way to where I'm some-what afraid if any two of 'em gets close enough to actually smell 'er at the same time, could have a brutal killin' on my hands."

I said, "You're kidding, aren't you, Bob?"

Evans shuffled back to his seat and came nigh falling onto

the piece of distressed furniture when he carelessly flopped down on it. Chair cracked and popped like it might collapse under his sizable bulk. Man propped one booted foot onto the corner of Sam Farmer's desk, then said, "Nope. Ain't no kiddin' here, boys. She has that effect on men. Gal might be the best-lookin' female-type person any of us have ever seen. Has that smell comin' off'n her. You know the one I'm talkin' 'bout. Makes the hair on a man's crotch stand up and wiggle. Swear to Jesus, gal has the amazing power to drive grown men to distraction—among other things."

Definite edge on his voice when Nate said, "Well, now, you gotta admit, that's a right strong assessment of the lady, don't you think?"

Evans knifed a keen glance at Nate, then said, "Well, friend, put it to you this way. Gal's got straw-colored hair hangs all the way down to an hourglass waist. Kind of figure would make a man want to slap his ole granny till her garters popped loose. Eyes the color of Mexican turquoise. Skin as smooth, and unblemished, as fresh milk."

Carlton grunted.

Nate squirmed in his seat, then said, "Describing a goddess of some kind, ain't you, Bob?"

Rueful grin etched its way across Evans's face. "Heard one of my boys say he'd be more'n willing to lay in the middle of Houston Street and let all four wheels of a loaded beer wagon roll over him just so's he could get a look up her skirt and maybe get a sniff of whatever that gal's got hid up there."

"You able to confirm any of the stories she told about bein' whored out by the Coltrane boys?" I said.

Evans shrugged. Shook his head. Said, "I ain't been able to confirm a single word outta that gal's mouth. About anything."

Carl rolled his eyes, stared at the ceiling, then said, "Has anyone tried to actually get at Miss Cassidy since Sam Farmer informed the U.S. marshal in Fort Smith of her whereabouts?"

Evans sat his cup on the desk, leaned back in the squeaking

chair, and laced his fingers behind his head. "Nope. Ain't no one as can actually even get close to her. Have to go through one or two of us city policemen to start. And, of course, then there's her brother."

Shot Carl and Nate a quick glance. "Brother?" I said. "What brother?"

Evans totally missed the incredulity in my voice. Scratched his muscular belly, then ruffed the thatch of hair on his head with one enormous bearlike appendage. "Yeah. Antsy little son of a bitch named Matt. Just kinda showed up a day or two after we put the girl up at the hotel."

"Just showed up. What's that mean?" I said.

"Exactly what I said, Marshal Tilden. Just kind of appeared in the Cassidy gal's room one mornin'. Swear it's almost like he grew up outta the carpet or somethin'. Been madder'n a teased banty rooster since the minute he showed his face. Boy gets so excited ever' time another man manages to be within ten steps of the sister, you'd think he was about to commit murder on 'em. Hell, feller with a dirty mind might even think there's somethin' goin' on 'tween the two of 'em."

Carl crossed his legs, then flicked at a gob of mud on the heel of his boot. Knew he and I were thinking the exact same thing, but didn't want to say anymore than absolutely necessary before clearing it with me.

After several seconds of awkward silence, my friend finally said, "Well, now that's right interestin', Bob. Boy showed up a day or two after the girl, huh? Puts on his raking spurs when any of your guys get too close to 'er?"

"Oh, hell, yeah. Silly wretch sets to hoppin' around like a Louisiana bullfrog in a hot skillet. Goes to yelling and hollerin'. He's a monumental pain in the rump, Marshal Tilden. Cain't say as I blame him for wantin' to protect his sister, but, tell you for certain sure, I don't envy you boys a bit havin' to put up with his angry, belligerent ass all the way back to Fort Smith. Probably make all y'all sit as far from the gal as you can get and still be on the same coach. That is, if he'll let any of you sit on the same coach with the two of 'em to begin with."

Feller in the checkers klatch said, "Matt Cassidy ain't just antsy, marshals. Son of a bitch's crazier'n a toe sack fulla yeller jacket wasps, you ask me. Ole Bob here's bein' charitable 'bout that boy's state of mind."

Officer pushing the red men around on the checkerboard added, "Crazy bastard's got loco camped out behind his twitchin' eyeballs, sure as Hell's hot and icicles is cold. He don't just *act* like he's a few sacks of seed short of a full load. His wagon's half empty, you ask me. Moonstruck son of a bitch has actually threatened more'n half of us with a killin' if we don't stay away from that good-lookin' twitch of a sister of his."

Third man said, "Yeah, Bucky's right. Gal's good-lookin' as hell. Any man's breathin' would give a bunch to see'er nekkid, but she ain't worth dyin' over, that's for damn sure. Personally be glad when the gal's gone. Don't even care to sit outside her door myself. They's just somethin' 'bout them two kids gives me the jittery creeps."

Got to my feet. Said, "Third floor of the El Paso, that right?"

Evans blew a smoke ring the size of wagon wheel, then said, "Yep. Last room at the west end of the third-floor hallway. Number three-twenty. Window looks out over Third Street. Cain't miss it. Put 'er there 'cause there ain't but one way in and one way out."

"Who's on watch right now?" Nate said.

Evans squirmed in his chair. Scratched a scruffy chin, then said, "Think I've got Tinker Bloodsworthy camped outside the door for the next couple of hours. You boys stroll by tonight, just tell 'im I said it was okay for you to go in. Decide to wait till tomorrow, I'll see you up there myself."

As we gathered our goods and headed for the boardwalk, Nate turned to Bob Evans and said, "Might wanna put two men on the Cassidy girl's door till we can get her outta town, Bob. There's mighty bad men lookin' to kill this kid, no matter how good-lookin' she is."

Threw my possibles bag over one shoulder. Said, "Think we'll mosey on over and take a room at the El Paso. Get one on the third floor if we can. Talk with the girl tomorrow morning when my mind's a bit clearer. Been a long, bad day and I'd rather be sharp when we interview her."

Evans followed us onto the boardwalk. Four of us stood beneath the shelter of the front porch and stared into the pouring rain. Other side of the street, back entrance of the Theatre Comique was little more than a dull blur. Storm appeared to have abated a mite, but not much.

Evans pushed his way up to me before I could get away, "Got any idea who's for sure after the girl, Tilden? Could help if I knew who we should be on the lookout for."

"Know exactly who's after her," I said. "The Coltrane brothers, Jesse and Leroy. Evil skunks are some of the worst of the worst up in the Nations. Could have several of their friends along with them as well. Just never know when it comes to the Coltrane boys."

"Mean we could be looking at a visit from more than just these Coltrane brothers?"

"Might be as many as half a dozen of their gang when they're all gathered, Bob. Maybe more. No definitive numbers that I'm aware of. But rumors do persist that Jesse and Leroy sometimes travel in the company of extremely bad men like C. W. Jemson, Bronson Staggers, Amos White, Jasper Neely, and others just as wicked. Have no way of knowing for sure who might come along for the ride till they actually show themselves."

Sounded like squirrels breaking walnuts in his mouth, when Evans gritted his teeth. Rubbed his brow with one finger, then said, "I'll send another man over right behind you fellers. Sure wouldn't want anything happening to Miss Cassidy whilst under my watch. Want that gal away from here quick as possible, to tell the righteous truth."

Stepped off the boardwalk, but Evans pulled me back out of the street. Clung to my sleeve and said, "There's one other thing, Marshal Tilden."

"Yeah."

Evans got up so close thought for a second there he just might go and kiss me. Sounded like the prophet of doom, when he hissed in my ear, "If'n I 'uz any of you boys, I'd be right damned careful around this particular little gal."

Must admit his unexpected warning surprised me some. Said, "Yeah, and why's that, Bob?"

"She's one witchy woman, Tilden. True enough she's young, good-lookin' as hell, and all that, but there's something on the scary side 'bout the gal, too."

"Scary?"

"Yeah. Can see it in her eyes, you take the time to really look. Made my blood run colder'n well water in January ever' time I've been around 'er. For some reason, she reminds me of a crazy woman lived back in my hometown. Leastways, folks always said she 'uz crazy. Know unsolicited advice ain't worth no helluva lot, but you'd best be mighty careful around Miss Daisy Cassidy."

Slid away from Evans and back out into the downpour. Over one shoulder I called out, "Another man sitting outside the room's a good idea, Bob. Coltrane brothers are some ornery, vicious, cold-blooded bastards. Those who choose to run with them are just as bad, or maybe even worse."

Behind me I heard Carl say, "Hayden's right. Coltrane boys are fully capable of killing Daisy Cassidy, all your men, and us, Bob. 'Specially if you give any of 'em half a chance and the ability to get behind you. Best tell all your boys that they should be especially wakeful till we can get the girl out of town."

When my feet hit the muddy slog of Fort Worth's Rusk Street as we headed for the El Paso Hotel, swear to Jesus I had the sinking feeling of having stepped off into a pit of poisonous snakes. Suddenly got the shivers, along with a prickly sensation that crawled up and down my spine like foamy waves on a wind-tossed lake.

Got to thinking as how maybe a few drops of frozen rain might've dribbled off my hat brim and slipped behind the collar of my shirt. But then, the hair on my arms stood, and a numbing cold seemed to seep into my bones. Tried to shake off Officer Bob Evans's foolishness about Daisy Cassidy, but for some odd reason his words kept gnawing at my insides and ringing in my ears like Sunday morning church bells.

"She's one witchy woman, Tilden. True enough she's young, good-lookin' as hell, and all that, but there's something on the scary side 'bout the gal, too . . . Can see it in her eyes, you take the time to really look. Made my blood run colder'n well water in January ever' time I've been around 'er . . . Know unsolicited advice ain't worth no helluva lot, but you'd best be mighty careful . . ."

Man hadn't really said a lot, but by the time we reached the El Paso's lobby, he'd sure enough cocked my pistol.

14

"He's a Back-Shooting Son of a Bitch . . ."

NATE COMPLAINED OF a stomach that he said was trying to gnaw its way through the waist of his pants and belt buckle. So, we threw all our gear in the floor of the hotel room and headed across Third Street for the restaurant in the White Elephant Saloon.

Reporter for the *Fort Smith Elevator* once referred to the Elephant as "the most magnificent com-bi-nation gambling house, restaurant, and saloon in the entirety of the whole nation—bar none." Man's somewhat sensational opinion couldn't be dismissed as much in the way of a stretcher, you ask me.

As we approached the joint, sounds of music, laughter, and good times to be had seeped from beneath the Elephant's bloodred batwing doors. Once inside, the eager visitor immediately found himself confronted by an impressive, carpeted staircase that led to the second floor and the most elaborate gambling setup in the whole of Texas.

Nate stood just inside the door, rubbed wet hands together,

grinned like a hungry raccoon, and said, "Hot diggity damn, boys. Place looks even better'n it did the last time we were here. Been hopin' for a return visit for a whole year."

Off to the left, across an expanse of lustrous hardwood floor, the longest, most elaborate bar for five hundred miles in any direction gleamed like a freshly polished decanter of the best whiskey hard-earned money could purchase. Men who wanted to eat, drink, keep company with willing women, or put their fat pokes at risk would've been hard-pressed to do any better than Luke Short's elaborate mixture of an eating, drinking, and gambling emporium. On that particular storm-tossed night in Fort Worth, anyway.

We scraped our muddy feet on a thick chunk of braided hemp rug that was especially laid out for that particular purpose. Let ourselves drip a bit before we slipped out of our rain slickers and other gear.

Carlton appeared truly taken by all the noise that flowed down onto us from the joint's elegant staircase, like the water falling in the street outside. Knew from our previous raid on Fort Worth that the table right on the edge of the landing above was piled a foot deep in gold coin. Whole glittery she-bang was easy to see from where we stood. Impressive. Mighty damned impressive. Remember standing there, as lightning flashed across the heavens behind me, and trying to imagine the Elephant's impact on a first-time-to-visit, south Texas brush popper on his premier trip to the Kansas railheads, or the local Fort Worth cattle yards.

Inviting sounds of gambling and easy companionship washed right over us. Above us, I could hear the heavy marble in a roulette wheel as it spun around, bounced, and clicked into place, along with the musical clacking of at least one wheel of fortune being touted by a barker who must've drawn quite a crowd. Friendly, metallic, rinky-tink-tinkle of a piano ebbed and flowed over the rest of the sociable noises that rolled down those stairs and beckoned to the prospective, tight-fisted, leather-pounding gambler to come on up and put his hard-earned fortune on the line.

Good-looking gal from the restaurant, who reminded me

some of my Elizabeth, took our rain gear and hats. She flashed Nate a smile that would've brought most men to their quaking knees. Boy's mind was somewhere else at the time. Had a damned fine meal that night. Back in them days, a man couldn't beat Fort Worth's beefsteak with a stick. Three of us were more than satisfied when the evening's repast came to an end.

Rubbed our stomachs as we stepped up to Luke Short's forty-foot-long, solid-mahogany filigree bar and ordered a drink to finish off a damned fine feed. Think we might've been well into our second beaker of Gold Label rye when Carlton leaned over and kind of secretlike said, "Take a gander in the mirror, Tilden. See them fellers sitting at the table over in the corner behind us?"

Puckered up and took a nibbling sip from my glass, then said, "Which corner?"

"Farthest one from us. One on our right. Far back as you can go. Kinda behind the piano."

"I seen 'em, Carl," Nate said. Storms suddenly looked right determined, when he threw his drink down in one quick swallow, thumped the glass back onto the bar, then rubbed chapped lips on his sleeve.

In an effort to get a look at whatever my friends might've seen, or thought they'd seen, I glanced into the Elephant's pride and joy—a gigantic, beveled slab of reflective, highly polished glass that covered the entire wall behind the joint's elaborate back bar. Spotted three shaggy, rough-looking types crammed into the corner like a bunch of hungry wolves all huddled up and checking out the sheep before they jumped out of hiding and killed one of them.

Feller in the middle of the group had his back wedged into the corner like he thought Jack McCall might return from the dead and put a bullet in the back of his head. Bearded, moustachioed, hook nosed, with long, stringy, gunmetal gray hair poking from under his hat, the squint-eyed piece of scum looked somewhat familiar. Scratched an itchy spot in my brain for several seconds. Even so, couldn't quite put a finger to a name for him.

Carl said, "Uh-huh. That's him alright, Tilden. The one and only C. W. Jemson. He's a back-shooting son of a bitch extraordinaire."

"Yeah, well, 'course I've heard the name. Didn't really know the man well enough to recognize him though. Ugly bastard, ain't he," I said, then took another run at the amber-colored liquid in my glass.

Carl leaned over on one arm, hunkered up next to me, and twirled his drink around in the wet spot beneath it on the bar. "Skinny twist of rusted barbed wire on Jemson's right hand is Bronson Staggers. Hear tell he covers Jemson's backside if'n they have difficulties requiring the quick death of them folks impertinent enough to get in their way. Piggy-lookin', fat-gutted slug on the left is Jasper Neely. Man'd just as soon rip out your guts as spit."

Eyeballed the mirrored images again, then said, "Empty chair at the table, Carl. You reckon Amos White's around somewhere close? Or maybe one, or both, of the Coltrane boys?"

Sounded like a dog growling when Nate said, "Even if White ain't nowheres to be seen, Hayden, I'd be willing to bet the ranch, if'n I had a ranch, that Jesse and Leroy Coltrane are in absolute fact somewhere nearby. Probably out askin' questions. Prowlin' around tryin' to locate Daisy Cassidy."

For fifteen or twenty seconds no one spoke, as we chewed on our drinks and studied the three thugs in the corner. Finally Carlton said, "Ain't got no official wants or warrants on any of them skunks, as I'm aware of. But, hell, we could slap 'em with a John Doe, then drag 'em all back to Fort Smith for anything you can dream up, Hayden."

"Damn right," Nate said. "No longer'n we've been standing here, pretty sure I've seen every one of them bastards expose his nasty-assed self at least twice to the cute little waitress that's been carryin' them drinks."

Couldn't help but grin. "Well, not sure that'd stand up, Nate. Might work if we were back in the Nations, at a watering hole in west Arkansas, or, better yet, a saloon in Fort Smith. But, being as how we're in the great Lone Star State, would bet that wagging your hoo-haw at a barmaid might not count for much in Judge Parker's court."

Nate crooked a finger at the Elephant's slick-pated, rail-thin bartender and pointed to each of our empty glasses for a refill. Appeared a bit on the anxious side when he dropped money on the bar, then said, "Well, whata you wanta do, Hayden? Ain't gonna just stand here and guzzle whiskey all night long, are we?"

Placed a calming hand on my friend's shoulder. Could tell he itched for a fight. Man had been keyed up ever since the horrific death of Rachael Little Cloud. Nate hadn't contributed much to that dustup, but he walked with a hitch in his git-along that constantly reminded him of the sorry event.

"Why don't we just stroll over and have a friendly talk with ole C. W. and his compadres," I said. "Kinda shake the tree a bit. See what falls out when we rattle 'em around some, as it were."

Could see Carlton smiling back at me in the mirror, when he said, "Now, there's a plan. 'Course, no matter how we handle this, them boys could get just a wee bit on the froggy side. Go to hoppin' around, pullin' pistols, shootin', and such."

Nodded my agreement. Said, "Their kind of man does get nervous for little or nothing."

Carl snorted, then said, "Hell, we just might be forced to drill a couple of 'em, Tilden. Maybe even kill one or two. Damn near a certainty if we provoke 'em in just the right way. Kill hell outta all three of 'em, we'd be doin' the Indian Nations—along with the states of Texas, Arkansas, Louisiana, and Mississippi—a by-God service, you ask me."

Nate slapped his empty glass down on the bar again. "Now that's a helluva good plan. Discombobulate 'em a bit. Like it. Let's get on over there 'fore they have a chance to jackrabbit on us. Move in on 'em and do 'er just like you said, Carl. Brace 'em where they sit. Any of 'em goes to reachin' and grabbin', we kill the whole sorry bunch. Bet that'd put a sizable crimp in whatever the Coltrane boys have planned for Daisy Cassidy."

Slipped the hammer thong off my belly gun, lifted the weapon, and let it settle into the well-used, oiled, leather sheath on its own. "Best limber up all your shooters, boys— belly guns and hip pistols. Sure wouldn't want to waltz over there and have Jemson and his friends get all chute crazy and not be able to get our weapons up and out for the kind of gun work we might have to do in a few minutes."

Carl grunted. "Good idea. Jemson might not know you, Hayden, but he's sure to recognize me 'fore we can get all the way across this room. Best all be ready for whatever they might want to throw at us. But, you know, sure wish I had my shotgun."

As surreptitiously as possible, Carl and Nate followed my lead. Loosed all the iron around their waists and got themselves primed for a fight. Didn't take much effort on Nate's part. Boy had blood in his eyes and murder in his heart. In a matter of seconds, everyone appeared ready. Three of us turned away from the bar at the same time.

"I'll go at them head on," I said. "Carl, you take Staggers. Nate, you keep an eye on Neely. We'll just stroll over. Ask them some questions. See what happens. Any of them goes and gets froggy, don't hesitate."

"Damn right," Nate hissed.

Quirky smile played across Carl's lips. "Don't know 'bout you, but I'm screwed down and riding deep in the saddle, Tilden. Ain't gonna find me sitting on my gun hand. So turn 'er loose and let 'er buck."

We stepped away from the bar as one man. Threaded our way between tables, chairs, and a packed crowd of noisy, happy, drunk, or near-drunk people, as we quickly moved across the room.

Jemson spotted us less than halfway there. Saw him shift in his chair. Leaned slightly toward Bronson Staggers. Whispered something to Staggers behind one hand, then reached over and patted Neely's arm. Swear 'fore Jesus the three of them looked like shocked puppies that had just discovered the first porcupine they'd ever seen sitting in the middle of their table.

Made my way right up to a spot directly across the table from Jemson. Came to a rocking halt and flashed a friendly, although blatantly insincere, smile. Couldn't have been more than five feet from the man. Hooked my thumbs on either side of the buckle of my pistol belt in an effort to try and put him at his ease. Hands on the grips of their weapons, Carlton and Nate took their positions, either side of and slightly behind me, and waited.

The raggedy-bearded Jemson pushed a Montana-peaked hat to the back of his grease-encrusted head with two fingers. Let the hand slowly, deliberately drift back down to the table-top. He glanced over at Carlton and said, "Helluva thang, boys. A man can ride all the way down to Fort Worth for a bit of fun and relaxation, and lo and behold if some of Parker's favorite henchmen and killers don't show up to ruin his much needed recreation. You law-bringin' bastards are a long way from home, ain't you, Cecil?"

Carlton grinned, let out a contemptuous snort, then said, "Could say the same of a low-life *bastard* like you, C. W. Appears you boys are a right far piece from your regular stomping grounds up in the Kiamichi Mountains. Might find it a bit harder to rob, murder, and pillage amongst these Tex-icans. Folks around these parts don't particular take kindly to such behavior."

Jasper Neely's piglike snout twitched, he grunted, then said, "You sons a bitches got no reason to go a-causin' us any trouble. We ain't in the Nations right now, by God. Ain't botherin' nobody. Jus' havin' a sociable drink with friends. Relaxicatin' in the finest waterin' hole 'tween Tuskahoma and San Antone. So, why don't y'all hair-covered walkin' assholes shuffle butt yourselves on outta here and leave us the hell alone."

I hadn't heard much, but it was enough. So, I said, "Damn, Jasper. Case you haven't noticed it, these badges we're lugging around signify that the three of us are deputy U.S. marshals. Comes to the heavenly climes of law enforcement, we're a special breed of lawdog."

Carl took up the thread and added, "Our commissions allow

us to go anywhere in the United States, or its territories, in pursuit of those who provoke our attention. Right now, we're looking for the Coltrane brothers—Jesse and Leroy. Rumor has it you boys might've spent some time of late running with those murderous skunks. Wouldn't happen to have seen either of them, have you?"

Bronson Staggers's cold, hard stare zeroed in on me. Man had his hands hidden beneath the table. Made me a bit uncomfortable because I couldn't tell whether he was holding or not.

"We ain't seen the Coltrane boys. Either of 'em," Staggers said. "Not sure I'd tell a trio of shit-kickin' stargazers like you even if'n I had."

Jemson looked thoughtful and a bit perturbed at the same time. Rubbed his stubble-covered chin with the back of one hand. "Maybe I missed it, but I don't think you mentioned Benny, Marshal. Would indicate to me as how you boys ain't lookin' for Benny. Why come is that? Coltrane boys never do anythang lest they do it together. Puzzles me a mite that Benny's name ain't come up?"

"Already have that runny pile of cow flop in custody. He's sittin' on his bony bohunkus in the basement dungeon back in Judge Parker's courthouse in Fort Smith." Nate's words sliced through the air like a freshly sharpened hay sickle.

Subtle change spread over Jemson's outward demeanor. "That a fact."

"Is indeed," Nate continued. "If we can't find his brothers, poor ole brainless Benny'll likely have to stumble up those long, terrible, lonely steps to the Gates of Hell gallows alone. Face judgment 'fore a crowd of thousands of spectators, all of 'em eatin' roasted corn on the cob and waitin' to get a gander of him when he hits the end of Maledon's oiled hemp noose, then messes all over hisself like a week-old child."

Staggers's face and neck flushed. Man squirmed in his chair like his pants might burst into flame. "Didn't have to go sayin' nothin' like that, damn your sorry soul. Sweet Jesus. Just ain't nothin' worse'n hangin', you ask me. Sure would hate to hear as how the Coltrane boys done got theyselves strung up. What the hell you Parker bastards think they went and done, anyhow?"

A nail-biting tension, soaked in a river of rising blood, kept edging up with every back-and-forth exchange. Staggers went to twisting his neck from side to side and blinking way too fast. Jemson kept rubbing at his jaw and chin like no-see-ums were eating him alive. Neely had begun to sway in his chair in the manner of a Baptist revival attendee caught in the slow rhythm of unheard music.

Reckoned we had just about twisted their tails enough. Backed away from the table a step. "Way we heard it they murdered an entire family, name of Cassidy, up in the Nations near Dutch Crossing. Even men as evil as the Coltrane boys can't go killing regular folks just for the fun of it and think they can get away with such a barbarous act."

Staggers twisted in his chair and mumbled, "Don't believe a word of that load of horseshit."

"Doesn't matter a single whit what any of you believe," I said. "We have warrants for them, and you can bet the ranch we'll serve them. So, you boys run across Jesse or Leroy, best let them know we're on their trail and that we will catch them. And, once we've caught them, we'll see they hang. Want some advice, I'd recommend you stay as far from Jesse and Leroy as you can get. Close proximity at this particular time could lead to an early grave."

"Heard 'bout the way you catch folks, Tilden," C. W. Jemson, growled. "Not many as you go out lookin' for come back breathin'. Yeah, I know you. Know you fer the cold-hearted killer you are."

Carlton glared across the table like he might reach over and snatch Jemson's hooked nose right off his face. "Why don't you go on ahead and say something else stupid and arrogant, C. W. That way I'll feel more'n justified in reachin' over this table, jerkin' your sorry ass outta that chair, and slappin' you nekkid."

Placed a hand on Carl's arm, then flashed another tight, grinning smile at Jemson. Let a bit of steel creep into my voice when I said, "Trust me when I tell you, C. W., might be right dangerous to keep company with the Coltrane boys for any time in the foreseeable future. But if you should run across either of them, be sure to deliver my message exactly the way you heard it."

Jemson's thin, cruel lips curled away from yellowed, tobacco-stained teeth. Nervous twitch in his pockmarked cheek when he said, "Well, now, we'll just sure enough do that, Marshal. You star carriers can depend on our complete cooperation. Yessir, its always law and order top to bottom for me and the boys here. That's us, for sure and certain. Born to help the law, by God."

Backed away from Jemson and his lethal friends, then turned and hoofed it for the Elephant's front entrance. Carlton followed. Nate was the last man out. He didn't give his back to those brigands until he'd darted through the Elephant's café doors onto the boardwalk, then he drew both pistols.

15

"Already Got a Bead on the Silly Idiot . . ."

I HIT THE White Elephant's batwings so hard those swinging, café doors sounded like pistols going off when they slapped against the outside wall. Had a gun in each hand. Quick as I could, turned left, out of the brilliant wedge of light that cascaded onto the boardwalk from the doorway. With Carl and Nate in tow, we headed north along Main Street fast as we could heel it.

Inky, thick layer of lightning-tinged cloud cover, no moon, and sheets of drifting rain contributed to a murky, sinister night. Remember it as being so dark Fort Worth's flickering, yellow-tinged streetlamps, though fairly close to one another, provided little in the way of helpful illumination. Only other available light shimmered over and around the saloon's front entrance, lay in pools on the boardwalk, or lamely oozed from the curtain-poor windows of other still-open businesses along the west side of the street. Way I had it figured a man could stand in the covering shadows and not be seen by someone within spitting distance who found himself caught in the poorest puddle of available lamplight.

All those thoughts buzzed across my heaving mind, as I pulled to a halt about thirty feet down the boardwalk from the White Elephant's entrance. Decided to take my stand out front of Ella Blackwell's Shooting Gallery. Joint was damn near right next door to Luke Short's place. Only thing separating the two businesses was a narrow, midnight-black alleyway.

Twirled around, pointed toward the entry of the shooter's paradise with one of my pistols and said, "Get up inside Blackwell's entrance far as you can, Nate. We don't want those skunks to see all three of us if they do come pouring out of the Elephant, grow a crop of smarts for the first time in their benighted lives, and manage to spin around our direction."

Carl took a spot on my left, nearest the street. A cocked weapon in each hand, he leaned against a porch pillar and sucked at his teeth. Sounded as calm as a horse trough in a drought, when he said, "You really think those idiots'll step out shootin', Hayden? Mean, hell, that'd be mighty stupid. Leave the ignert churnheads standin' right out in the light. Make perfect targets."

"Figure if they have any idea at all where the Coltrane boys are, Carl, they're gonna come fogging through the Elephant's front door behind a curtain of hot lead. Besides, think you might've jerked Jemson's tail a bit harder than necessary. May have even insulted him a mite."

"Doubt that. Not sure you could insult anybody that stupid. 'Course, suppose anything's possible. But, maybe they'll just let it all slide. Slink out the saloon's back door. Vanish into the night to do whatever evil it is men like those three brigands do when no one's watchin'."

Backed up against Ella Blackwell's sheltering door frame, could barely see Nate when he rolled the cylinder of one of his weapons across an extended forearm and said, "By God, I doubt that, Carl. Have my doubts that snaky, vicious skunks like Staggers, Jemson, and Neely will let our visit pass. Fact is, way I've got it figured, them no-accounts should be hittin' the door just about right now."

Those wildly prophetic words had barely fallen from Nate Swords's lips when the White Elephant's fancy, bloodred batwings exploded in a bullet-rendered cloud of gore-colored flying wood splinters and hot lead. Thunderous explosion was followed by a roiling cloud of spent black powder and splintered fragments of the wooden doors that showered down into the muddy thoroughfare.

Directly across the rain-soaked quagmire that was Main Street, people out front of the Empress Saloon and Beer Hall went to hollering and running in every direction imaginable. Next day we would discover as how the Jemson gang's initial salvo gouged half a dozen holes in the popular watering hole's front façade.

Heard scared, surprised folks inside the Elephant as they yelled, turned furniture over, and ricocheted off the walls in an effort to hide themselves, or get away from the promiscuous blasting. Heavy footsteps rumbled all through the building as terrified revelers heeled it for the nearest exit.

Remember thinking as how there's just nothing like the fear of brutal, impending death to send normally reasonable, thoughtful folks into a blind panic. Turn the stoniest amongst us into shrieking children, searching for the comfort of parental protection.

Brought both my pistols to bear on the White Elephant's bullet-ravaged, smoky entrance and waited. Didn't take long for the ball to open and really get rolling.

Stooped in a gunman's crouch, both arms extended, hands filled with a brace of Remington pistols, Bronson Staggers leapt through the demolished entryway first. He landed in the middle of the now sharply defined pool of iridescent light left by the missing doors, then swung around to his right, away from us.

Plain as rat pills in a sugar bowl, the ignorant, squint-eyed wretch couldn't see for more than a few feet. So, typical of his type, he went to firing at anything he could hear, or thought he could hear. The few people bold enough, or unthinking enough, to be out on the street yelped, screamed, or swore, and dropped behind the nearest available cover.

Kept my gaze fixed on Staggers. From the side of my mouth and under my breath, said, "You got him, Carl."

Flicked a quick, corner-of-the-eye look at my friend. He had turned sidewise like a New Orleans pistol duelist. Left hand braced on his hip, right arm straight and level. Solid as the biggest limb on a hundred-year-old live oak.

Though but a few feet away from him, barely heard it when Carl hissed back, "Already got a bead on the silly idiot, Hayden. He's a dead man soon's he turns back around our direction."

C. W. Jemson hesitated in the saloon's devastated doorway, then hopped out onto the boardwalk like some kind of enormous, demented, heavily armed jackrabbit. A clearly inebriated Jasper Neely wobbled out last and swung to his left and directly into our line of fire.

In the manner of an inquisitive dog, could see Neely tilt his head to one side, then squint, as he tried to penetrate the light and get a look into the darkness where we stood and waited. Given the spot they'd chosen to take their stand, not a one of the witless morons could see more than three feet in any direction.

An edgy Jasper Neely swung his weapons back and forth at the impenetrable darkness surrounding him. Man had the bug-eyed, terrified appearance of someone scared right up to the precipitous edge of screaming insensibility.

Red faced and shaking all over, Neely set to hollering, "Where are you? Show yourselves, you cowardly, star-totin' bastards."

Idiot bystander, somewhere off to my left, across Main Street near the Merchants Restaurant, yelled, "What'n the blue-eyed hell's a goin' on over there? What's all the shoutin' and shootin' about?"

Another less-that-bright, anonymous gawker bellowed, "'Pears theys the makin's of a killing out front of the White Elephant. Somebody best call the law. Go on now, run for the marshal's office and be damned quick about it."

Neely did a sudden shift and thumbed off three or four quick shots in the general direction of the disembodied voices. Heard what sounded to me like a man yelp out from being hit.

Brought both my weapons up and said, "Guess we'd best put a stop to this dance, boys. Wouldn't want these lunatics to mess around and accidentally kill somebody."

Six well-aimed shots, touched off at almost the exact same instant, delivered a near deafening, cannonlike torrent of blue whistlers that sliced through C. W. Jemson, and his pair of liquor crazed toadies, like a busy butcher's favorite, well-honed meat cleaver.

River of bright, reddish-orange, blue-edged flame carved trenches in the darkness and squirted six feet from the muzzels of our pistols. Flashes lit the street as surely as streaks of ice-pick lightning and, for about a second and a half, turned blue-black night into something akin to a lurid form of startling, nightmarish daylight.

Curtain of sizzling lead we threw at Jemson and his boys shredded the three gunmen like we'd run them down with a sodbuster plow. Hard behind our blasting, a thick cloud of spent black-powder smoke rolled along the boardwalk and away from us like a wave on a storm-tossed ocean. Carried on a slight breeze, the dense screen of smoke came nigh on to completely obscuring our view. Still and all, I could see more than enough.

Neely's block-shaped, anvil-thick head exploded in a plume of misted gore, bone fragments, and shredded pieces of his hat. Second chunk of hot lead stood the man straight up, then put him back on his heels. Useless arms plastered to his sides, he went rigid, but somehow fired two shots into the plank walkway at his feet. Then, knees locked, he toppled sidewise and went to ground like a hewn tree.

At the same instant, our death-dealing barrage caught C. W. Jemson in the side, twirled him around like a kid's wooden top and dumped him in a mud hole near one of the Elephant's hitch racks. Almost flat on his back, the man still had the amazing wherewithal to rip off four or five more shots of his own. While noisy, his efforts proved ineffectual. Seemed as though he fired at everything in general and nothing in particular—the old spray-and-pray method of gun-fighting. Poor wretch ended up killing a defenseless, unarmed horse tied at a hitch rack out front of the Club Room Saloon a block away, before he finally stopped moving.

A wounded Bronson Staggers went down on one knee. Thought sure the man was dead, finished, and just didn't know it. But, some way or another, he managed to twist around at the waist and get off a pair of shots that cut through the murky night and buzzed within inches of my ear like angry hornets.

Air still sizzled like coppery-smelling bacon frying in a hot skillet when I once again caught view of a shadelike Carlton J. Cecil from the corner of one eye. He leveled up on the dying Staggers, took aim, and fired again. Saw the hammer on his pistol fall.

Blast sent a 255-grain, .45-caliber chunk of lead that caught the shot-to-pieces Staggers dead center of his chin. Slug blew the whole bottom of the man's mouth to misty smithereens. Fist-sized wad of teeth, bone, and shredded flesh flew into the air like a handful of bloody confetti.

Heavy bullet punched on through ole Bronson's windpipe and severed his spine, just below the spot where his head was attached to his neck. Slug exited in a torrential, mistlike storm of flying blood droplets, bone chips, and body parts. Man went rigid, then rolled onto one side like a two-hundred-pound burlap bag of feed pushed off a general store's loading platform. Didn't even twitch.

Then, of a sudden, the corner of Fort Worth's Third and Main Streets got so quiet a body could literally smell the odor of dead silence. There, for a few seconds, got quieter than snow falling on a feather bed. Would've sworn I could hear my own eyes blinking.

Kept my gaze glued to the fallen trio and didn't bother to look over at my friends when I said, "Everybody all right? Either of you boys hit?"

Carl just grunted. Heard him spit, then set to reloading his weapons. Spent shell casings bounced off the boards beneath his feet, then rolled into the street.

Nate said, "Finer'n frog hair, Hayden. Feel better right now than I have since we left Atoka. Just might feel better'n I have in a month or so. My side's even stopped hurtin'. Just ain't nothin' like killin' a skunk to brighten a man's outlook. Killin' three of 'em just might keep me grinnin' for nigh on a year."

"Glad to hear it."

"Just one thing though," Nate said and holstered both his pistols.

"And what's that?" I said.

"Sure 'nuff gets right hot travelin' with you'n Cecil, Tilden. Can't say as I've ever been involved in a pair of toe-to-toe shootings this close on top of one another in all my time as a lawdog. Tension following you boys around sure goes a long way to keepin' a feller on his toes."

Carlton shoved both his weapons into their holsters, then rubbed the back of his neck. Torqued his head from side to side, then twisted it back and forth, as though trying to stretch out a crick the size of a yellow-meat watermelon. "Well, don't get too used to such shenanigans, Nate. Bein' around Tilden's usually about as boring as trying to talk Chinese to a wooden Injun. But the man does have these moments when he sure 'nuff drives the dogs out from under the porch. Definitely has a way of gettin' my attention, tell you for certain sure."

Approached the bodies of Jemson, and his stupider-than-stinkbugs amigos, with all the care that men who'd kill you for the fillings in your teeth deserved. Here and there, the lame-brained, the dim-witted, or the just downright inquisitive crept from their hidey-holes and began drifting toward the bloody scene.

One man pointed and, under his breath, declared, "Aye God, them's teeth yonder, Kyle. See 'em. And 'at 'ers part of this poor bastard's jawbone. My God, look at that mess. 'S enough to make a feller wanna retch."

Another sagely shook his head, then said, "Do believe that's a big ole chunk of this 'un here's skull plastered to the porch pillar. Lord, Lord. Glob of goo still has the hair growin' out'n it."

And a third announced that, "Sweet merciful Jesus, they's blood all over hell and yonder. Cain't say as I've seen this much blood since the Big War. Maybe as far back as Pea Ridge."

Holstered one weapon, unpinned my badge, and held it up so everybody and sundry could see it. Loud as I could manage, called out, "We're deputy U. S. marshals, folks. Best if you all kept your distance from these men. Better for everyone involved if you just stayed inside. Still a very dangerous situation out here, and we don't need your help."

Sure surprised hell out of all of us when C. W. Jemson lived up to that warning, brought one arm out of his mud hole, then fired a final, air-burning shot that carved a hissing path between Nate Swords and me. Lightning fast, Nate drew and ripped off at least three more booming rounds that thumped the walkway so hard a thin puff of drifting dust rose up around our feet from between the cracks between the boards.

Think all of Nate's well-placed rounds hit Jemson somewhere. Man's body jerked, flopped, and rolled around in the muddy, bloody puddle like an unseen attacker was beating on him with a long-handled shovel. After everything calmed down again, felt pretty sure we didn't have to worry much about anything else in the way of response from Jemson or his friends.

Was standing near the limp body of Bronson Staggers when I felt someone at my elbow. Bob Evans eased up next to me, shook his head as though he might well be the weariest man living. Knuckled one eye, then said, "Damn, Tilden, been working at this job for about a year now. Never seen anything to match this dance."

"Gun work can get right bloody, Bob."

"Yeah. Sure 'nuff. 'Course I'm well aware that cowboys, gamblers, and such do have their disagreements. Some of 'em have even been known to shoot each other every once in a blue moon. And, in spite of every thing we can do, once in a great while they even manage to kill one another. But I swear to Jesus, ain't never seen a triple killing before. This 'un here sure 'nuff one helluva mess. Blood, bone, and pieces of rended flesh all over creation. Boardwalk looks like the floor of a Chicago slaughterhouse."

Shaking his head in disbelief, Evans, and two of his fellow Fort Worth policemen, walked the scene, examined the bodies, and asked more questions than there are fiddlers in Satan's favorite playground. Watched and offered all the information I could in an effort to satisfy their necessary, but often clumsy, inquiries.

Couple minutes into Evans's investigative dance, I leaned against one of the porch pillars and stoked myself a nickel cheroot. Shook the lucifer to death and thumped it into the soggy street. Tried to stay out of the way while Carlton and Nate laid out a detailed explanation of the events that surrounded what we'd been forced to do and how it all came to happen in the first place.

While I puffed at my stogie, the rain slacked off some. Clouds the color of buckshot mud and gunmetal parted. A clipped fingernail slice of silvery moonlight sliced through the gash and bathed the entire street in an eerie, muted, hoary glow. For the first time since our arrival in Fort Worth, a body could actually see from one side of the street to the other.

To this very instant I could not for the life of me tell anyone why, but at some point during all the walking, talking, and testifying, I glanced up at a corner window on the El Paso Hotel's third floor. Stunned the hell out of me when I spotted the backlit silhouette of a young woman.

Appeared to me that gal was as naked as the day she got birthed. Couldn't really see the details of her face, just the unclothed shape of an obviously nude body. She clasped the edge of a heavy curtain panel in each of her fisted hands. Would've sworn she was hanging in midair, like some untethered, floating spirit, staring down at the gory carnage that decorated the blood-soaked street at my feet.

Not sure why, but it suddenly came to me as how, beyond any shadow of doubt, the anonymous woman was none other than the elusive Daisy Cassidy. Had an eye clamped on that little gal's shadowy outline for less than ten seconds. Was stunned when I realized that she was laughing—head back, in full hoot. Cackling like a person completely addled in their thinker box. Unexpected, eerie scene sent an icy chill down my cold, damp spine.

Gal's ghoulish conduct was enough to make the hair stand up on a stuffed grizzly's hump. And I swear before Jesus, the kerosene lamp's flickering light behind her that should have been a muted yellowish-gold in color poured around her ethereal outline like a blood-tinted shroud.

Hair prickled on my neck, when I got to thinking as how I could hear the devil himself laughing, and that I'd been given a free glance into the open maw of a pustulous Hell. Then, with the muted, dying sound of Satan's insane, grunting laughter echoing in my ears, she suddenly snatched those curtains closed and vanished like a puff of smoke.

Set me to wondering if maybe Daisy Cassidy had seen me take notice of her chilling behavior. And for the first time, in that very instant, I realized there may well be something going on that Carl, Nate, and me didn't have any inkling about. Something darker, even more sinister, and vastly more wicked than any of us could have imagined. Something destined to cause the spilling of a lot more blood.

16

"No Point Diggin' at This Pimple."

NEXT MORNING, A copper-colored sun crawled into the Texas heavens and set to baking everything in sight. A cloudless, crystalline sky turned so blue it hurt a body's eyes just to gaze on it. Steady, overheated wind swept up from the south. Before a tobacco-chewing brush popper could spit, everything commenced drying up. Carlton declared as how it wouldn't take long before birds started building their nests out of barbed wire.

Fort Worth buzzed like a whacked hornet's nest with news of the previous evening's blistering gunfight. Knotted crowds of people filled the still-muddy thoroughfare, between the El Paso Hotel and the White Elephant, like an empty bucket dropped in a Ruidoso well.

Men, women, and wide-eyed kids took turns examining the bloodstained boardwalk as though they'd discovered a long-hidden treasure. They stepped off the distance between the spots where the shooters stood. Loudly cussed, discussed, proclaimed, and rehashed the details of the horrible scene.

Some acted out the various parts of the killers and those killed—whether they knew what in the blue-eyed hell they were talking about or not.

Others, folks with an extra three dollars burning a smoking hole in their pockets, stood over the bloodied boards, pointed, and had their solemn-faced likenesses preserved for posterity by a local photographer. Industrious gent used a big-box camera perched on a set of spindly wooden legs. Contraption required the efforts of two men just to move it from one spot to another.

Carl, Nate, and I took breakfast in the hotel's dining room that morning. Place proved right homey. Lip-smacking aromas of baked biscuits and frying bacon, alongside heaping mounds of grilled steak and eggs, put me in mind of Elizabeth's kitchen. Between the three of us, think we might have consumed nigh on two dozen of those cackleberries, along with the better portion of two slabs of bacon, three or four pounds of steak, ten or twelve biscuits, and half a gallon of flour and sausage gravy.

We had the best window seats in the joint during all the growling, grunting, and slobbering. Could easily observe most of the foolishness going on over next to the White Elephant while we ate. Have to admit, it was one hell of a show.

Bob Evans dropped over about the time we'd almost finished our meal. He slid into the only available seat and went to asking questions again. Carlton finally got all he could stand, pushed the remnants of his third plate of steak, bacon, and eggs aside, clattered a coffee cup into its saucer, and snapped, "'S damned 'nuff, Bob. We've gone over the whole dance twelve or fourteen times since last night. There simply ain't no more to tell."

"Well, I know, Marshal Cecil, but . . ."

Carlton held an authoritative hand up in Evans's face. "Look, I'll say this one more time and that's gonna have to be the end of it. We confronted them three sidewinders in the saloon. Spoke with 'em for maybe five minutes. Maybe some less. Then we headed for the street. Cowardly sons a bitches blew the Elephant's batwings off their hinges 'fore they followed us out. Went to blastin' at everything any of them belly-slinkin' snakes thought they could see or hear."

"Yes, yes, I know . . ."

Carl waved Evans into silence again. "No choice in the matter. Had to kill 'em, Bob. If we hadn't, Jemson and his friends might well have put more of your citizens down than that one poor pilgrim who got hit. Man's fortunate as hell he ain't dead, you ask me. Hear tell as how he's missin' part of one ear, but he'll get over that. Inch or two over, somebody'd be burryin' the poor gotch-eared sucker later this afternoon."

Nate eyeballed the perambulating carnival and doodah show out in the street. Wearily shook his head, then said, "Carl's right, Bob. Sure you won't need a story any more detailed than what he just gave you to satisfy Marshal Farmer when he gets back from Waco. No point diggin' at this pimple. Just ain't nothin' else there. You've got three dead men, all of 'em notorious for their sorry behavior from one corner of the Nations to the other. 'S all you need to know."

"Yeah, but we don't have any outstanding . . ."

I reached over and squeezed Evans's arm. Said, "True enough we didn't have any active wants or warrants on Jemson, Staggers, or Neely at hand last night when the unfortunate confrontation took place. No paper on them in Arkansas, the Nations, or Texas existed insofar as we were aware of—at the time."

Evans nodded. Let out a long exasperated sigh. "Boy howdy, Marshal Tilden, but I do hate to hear that."

I slapped his shoulder, then leaned back in my chair. "Well, now, hang on, Bob. Earlier this morning I wired Mr. Wilton back in Fort Smith. Through some quick and concentrated effort on his part, he discovered that all three of the dead men have arrest dodgers and rewards posted on them for a double murder in Bienville Parish, Louisiana. Appears Jemson and a few of his dearest friends made a raid over that way about a year ago. Killed a popular sawbones name of Thibodaux during the course of a bank robbery. Documents to that effect are being forwarded to you as we speak."

Of a sudden, Evans appeared to relax like an untwisted banjo string. He ran one finger across a sweat-covered brow.

"Damn. Gotta say I'm right glad to hear that, Marshal Tilden. Sure clears the way for me when I have to explain this blood-soaked hairball to Marshal Farmer. Ain't had a gunfight in the streets of Fort Worth to match this one. Not as I can recall anyway. Ever."

Patted the distressed man on the shoulder again. "Always glad to help in any way we can, Bob. Now, you reckon we can drop all these questions and get on with other business?"

"Oh, sure. Just tryin' to be thorough. You understand, don't you, Marshal Tilden?"

Pushed back from the table. Dabbed at crumb-covered lips, then dropped the napkin in my plate. Said, "Absolutely, Bob. But right now, think it'd be best if you escorted the three of us up to the third floor and introduced us to the enigmatic Miss Daisy Cassidy. Want to get this travelin' shootin' match headed back toward Fort Smith tomorrow morning, if possible."

Man almost fell all over himself getting to his feet. Came near knocking his chair over when he stood. "Oh, sure. You bet. You fellers just follow me. More'n happy to take you fellers upstairs my very own self."

We trudged our way to the third floor. Trailed Evans down to the end of the narrow hallway. He introduced us to the men he'd stationed outside Daisy Cassidy's door that morning—couple of fellers named Boo Higgins and Carter Dillworthy. After everybody shook and howdied all around, the guards dragged their chairs aside and made way as we stepped up to the door.

Evans knocked. Stood right next to him, and I swear the man acted as though he was afraid someone might actually answer. He knuckled the door several times before we finally heard a female voice call out, "Do come in, gentlemen."

Had to move out of his way, as Bob Evans motioned us inside, then quickly turned on his heel and headed for the staircase. Over one shoulder he waved and called out, "Good luck, boys. Want my advice, don't believe anything you hear and keep your hands on your pistols."

As I pushed the door open with one finger, heard Carl say, "What the hell'd he mean by that?"

We stepped into the first of a suite of rooms so poorly lit it took several seconds for my eyes to adjust to the hazy darkness. Thin ribbon of sunshine entered by way of an inch-wide gap between heavy drapes covering the window that overlooked what I felt sure was the corner of Third and Main Streets. Same window I'd seen a nude, cackling Daisy Cassidy standing at the night before.

A brocaded armchair appeared to have been strategically placed directly in front of that selfsame window. Seated, as though on a ceremonial throne, a shadowy, imperial-looking young woman waved us inside with the motion of one regal hand.

Clad in a high-necked, long-sleeved, dove-gray dress that sported a frilly, chin-tickling white blouse, Daisy Cassidy could have easily been taken for any brush popper's vision of a cow-country queen, or, at the very least, a princess. In spite of her obvious, near-overwhelming beauty, something tactile, almost feline, and decidedly sinister seemed to envelop the girl like an undertaker's blackest shroud. Vision proved somewhat disconcerting to say the very least.

Boy, who looked like he couldn't have been much more than fifteen or sixteen years old, stood at attention on the girl's right hand. Dressed in a dark, three-piece business suit, the youngster rested one hand on Daisy Cassidy's seat back in a kind of formal, stylized, ready-to-have-his-picture-taken stance. Entire scene had a pompous, overly formal, carefully staged look about it.

Then, you know, out of the clear blue, a niggling thought darted across my mind. Got to thinking as how the pair of them bore absolutely no physical resemblance to one another. In point of pure fact, their outward appearances could not have been any closer to exact opposites. Where Daisy was fair and blond, Matt Cassidy had a dusky, ebon-haired, eyes-drawn-up-like-birdshot, sullen look about him. Honest to God, the kid appeared about as Indian in his lineage as any man or boy I'd ever seen, or perhaps a breed of some sort at the very least. Additionally, young Master Matt instantly struck me as being mad enough to start foaming at the mouth with little or no provocation on our parts.

Carl leaned over and whispered, "What the hell you think these two are trying to pull here, Hayden? This entire cooked-up scene looks like a couple of kids working real hard at trying to fool the grown-ups."

Removed our hats and moved to the center of the room. Closer we got to Daisy Cassidy, the greater her impression on all of us. Girl proved exactly the stunner Bob Evans had described and more—an incomparable beauty. In spite of that, there existed something about the girl's astonishing good looks that took a backseat to an eerie, difficult-to-fathom strangeness that crinkled around catlike eyes and danced over the carefully crafted tightness at the corners of her full-lipped mouth.

Daisy Cassidy forced a counterfeit, snaky-looking smile and said, "Gentlemen."

I nodded her direction, then got right to the point. "Miss Cassidy, I'm Deputy U.S. Marshal Hayden Tilden. These are my associates, Deputy Marshals Carlton J. Cecil and Nate Swords. We have come to act as your escorts and protectors for the trip back to Fort Smith tomorrow morning. As a courtesy, just thought we'd stop by, introduce ourselves, and let you know that all the necessary arrangements have already been put into place. M.K. & T. Flyer going north pulls away from the passenger loading dock of the depot at ten. We will see the both of you downstairs and accompany you on the short jaunt to the station."

Swear before Jesus the boy looked like I'd slapped him, and he fidgeted like a frog in a hot skillet.

A fleeting look of stunned disbelief flashed across Daisy Cassidy's beautiful face. But she quickly regained her composure and said, "Most sorry to have inconvenienced you and your colleagues with a grueling trip, Marshal Tilden. But your journey has been in vain. I have not the slightest intention of going back to Fort Smith."

First words out of her pouty mouth and I had no doubt, Daisy Cassidy was as smart as the proverbial whip. But a curious and oddly foreign feeling leached off the girl's decidedly defiant words. Couldn't put a finger on exactly why, but the sound of that girl's voice, and her condescending demeanor, made my skin crawl.

Before I could stop him, Carlton snapped, "And why is that, miss?"

Girl blinked as though somewhat taken aback, but didn't hesitate, or back away. Carl's question still hung in the air when she said, "Because my very life is in jeopardy if I do, sir. As you may or may not know, Jesse Coltrane has sworn to kill me. I personally witnessed the horrors he perpetrated upon my family, and the man will do whatever he deems necessary to see that my rendition of the story of his murders never sees the light of day. I fled our home for the safety I've found here in order to get as far away from that horrid scene as possible."

"That's not exactly the version of your appearance in Fort Worth made privy to us, Miss Cassidy. It was our understanding that you were forced here under great duress," I said.

She eyed me like a tumblebug that needed killing. "Well, whatever you might've heard from local law enforcement, Marshal Tilden, I am here through my own efforts and am not going back."

I nodded, then said, "Suppose it is possible, as our information is third- and fourthhand, that we were misinformed. Marshal Farmer might well have misunderstood your reported situation when you first arrived in town. Or maybe he simply misinterpreted what you told him."

A counterfeit smile etched its way onto the girl's face. "I think you are correct, sir. Nonetheless, I will not be stampeded into a trip back to the Nations by those who have no real understanding of my situation."

"You have our guaranteed assurance that you'll be perfectly safe as long as you're in our care, Miss Cassidy. Deny our assistance and you might not live out the week," Nate offered.

Like a starving tomcat with its back arched and ready for a spitting scratch fight, the boy snarled, "She's told you we ain't goin' back, you ignorant wretch. There's no more to be said about it."

Nate's glare narrowed up on Matt Cassidy like the sights on a Sharps rifle. Could see the beginnings of a heated disagreement in the making. An argument the Cassidy boy would surely lose if he pushed Nate Swords too far.

I said, "You're almost right, Matt. It is Matt, isn't it?"

Boy trembled, as he leaned away from the conversation. Sounded suspicious when he said, "Yes. That's right. Matthew Cassidy. Daisy's brother. Matt Cassidy. Yes, that's my name."

"Well, Matt," I said, "You were absolutely correct when you intimated that there's no need to debate this question any further. You're both going back to Arkansas with us tomorrow morning. Won't be any of this 'oh, we won't be making the trip' stuff. You were ensconced in these rather nice digs at the expense of the federal court in Fort Smith. Your sister must return with us to testify at a grand jury hearing into the murders of your family. I have John Doe warrants in my pocket, and if necessary, I'll place the pair of you under arrest and shackle you hand and foot for transport. Do we understand each other?"

Color of barely controlled anger bubbled up Matt Cassidy's neck and reddened his ears. Boy appeared about one heartbeat away from popping a major blood vessel when his sister raised a hand and shushed him into silence.

"Please forgive the impetuousness of my younger brother, gentlemen," she said.

Then, she glanced at the boy, appeared to grit her teeth, patted him on the arm, and with a tight grin on her face, turned back to us. "Of course, you're absolutely right, Marshal Tilden. Cannot imagine what I was thinking when I said that I wouldn't go back to Fort Smith with you. Tomorrow morning we'll be packed and ready to leave at your convenience. I trust you'll send someone by to pick us up for the trip to the depot?"

"Indeed. We'll engage the services of a gentleman named Fletcher Turnbow. Mr. Turnbow owns a wagon yard and livery about four blocks south of here on Main Street. He has transportation more than adequate to meet your needs."

The girl stood. Hands daintily clasped to one side, she

flashed a cold, thin-lipped, dismissive smile. Said, "Well, then, if you'll excuse us, my brother and I will see to our belongings and prepare for the trip." Then she stepped forward, shook my hand, moved to Carl, and on to Nate. She threw us a final, wooden nod and headed for the suite's bedroom.

The brother kept his position and glared at us.

Barely detectable hitch in Daisy Cassidy's step as I called out to her back, "As Marshal Farmer's policemen will remain posted outside your door tonight, miss, I would recommend that both of you keep to the room." Didn't even hear the door as she pushed it closed behind her.

Carl slipped his hat on and mumbled, "Appears Her Royal Highness has left the room, and we've been summarily dismissed, gents."

When we hit the first-floor landing near the hotel's desk, Nate pulled us to a stop in the lobby and said, "Is it just me, or did you boys come away from that meeting with the feeling we'd just witnessed some sort of unsettling game?"

Carlton cast a darting glance around the hotel's reception area. "Not sure how to feel about the whole dance myself. But I'll tell you one thing, boys, those kids are hiding something. Ain't a single thing about the pair of 'em seems right. Be willing to bet the family manse they ain't brother and sister, tell you that for sure."

Spent the rest of that afternoon in the hotel's bar, or down at Turnbow's wagon yard. While we checked over our mounts, ole Fletch flashed a snaggle-toothed grin and said, "Aw, hell, yeah. I'll get that little gal and her brother to the depot in high style. Won't even charge you fer the trip, bein' as how you fellers kept these animals a yern with me. Be my pleasure."

By the time the sun went down, came to feel pretty good about getting on back to Fort Smith. Looked forward to heading home to Elizabeth quick as I could. But, as sometimes happens, not long after I drifted into a dreamless sleep that evening, fate stepped in and reared its ugly, unruly head.

17

"Hit Poor Boo With That Hatchet . . ."

SWEAR I MUST have been a lot more worn down by the previous week's events than I thought when my head hit the pillow that night. Plunged into the pitch-black well of deep sleep, and guess I didn't even so much as twitch for about an hour or so. Then, I tossed, turned, and spent the rest of that night plagued by a nightmare that never seemed to end.

Can't say as I remember all that much in the way of details about the unearthly vision. Can recall as how it had something to do with being pulled into a sucking, howling, bottomless pit by a grasping, vinelike morass of human arms—women's arms. Then, about half a second before I felt like a calamitous ruination was most assuredly descending upon me, a thunderous pounding at the back of my dozing brain snapped my more-than-willing eyes open quicker than Heaven's golden gate could slam shut on hated Judas.

Blinked myself to something akin to wakefulness just as the shadowy figure of Nate Swords, dressed in nothing but a pair of balbriggans and run-down boots, stumbled across the room. Pistol in hand, he caught his toe on something, swore, then jerked the door open.

Sounded right snappish when Nate said, "For the love of sweet Jesus, it's the middle of the night, Bob. What the hell you want?"

Bob Evans stood in the doorway and went to yammering like an escapee from the lunatic ward of one of those hospitals for the criminally insane. But none of what he was saying seemed to make any sense.

Sat up. Shook a mess of nightmarish cobwebs out of my head. Climbed out of the bed as Nate moved to a nightstand. He turned the wick up on a kerosene lamp to put a bit of light on the situation. Honest to God, in that lantern's flickering, reddish-yellow glow, Deputy Town Marshal Bob Evans had all the outward manifestations of a man who'd just seen a ghost. Or maybe something real that had proved way beyond his ability to understand it.

"Hurry. You fellers need to hurry. Don't have to be fully dressed," Evans said and sucked air as though drowning. "Just get yourselves decent. Come on. Have something you've gotta come see."

"What?" Carlton growled and rolled to a sitting position on the edge of the couch where he'd been sleeping. He ran a hand through a head of thick, matted, red hair and said, "What on God's earth could you need to show us at this time of the night, Bob?"

Carlton pushed both elbows backward until I heard his spine make cracking noises, then added, "Hell, feels like I just got to sleep a few minutes ago. Now you come bustin' in here running off at the mouth like a man who's left the better part of his brain out in the hall somewhere."

Evans's dark-eyed, panic-stricken glance shot from one of us to the other, as if he were looking at ghoulish specters straight out of Beelzebub's sulfurous pit. "Swear 'fore Jesus, there's just no point trying to describe what I'm here for. Get yourselves dressed. Right now, dammit. Hurry. Hurry."

Well, we couldn't work fast enough to suit him. In fact, none of us had managed to get ourselves anywhere near completely outfitted, when he said, "That's enough, for the love of sweet Mary. Come the hell on."

Still working like a field hand at getting my pants up, as I followed ole Bob up to the third floor in my sock feet. Hadn't gone far when I realized that he was leading us toward Daisy Cassidy's digs. Couldn't really see much. Just no way for me to get a decent look around the man's sizable bulk in the narrow, poorly lit hallway.

Had to push our way past several of the city policemen we'd seen in Sam Farmer's office when we first arrived in town. Seemed as though every lawman in Fort Worth, and a good many of their closest friends, had wedged themselves into that jam-packed passageway. Couple of spots were so choked with milling, mumbling people we had a real problem getting by.

Finally, Nate, Carl, and I bunched together on one side of the open door to Daisy Cassidy's room. Evans backed up against the opposite wall as far out of the way as he could get.

Heard Nate suck in a ragged breath. Carlton coughed and backed away from the horrific sight Evans's calculated sidelong move revealed.

Blood-soaked scene came near stunning me to the bottoms of my bootless feet. Hadn't laid my eyes on anything quite so horrific since the time Dennis Limberhand led us all over hell and the Indian Nations looking for those murderous Crooke boys.

Boo Higgins and Carter Dillworthy sat in chairs opposite each other beneath the ghoulish glow of a couple of flickering wall sconces. Higgins had the seat on the far side of the hotel room's door closest to the street below. Man sported the bloody-handled head of a hatchet buried in his skull just above the right ear. Better part of the leaked brain matter and oozing body fluids that sizable hole in his busted noggin had released rested on one shoulder. Stuff was pooled up in a shimmering glob of reddish-gray viscera the size of a number-three grain scoop.

Just right of where a trembling Bob Evans stood, the vacant-eyed Carter Dillworthy sat bolt upright and stared across the narrow hallway at his butchered friend. Near half the massive blade of a knife protruded from Dillworthy's upper right chest. Crude, wooden handle of the big sticker sported the emblazoned words MIGHTY OAK. A glistening river of sticky blood ran from the ragged wound, saturated that side of his shirt and the waist of his pants. Then, the grisly stream coursed over the edge of the ladder-backed chair's woven seat and dripped into a growing puddle on the hotel's carpeted floor.

Carlton slapped me on the arm, coughed again, and pointed at Higgins. "These killings must've happened mighty fast, Hayden. Appears to me as how neither one of these sad wretches had much of a chance to move out of harm's way 'fore he got sent to his Maker."

"Poor jokers evidently trusted whoever did this," Nate said and stared at the ceiling. "Nobody in his right mind would sit still to be murdered in such a fashion, unless he knew and trusted the person what done the deed and let 'em get close enough to pull off such an atrocity."

More to myself than anyone else, I said, "Then again, they could've just been asleep, or almost asleep, when the attack occurred. Might not have been paying strict attention. Maybe they were bored and someone just snuck up and caught them flat-footed, unawares."

A clearly distressed Bob Evans snaked out a tentative hand and placed it on Carter Dillworthy's shoulder. As Evans started to speak, the brutally stabbed Dillworthy's head jerked up. Man sucked in a tremendous lungful of air, then groaned.

"Sweet Jesus," Evans squawked, snatched his hand away as though he'd just touched liquid iron, and jumped back a full step.

The wooden-handled knife, jutting from Dillworthy's body, rose and fell with the rapid heaving of his chest. "Wha . . . Wha . . . What the hell?" he said and made a hesitant, awkward, grasping move toward the blade.

Evans quickly stepped forward, grabbed Dillworthy's hand, and pushed it aside. Wild-eyed jasper had assumed the appearance of a man completely baffled, when he said, "Don't touch it, Dill. Don't dare touch that pigsticker. Might make the situation even worse'n it is now. Doc's on his way. Should be here soon. Maybe he can get the damned thing free and not do too much more in the way of damage."

Dillworthy stared down at the knife like a baffled child. "Yeah, but . . ."

Evans patted his friend's shoulder. "No. You go pullin' a blade that size loose now and you might well bleed slap out, right where you're sittin'."

Dillworthy's stunned, buglike gaze rubbered up to Evans, then from one of us to the other, back down to the knife, and finally landed on Higgins. "He's d-d-dead, ain't he, B-B-Bob?"

Evans nodded. "Sure as hell seems so. 'Course we thought you were a goner, too, Dill. Would be something of a shocker if ole Boo was to go and sit up. Snatch that hatchet out of his own head. Such a sight would sure 'nuff send me to church Sunday morning, and that's a fact."

Leaned over to a point where Dillworthy could see me and said, "Who did this to you, Carter?"

Took some doing, but with a gurgling froth oozing from one corner of his mouth like an ever-widening, pink river of bubbles, he said, "That d-d-damned gal. Was sittin' here tryin' to keep my eyes open, you know. B-B-Bored slap silly. Of a sudden, she jerked . . . the door to the room . . . open. Come a flyin' out . . . like some kinda b- b-broom-ridin' banshee."

"Daisy Cassidy? You mean Daisy Cassidy?" I said.

"Yeah. Gal jumped into the hall . . . like a b-b-branded bobcat. Hit poor Boo with that hatchet . . . quicker'n a b-b-body can spit."

Glanced at Carl and Nate. They both looked dumbfounded and shrugged.

"You're certain?" I said.

"H-H-Hell, yeah. Happened so fast I d-d-didn't even know what she'd done 'fore she was on me like st-st-stink on cow flops with this here knife." He gingerly slid an inquisitive finger up and down the blade's rough hilt. "S-S-Shit. Little gal went and stabbed the bejabberous h-h-hell outta me 'fore I could even react. Who'd a thunk it?"

A clearly unsettled Bob Evans patted his friend's shoulder again. "God forgive us, but we thought you were deader'n a drowned dog, Dill."

Like a chicken charmed by a snake, Dillworthy gazed at the knife's hilt, as it rose and fell with his labored breathing. "M-M-Me, too. She musta hit somethin' as p-p-paralyzed me, Bob. Couldn't get my b-b-breath, doancha know. And then, Lord G-G-God help me, I couldn't m-m-move. Felt as how I'd been turned to stone, or somethin'. Still havin' trouble b-b-breathin'."

Evans stared at his badly wounded friend and shook his head in bug-eyed disbelief.

Dillworthy tilted a wobbling head back against the wall and groaned. Sounded a thousand miles away when he said, "Tell you true, boys, they was . . . a time or two there, th-th-thought I'd already gone on up to Heaven. Swear 'fore Jesus, I seen my gr-gr-grandpap. That old man's been d-d-dead n-n-nigh on thirty year. Then you touched me, Bob. Felt like some kinda hot, nerve-tinglin' spark shot through my whole b-b-body when your hand hit my shoulder. Sure 'nuff brung me b-b-back from wherever'n hell I'd went."

Didn't look around when I heard Nate say, "The kids are gone, Hayden. Ain't a sign of 'em in the room."

Squatted down in front of Dillworthy. "You have any idea where the Cassidys were headed, Carter?"

"Know exactly where they were g-g-goin', Marshal Tilden," he said.

"You're certain?"

Dillworthy's head bobbled around on his neck as if it were mounted on a piece of spring steel. Thought for a second he'd passed out. But then he appeared to snap back to reality and hissed, "P-P-Pretty sure that gal thought she'd gone and k-k-kilt me. Heard the pair of 'em whisperin' back and forth as they went sneaking off down the hall. They was arguin' 'bout what to do and where to go."

"Arguing?"

"Yeah." He took a long, gurgling breath to steady himself, then added, "Seems the boy, M-M-Matt, wanted to scoot on back to the Nations. But that gal, that D-D-Daisy Cassidy, she told her little brother they had to get on down to Turnbow's w-w-wagon yard, find some horses, and hoof it on to Morgan's Cut, quick as they could."

"Morgan's Cut?"

"Y-Y-Yeah. Out on the Brazos. Half-assed, jerkwater wide space in the Abilene stage road. 'Bout forty miles west of Fort Worth. Not much there. Only one saloon. And it's a damned disreputable joint where the dregs of humanity hang out. Couple a stores, if they're still up and r-r-running. Crossroads meetin' place for the low, and them as are goin' lower, more'n anythang else."

"Why the hell would she say something like that?" Carlton wondered. "Better yet, how'd she even know about a spot like Morgan's Cut?"

Dillworthy moaned, wagged his head back and forth like a sick dog. Thought sure he'd said all he could. But then, between hisses and slobbers, he added, "Heard her say as how they had to get their hands on some horses. Hit the trail 'fore anybody f-f-found out what they'd gone and done. Needed to get there . . . quick as they could . . . meet up with somebody . . . name of Coltrane."

"You're certain that's what you heard? No doubt in your mind?" I said.

Dillworthy's eyes rolled up in his head. Violent jerks racked his body several times. One shudder hit him so hard felt sure he might go and fall right out of the chair. Thought for a second or two he would pass out again, or get called to the great beyond before he could finish telling us what we needed to know.

Several seconds of ragged breathing and more moaning passed before the cruelly stabbed man gasped as though strangled, then hissed, "Certain as a man with n-n-nigh on five inches of sharpened steel stickin' outta his chest can be, Marshal."

Nate looked incredulous when he said, "You heard 'em

talking? You actually thought you were dead and still heard 'em talkin'? That what you're sayin', Dill?"

Dillworthy blinked fifteen or twenty times real quick, like he'd lost control of his eyelids and couldn't stop them flapping. Looked some confused, lost, but said, "Yeah. They 'uz only . . . a few feet away. Heard everthang. Swear 'fore Jesus . . . swear it."

Natc held a hand up as though to slow the conversation. "Okay. Okay. Don't get your balbriggans all knotted up."

More than a bit wild-eyed by then, Dillowrthy snapped, "Even heard what all my . . . g-g-good friends and b-b-boon companions said . . . later when they finally showed up."

Man closest to Dillworthy let out an audible gasp, then stared at the hallway floor.

"Yeah. Y'all 'uz millin' around and talkin' 'bout how I 'uz crow bait. How I'd done gone . . . and sh-sh-shook hands with eternity and all. G-G-Give up the ghost. Quit this earth. Deader'n Hell in a Baptist preacher's . . . b-b-backyard. Whole time . . . I 'uz just screamin' like a son of a bitch inside. Nobody could hear me. God Almighty, nobody could h-h-hear me. It were awful."

Didn't have the slightest idea what to say to that. So I got to my feet and turned to Evans. "Have any idea how long ago this all took place, Bob?"

Evans ran one hand up under his hat and scratched. "Oh, couldna been much more'n half an hour, Marshal Tilden. Little longer, maybe." He pointed a shaking finger at Higgins. "I sent poor ole Boo, there, up to spell Hardy Forrest—maybe forty-five minutes ago. Had another man who 'uz supposed to relieve Dill, but he didn't show on time. He come up late and found both of 'em all butchered up like this. Damn near scared him slap to death. Wouldn't even come back up here with us. Still down at the office blubberin' like some kinda escaped loony, I suppose."

"God Almighty," Carlton said. "You mean this poor son of a bitch might've been sittin' here for near half an hour, or more, the way we found him? With that big ole knife juttin' outta his chest and all?"

Evans knuckled a stubble-covered chin, shrugged, then nodded. "Sure as the devil's an awful thought, ain't it? But, yeah. Guess that's the way of it."

Carlton shook his head, then toed at the carpet beneath his feet and stared at the floor. "Damn. Thought I'd seen some strange stuff over the years we've traveled together, Tilden, but this here takes the by-God cake. Woulda swore that man was stone-cold dead when we walked up."

Dillworthy coughed. Spotty stream of spittle and blood trickled out of the corner of his mouth and onto an already gore-covered shirtfront. "Ain't n-n-none of you boys any more surprised that I'm alive th-th-than me," he said, flashed a weak grin, then coughed again.

Nate rubbed the back of his neck. Shook his head, then said, "Oh, I dunno. Couple years ago heard tell of a feller what got hisself shot up through and through the chest, was over in Okmulgee. Everbody what looked him over declared as how the poor fool was deader'n a pitchfork handle."

"His name was Reggie Crawford," Carlton offered.

"Yeah, Reggie Crawford," Nate said. "Talked with folks from around those parts who claimed as how they listened for a heartbeat, felt for a pulse, even held mirrors up to his toothless mouth. Nothin'. Middle of July at the time. So, they went and put 'im on top a slab of ice in the nearest icehouse. Covered the poor feller head to foot with a layer of straw and horse blankets. He laid there for nigh on two days."

"Think I remember hearin' 'bout this one myself," I said.

"Most probably you did, Tilden. It's a well-traveled tale," Nate continued. "Anyhow, way I heard it told, the poor joker come conscious in the dark. Colder'n Hell with the fires doused. Sat up and went to screaming like a lunch whistle at a sawmill. Scared the bejabberous hell outta people outside what heard 'im. Even so, somebody finally got up nerve enough to open the icehouse door. They got him out. Warmed him up, patched him up, and last I heard, he's still alive and kickin' to this very day."

"Yeah," Carlton said, "that's all well and good, but can

testify from personal knowledge, if you put the poor goober's scrambled-up brain in a horned toad, it'd jump around in circles, backward."

About then, a short, dark, intense-looking gent wearing a threadbare, pin-striped, three-piece suit, white shirt, short-brimmed hat, and carrying a black leather bag pushed through the crowd and muscled his way up to the scene. Snatched his pince-nez glasses off, got in Bob Evans's face, and said, "Need to move some of these people the hell and gone out of here, Bob. Sweet merciful father. No way I could possibly help anyone with all these gawking ignoramuses clogging everything up from here to halfway down to the street. Go on, Bob, get them the hell out of my way."

Evans tipped his hat. Said, "Sure 'nuff, Doc. I'll move 'em on down to the other end of the hall. Maybe then you'll have enough room to work and can keep ole Dill from pass-in' on."

I figured as how our presence was no longer needed. So, we scurried back to our room. Got ourselves fully dressed, then hoofed it downstairs. Stood around in the El Paso Hotel's bar for another thirty minutes or so. Had a stiff drink while we waited.

Well, it surprised the hell out of everybody in the place when the doc came down leading Dillworthy by the hand like a small child. Personally must admit, I found it unimaginable that the poor, stabbed-up joker was still alive and could walk at all. The doc had him bandaged from neck to waist, like one of those Egyptian mummies in a traveling carnival you could see back in them days for a nickel. Dillworthy did stumble some now and again, as though he just might not make it to the hotel's front entrance.

Entire troop of Fort Worth's grim-faced police force followed along behind. Narrow stairway made it some difficult, as they lugged the hatchet-brained corpse of Boo Higgins down all wrapped up in a bedsheet. Creeping bloodstain on the upper end of the sheet made it right obvious that his demolished skull was still leaking right smart, though. Saw several people in the hotel lobby cover their faces with a kerchief and turn away. Can't say as I blamed them much. Was right gruesome.

Carlton leaned against the hotel's bar, took a sip from his drink, then under his breath, said, "Gets home to you right quick when a fellow lawman bites the dust, don't it? Bet every one of Marshal Sam Farmer's boys is silently thanking whatever god he prays to that he wasn't sittin' where Boo Higgins was earlier this evenin'. Know for sure I'm gladder'n hell it weren't me."

Half finished drinks in hand, we trailed Fort Worth's party of hurting lawmen out into Third Street. Stood beneath the hotel's veranda and watched as they disappeared up the sparsely peopled thoroughfare and slowly bled into the receding darkness.

Smoldering, square-cut cheroot, that looked like a rotten tree root, dangled from Nate's lips when he said, "We gonna follow along with 'em to the city jail, Hayden?"

"Nope. We've got other, far more important fish to fry, Nate."

Carlton slapped the grip of his belly gun, said, "Best get ourselves on down to Fletcher Turnbow's place, Hayden. If that old man's still alive, it's sure 'nuff gonna surprise the hell outta me."

Can't imagine why, but such a thought hadn't so much as crossed my mind. Of a sudden, though, I felt the urgent need for the three of us to get down to the wagon yard quick as we could heel it. Sat our empty glassware on the edge of the hotel's boardwalk and struck out for Turnbow's outfit like a trio of scalded dogs.

Along the way I said a silent prayer for the old man's safe deliverance from an evil he could not have imagined.

18

"COLTRANE BOYS DIDN'T KILL THE CASSIDYS . . ."

FOUND FLETCHER TURNBOW all balled up in a knot. Laid out in the corner of one of his horse stalls. Blood spattered all over hell and yonder.

"Good Lord, looks like somebody hit the old man in the head with a hay sickle," Carlton said through a tight-lipped grimace.

Nate reached into the stall's feed box and brought out an ax handle decorated on one end with a gob of hair and blood. Held it up. "Nope. Be willing to testify as how they used this right here on the old feller, Carl."

Dragged Turnbow out into the centermost open area of his barn. Hit him with a splash of cold water from a pail Carl found. He woke up and started coming back to life. Struggled and fought with us, at first. Old coot fisted Carlton in the eye before we could get him calmed down. 'Course we knew Fletch didn't mean to do it, but Carl yelped like a kicked dog anyhow. Did his very own share of swearing. Danced around the barn, one hand cupped over a split brow.

Second or so after he popped Carl, Turnbow hopped up

on wobbly legs. Codger was so bowlegged he couldn't have caught a pig in a water trough. Fists out like a sparring, bareknuckled prizefighter, he went to bouncing around on those saddle-warped legs of his. Cussed a blue streak that could have peeled red paint off a New Hampshire barn. His muddle-headed, anger-laced profanity made that musty barn's air crackle and smell like sulfur.

Bug-eyed, slobbers dribbled down the geezer's stubble-covered chin, when he screeched, "Kick your collective asses, by God. Yessir, sure as hell will. Want some? Come on and git some. Whip the whole damned bunch of yuh like a pack of yard dogs. Run all of yuh back under the porch, by God."

Took considerable doing, but we finally got Fort Worth's premier hostler calmed down a bit. Had to spend almost five minutes talking to him like he'd reverted back to early child-hood and needed his diaper changed.

Tried to clean him up with a piece of rag and some water, while he sat on an empty, wooden nail keg and tongue-lashed the entire seen and unseeable world. Think he had just about wore out every method of blasphemy privy to God and man-kind when he said, "Swear to Christ, Marshal Tilden, a body cain't trust a solitary soul these days. World's goin' straight to a festerin' hell on an outhouse door, you ask me. Can't even trust a good-lookin' woman or little kids anymore. Never can tell when one of 'em might go an' jump up and try to kill the hell out of you. Would lead a feller to believin' we're in the final days 'fore the Rapture comes."

"Straw-haired girl with the face of an angel do this to you?" I said.

Turnbow looked surprised and a bit puzzled, but nodded. "Well, kinda. Woke me up out'n a sound sleep, Tilden. Went to bangin' on my door like my barn was on fire or something. Hell, I 'uz dreamin' 'bout painted women of loose virtue and looser underwear," Turnbow said and dabbed at the wound on the side of his head. "Still pretty groggy when I opened the door, I guess."

"Have a dark-haired boy looked like he might be part Injun with her?" Carlton said.

"Yeah. That she did. But he didn't say mucha nothin'. Not at first, anyways. Just kinda hung back in the shadows and looked sulkified. All red in the face. Acted like he might go and bust out cryin' just anytime."

Nate leaned against a stall rail, pulled the makings, and set to building a hand-rolled. Puffed it to life, then said, "Attack you right off?"

"No. No. They both come inside. Gal said as how Marshal Hayden Tilden, from Fort Smith, had said I 'uz supposed to provide 'em both with a proper mount. Said they needed the horses fast as I could get 'em saddled. Said as how they had to be on their way quick as possible. Made out like you were gonna explain it all for me when morning come."

"You believe her, Fletch?" Carlton said.

"Hell, no, I didn't believe her. Told both of 'em as much, too, by God. 'Course, soon's I went to questionin' 'em that really ripped the rag off the bush. Words hadn't even got outta my mouth good and that boy started acting like he'd had some loco weed in his last bowl of porridge. Ranted and raved like some kinda madcap. Girl tried to calm him down. Then, she went and pulled a sack fulla money out'n this big ole canvas bag she 'uz a-totin'."

"Sack full of money?" Carlton said, as though amazed.

"Yeah. Yeah. Looked like some kinda bank bag, maybe. Bet she had ten thousand dollars in that poke, if'n she had a penny. Said if I couldn't see my way to doin' as you'd requested, she'd buy the horses. Pay fer 'em with cash money. Long as I could get 'em saddled and have the two of 'em on their way in ten minutes or less."

Nate grinned. "You get the job done, Fletch?"

Turnbow dropped the bloody rag into his lap, then fingered at the gash over his ear. "Hell, yeah, I got 'er done. Not quite as quick as she wanted, but I got 'er done. Walking them animals to the door to get my money, when that boy popped up in front of me with a stick of wood in his hand. Swung at me and missed."

"Missed?" Carlton said.

"Yeah. But then he chased me back yonder to the stall.

Hemmed me up and whacked me on the noggin. Felt like my head split open all the way down to my ass crack."

I shot a quick glance over at Carl and said, "Get our fantails out and ready to go. We need to be on their trail before they can manage to do any more damage to unsuspecting citizens they might happen upon along their path."

Refocused my attention on Turnbow, as Carl and Nate raced to our mounts. "Thinking right yet?"

"Guess so. Kid made one helluva dent in my noggin though."

"What's the quickest route to Morgan's Cut, Fletch?"

Still fiddling with the slash over his ear, when he pointed in no particular direction and mumbled, "Just head on back up Main to Weatherford. Turn due west. You'll hit the old Abilene stage road. Morgan's Cut's thirty-five, maybe forty miles out. Can't miss it, really. Spot where the Brazos crosses over the road. Wide, washed out spot there. Known to flood for no apparent reason there. Dangerous at times. That where you think they're goin'?"

"Yeah. Pretty sure. Put the spur to our animals, might even catch up with them before they can get there."

"Well, they ain't got much of a head start on you. Might've even done you a favor that'll help."

"How so?"

"Give that boy a big blaze-faced plug named Digger. Animal's right rear shoe's cracked and needs replacin'. Was gonna fix it today. Should be a snap to track 'im. Kid pushes Digger too hard, that shoe's gonna come a-flyin' off."

Patted the old-timer on his shoulder. "That's good to hear, Fletch. I'll put Carl on their track. Lot better at reading sign than me. He'll run them down. Now, are you gonna be all right?"

Turnbow flashed a tight, snaggletoothed grin, then nodded. "Take more'n a kid with a stick of wood to keep me down, Marshal. Be goin' like a barn burnin' by tomorrow mornin'. Garn-teed."

"Sure you don't want me to talk with Bob Evans and have the doctor come on down this way to check on you?"

"Oh, hell, no. Don't trust no sawbones any farther'n I could throw the two horses them kids made off with. I'll be fine. Just need to take a few minutes to collect myself's all."

As I turned and started away, Turnbow added, "You catch that gal, Tilden, tell her she owes me a hunnert and six dollars for them horses, saddles, and such. Sure would like to have my money."

Razor's edge of sunlight sliced across our backs as we stormed out of Fort Worth and hit the Abilene Road. Green, hilly landscape, typical of east Texas, falls away pretty quick once you get a few miles west of the area around Hell's Half Acre. Earth flattens out. Quickly becomes browner and more barren. Not much in the way of greenery except stunted bushes and the rare tree, here and there. Rode like red-eyed demons straight from the fiery pit, till the horses began to complain.

When the light got good enough, Carlton and Nate scoured the heavily traveled path looking for sign of our prey. Took near an hour of concentrated effort before they managed to pick Digger's trail out of the cobweb of tracks that confronted them in the baked soil.

Going along at a pretty good clip, an hour or so later, when Nate drew us to a stop atop a small rise in the road. Quarter of a mile away, only live oak more than ten feet tall grew within a few steps of the roadway. Appeared to me as how travelers often stopped there to seek respite from a sun that seemed to have the power to auger right through a man's Stetson and on into his skull.

Nate pulled his long glass. Snapped the five-segment scope out to its entire length, scanned the area in every direction. Handed the fully extended glass to me and said, "Look yonder, Hayden. Base of the tree."

"What is it?" Carl said.

Put the glass up to my eye. "Appears there's somebody sitting on the ground with his back to the tree, Carl. Horse not far away. Animal's standing hipshot. Got its right rear hoof up. Damn. Think that might well be Matt Cassidy down there, boys." Handed the glass back to Nate. "Whoever it is, Cassidy or not, he sure as hell ain't moving around much. Best kick on down and check it out."

"We goin' in hot?" Carl said, then pulled and cocked a pistol.

"Sure as shootin'. Shotguns and rifles probably best," I said and freed my sawed-off Greener from its bindings. "In the immortal words of Billy Bird, it's always better to be safe than sorry."

Guess we hadn't advanced much more than a hundred yards when Nate reined us to a halt again. Said, "Well, he still ain't movin'. And I don't see anyone else around. Either of you?"

Me and Carl agreed as how we didn't. So, we kicked hard and thundered up on the scene like a heavily armed twister. Didn't take long to see why the boy hadn't moved around any.

Stepped off Gunpowder's back with my shotgun in hand. Three of us spread out and crept up on Matt Cassidy at the same time. Maybe ten paces away when Nate stopped dead in his tracks, gagged, and almost lost everything he'd had to eat for breakfast and the tubful of victuals he'd scarfed down the day before.

Pool of sticky, blackened blood saturated the ground for two feet around the Cassidy boy's narrow behind. Someone had sliced the kid's stomach open from one side to the other. Pile of innards lay in a greasy heap between his outstretched legs.

Carlton kicked at the dirt and looked away. "Jesus," he said. "Ain't this a god-awful mess."

Eased up as close to the kid as I cared to get. Hit one knee and damn near fell over backward when he looked up at me. Face drained of color and twisted in pain, tiny rivers of tears streaked their way down his filth-encrusted cheeks.

Most pitiful thing I'd ever heard when he pawed at that mound of guts with useless hands and gasped, "Tr-Tr-Tried to fix 'em. Tried to pull 'em b-b-back. Cain't get 'em back inside where they belong."

Behind me, heard Carlton say, "Sweet Lord Almighty."

Waved at the kid with one hand. Said, "Don't, Matt. Don't do that. You're just making a bad situation a lot worse."

He held up a mess of his own entrails, shot a desperate, fleeting look my direction. "Can you p-p- put 'em back? Please. Oh, p-p-please, God. Can you p-p-put 'em back, Marshal?"

In spite of myself, shook my head and looked away for a second. "No. No, Matt. Think you're beyond human help. Not sure anyone could put you back together, son. Not now."

An agonized, wrenching groan oozed up from somewhere in the boy's thin, empty chest. "She's crazy. Nuttier'n a bag . . . of roasted peanuts. Said sh-sh-she didn't have n-n-no more use for me and opened my stomach up like she was guttin' a calf."

Nate eased up next to me. Dropped a canteen on the ground near the butt of my Greener. "Not sure we should give him water in such a condition, but I brought it anyway." He squatted next to me and looked at everything he could see, except the butchered remnants of Matt Cassidy.

Opened the canteen and handed it to the boy. "He's way past helping, Nate. Don't think a little water will hurt anything."

Cassidy kid took several long gulps. Still going at it when I took the water away from him.

"Daisy? Your sister?" I said. "She did this? She's the crazy one?"

He wiped bloody lips on a nasty shirt-sleeve. "Yeah. She d-d-done for me all right. Sure 'nuff. But sh-sh-she ain't my sister. I ain't Matt Cassidy. Ain't . . . nobody named Matt Cassidy. Name's Jacky White. Lived on the farm next to the Cassidy place."

Didn't see him but felt Carl behind me when he said, "You there when the Coltrane boys kilt the Cassidy family, son?"

No answer for a time. Thought maybe the boy had passed over. Of a sudden, he sucked in a long ragged breath. Said, "Coltrane boys didn't k-k-kill the Cassidys. D-D-Daisy done it. Well, actually, Daisy . . . and me. We done the sorry deed."

Carlton grunted like he'd been slapped across the face.

Nate shook his head and stared at the ground.

"Daisy? You're sure?" I said.

"We were together in one of her pa's fields when the Coltranes came. Doin' . . . well, sure you can guess at what we 'uz doin'. Spent most of our time together doin' each other." He groaned, closed his eyes, groaned again. Called on a god that evidently had other things to take care of.

"You were out in the fields, doing whatever you were doing, when the Coltrane boys came by the house?" I asked.

He grunted, nodded, then said, "Got back 'bout a minute . . . after they left. Daisy had some kinda fit . . . found out her pa'd run 'em off. Gal's m-m-murderous addled in her thinker box. Has a th-th-thing for that Jesse. Called me Jesse . . . in my ear . . . when we was a-doin' the big . . . wiggle, you know."

"God above. No. We didn't know that. Any of it," Carlton mumbled. "You're sayin' the gal's insane?"

"Hell . . . yeah. She grabbed . . . an ax. Went in the house . . . kilt her ma and baby brother. Come outside dripping blood. Scared me . . . sl-sl-slap to death. Handed me a p-p-pistol. Said I should k-k-kill her pa. He was out in his sorghum patch. God help me, I tr-tr-tried to get out of it. Daisy wouldn't listen. Made me do it."

Sounded unconvinced when Carl said, "She killed her mother and brother, then you shot Matthew Cassidy?"

"Had to. She said . . . we'd never again do any of what we'd been doing . . . if'n I didn't kill her pa the way she wanted. So, I took the pistol. Walked down to the field. Sh-sh-shot him in the head. Looked . . . right surprised a-layin' there . . ."

Nate sounded more than a bit angry when he snapped, "Why are you here, boy? We thought the Coltrane brothers did the killings sure as Hell's hot."

"'S what Daisy wanted people to think. She's chasin' Jesse. Cain't think of nothin' else. Bird-doggin' his trail. . . . Daisy says he's a-waitin' for her . . . at Morgan's Cut. Said they had previous made plans. If'n he come by and m-m-missed her, she was to head for Morgan's Cut, out west of Fort Worth. Even give her a map. So . . . we k-k-kilt her family . . . took all the money hid under the floor of the house . . . and headed out."

"She told quite a tale so you two could stay in Fort Worth, didn't she?" I said.

"Yeah. Quite a tale 'bout how she'd b-b-been mistreated. She actually believed Jesse would come. Not sure why . . . b-b-but she believed it. Believed it till you marshals . . . showed up. Then, she went m-m-murderous crazy again. Jesus . . . I'm cold."

Gutted boy's eyes rolled to the back of his head. A pink-ish, gray froth poured from both corners of his mouth. Went to flopping around like a beached fish. Seizure proved so violent, we had to jump back and move away to keep from getting sprayed with all the flying viscera. Guess he flailed around for near a minute before finally getting still again.

Think it was Nate who said, "Figure he's gone, Hayden?"

Took some doing, but I managed to get around to the White kid's side without stepping in his guts. Felt for a pulse by placing my finger under his jaw. Couldn't find one. Said, "Yeah, he's gone, boys. He's gone."

We didn't bother to dig a hole. Scrounged up every rock we could find and just piled them on top of the body. Took some doing and wasted nigh on two more hours of our time. Just couldn't bring myself to leave the boy laying out there in the big cold and lonely all gutted out like that and at the mercy of passing animals.

At first blush, I couldn't figure any way to grease the path to whatever God had in mind for Jacky White. Stood next to that pile of rocks, hat in hand, but just couldn't think of a single good thing to say for him. Then, I remembered a pas-sage my mother had me try to commit to memory. Piece by an English feller named Donne, I think. Not sure I said it right, but I tried.

Stared at that pile of rocks and said, "No man is an island, entire of itself; every man is a piece of the continent, a part of the main; . . . any man's death diminishes me, because I am involved in mankind; and therefore never send to know for whom the bell tolls; it tolls for thee." Picked up a handful of dirt and scattered it atop that poor boy's pitiful grave. "In the midst of all life we are in death. Earth to earth, ashes to ashes, dust to dust; in the sure and certain hope of the resurrection unto eternal life. May God have mercy on his soul."

Carlton placed a hand on my shoulder. "Time to go, Hayden. You did the best you could by 'im. Nothin' else for us to do here. Got bloody business, on down the trail."

Slipped my hat on. Stared at that pile of rocks. Said, "Think he told us the truth, Carl?"

"Why would he lie?" Nate offered. "Boy was standin' on death's threshold when we got here. He had to have known what was in store for him."

"Have to say I'm with Nate on this one, Hayden. Feel like an old dog that's been chasing his tail for years and finally realized that what he's been chasing is attached. Wild-eyed gal's sure as hell done gone and pulled the curtain on all of us."

"Knew as soon as we walked into that hotel room back in Fort Worth there was something wrong, Carl," I said. "Just never expected anything to match this."

Carl stared at his feet. Said, "If you'd a told me, when we left Fort Smith, that this chase would've worked out the way it has, pretty sure I'd of thought you'd lost your mind, and Elizabeth was gonna have to have you committed to the crazy house over in Benton."

"Either of you ever had to drag a woman back to Maledon's gallows?" Nate asked, then climbed onto his mount.

Question came as something of a surprise, but we both said "No" at the same time.

"Ever had to kill one?"

Again, "No" in unison.

Stepped into the stirrups, threw my leg over Gunpowder's muscular back. "Then again, according to the Book, there's usually a first time for everything."

As we turned our animals west again, Carl said, "Just have to wait and see what's waiting for us at Morgan's Cut, I guess."

19

"Gonna Brace 'Em Inside, or Call 'Em Out?"

DREW OUR ANIMALS up on the east side of a wide, shallow, water-poor wash that slashed across the Abilene road as if the earth had opened up on its own and left a dried out, scabrous wound. Hard against the far bank of Morgan's Cut, a single line of rickety, clapboard buildings and gauzy canvas tents shimmered in the glare of early afternoon sunshine. Pitiful, forlorn spot reminded me of Lone Pine, up in the Nations, and the fight with Mordecai Staine.

Ramshackle structure, dead center of several smaller but similar buildings, sported a large, obviously handmade wooden sign emblazoned with the words HICKERSON'S CANTINA— BESTEST WHISKEY 'TWEEN HERE AND ABILENE. Almost a dozen drooping bangtails stood tethered to the seedy tavern's hitch rails.

"You figure the Coltrane bunch is in there, Tilden?" Carlton said.

"No way to be absolutely certain, but I'd bet my house on it. Bet Daisy Cassidy's in there, too," I said.

Function of the other weather-beaten, dilapidated stores and shops roosting on either side of the notorious roadhouse proved unknowable, from our vantage point. They evidenced no billboards or markers to enlighten the passing traveler of their intentions.

Glanced over at Nate and could tell the sight affected him in much the same fashion as it had me. Watched as he limbered up his shotgun, attended to the death-dealing weapon's massive brass shells, then intently stared at the rough village less than a hundred yards from where we sat our mounts. Our memories of the blistering gunfight at Lone Pine remained fresh and near to the surface of our emotions.

He took a quick look my direction, flashed a nervous grin, then said, "Ever eat a deer-coo-kin, Tilden?"

Brought my big popper up and laid it across my saddle. "A deer-coo-kin, you say? Hear you right, Nate? A deer-coo-kin?"

"Yeah. Might well be the finest plate of victuals you could ever fork up and let slide down your gullet. Makes my mouth water just thinkin' 'bout how good one of 'em is. My grandpa could cook up a deer-coo-kin better'n anybody in Arkansas."

Carlton made a piggish snorting sound, flipped the loading gate open on his belly gun, then, as he rolled the cylinder and eyed each round, said, "Aye God, Swords, this ain't another one a them Arkansas, stump-jumpin'-bayou-family recipes you're always comin' up with is it? Like fried crawdads and other such lunatic ideas?"

Barrels of Nate's shotgun snapped into place with a loud metallic click. "Could be. Could very well be. Why? You got somethin' against my family's eatin' habits, Cecil?"

Carlton almost let the query pass, but couldn't keep his mouth shut. "Oh, hell, no. Just strikes me as a mite odd that this business with food always seems to come up right 'fore we're about to face the possibility of some fast-and-furious gun work. Can't remember as how I've ever heard you bring up the subject at any other time."

From behind a narrow-eyed gaze, Nate stared across Morgan's Cut. A sudden, disconnected, distant look played across the man's face as his smile bled away. "Damn. Believe you're right, Carl," he mumbled, as if talking to himself. "Never really thought of it just exactly that way. Somethin' about hunger and the expectation of the air being laced with gun smoke and hot lead just has the unique power to drive me to thoughts of hearth, home, and food, I suppose. Must be why the deer-coo-kin came to mind."

Left the horses beneath a sixty-foot cottonwood that hovered over the road on our side of the cut. Ground at the base of the tree was layered two feet deep in brown, sunbaked leaves. Figured there were roots as big as a grown man's leg spreading out atop the unseen earth in every direction from the tree's thick trunk.

Guns at the ready, we heeled our way into the arid streambed. Midway, Carlton said, "Well, Swords, we'll be right in the lion's den in a minute or so. You gonna tell us 'fore this dance starts or not?"

Water-smoothed gravel crunched beneath our feet, as we strode toward Hickerson's crude roadhouse. Could hear the subtle amusement in Nate's voice, when he said, "Why, what on earth do you mean? Tell you what, Carl?"

"Tell us what'n the blue-eyed hell a deer-coo-kin is, for the love of sweet Mary? Can't just leave a man hanging out here in the wind a wonderin' about such things, now can you? Wouldn't want to go to my Maker, in a few minutes, a wonderin' what'n the hell a deer-coo-kin is. Would hate to spend eternity with such an unanswered poser a-plaguing me."

"Oh, so now you want to know about deer-coo-kins? That it, Carl?"

As we stepped onto the west bank of the cut, Nate almost laughed when he said, "Okay, here's the deal. First, you field dress a deer. Rub the carcass down with every kinda spice you can lay your hands on, inside and out. Use whatever you've got. Don't really matter. Fill the carcass with a couple of chopped coons and enough chicken meat to fill 'er up, along with lots of salt and pepper. Any kinda root vegetables handy. Truss 'er up good and tight. Put 'er on a spit. Roast 'er till she's ready to eat. My God, makes my mouth water just tellin' you about it."

Three of us came to a rocking halt less than a hundred feet from the cow-country oasis's shabby, sunblasted front entrance. Heard Carl let out a low chuckle, then he said, "Sweet merciful father. So you take a deer, stuff it with some coons, couple a chickens, and some vegetables. Then you roast the whole deal over an open fire and you've got yourself a deer-coo-kin? That's what you're talkin' 'bout, right?"

Toothy grin creaked its way across Nate's face. Boy made loud, smacking noises, then licked his lips. "There you go, Carl. Aye Godfrey, that puppy's the best eatin' this side of a corn-fed, Kansas City T-bone. Guaranteed."

Carl pulled the hammers back on his big popper. Swept the front of Hickerson's with one final flinty gaze, then said, "Get back to Fort Smith we'll have you cook us one of 'em. Do it out front of Tilden's house. Have a picnic down by the river. Make a day of it."

"Sounds like a winner to me," I said. "But, right now, we've got to take care of this little problem."

"Gonna brace 'em inside, or call 'em out?" Carl said.

"No point calling them out. Might start shooting from the windows and doors," I said. "Best go on in after them, I suppose. Once we get inside, whatever comes our way, don't hesitate. You see a threat, either of you, drop the hammer on it. We'll argue about the consequences later."

Carlton didn't look at me when he said, "Don't see me sittin' on my gun hand, do you?"

Nate shot a corner of the eye look at me. "What about the girl, Hayden? If she's inside and comes up a threat, how should we handle it?"

"Well, near as I can tell that gal's had a direct hand in at least five brutal murders that bordered on butchery. Along with an indirect connection to the killing of her father. Wouldn't want her too close to me with a knife or hatchet in her hand."

My friends both nodded, but I could tell that despite their

firsthand knowledge of Daisy Cassidy's potential for bloody violence, they were still uncomfortable with the possibility of being the person responsible for sending a woman to Satan with a bullet in her head. Made me more than a bit uneasy when I recognized that reluctance so late in the chase.

"Do what you think best," I said. "But make damned sure you protect yourselves. And don't waver, shilly-shally, or let your emotions get in the way. Understood?"

Nate nodded.

Carlton grunted.

"Well, guess we'd best get this dance started," I said. "You ready?"

Nate grabbed the brim of his hat and pulled it down tighter. "I 'uz born ready, Tilden, and you know it. So, let's put the spurs to 'er and see which way she hops."

Carlton let out another animalistic grunt.

We took the steps out front of Hickerson's as one man. Pushed our way through a rickety set of batwings that complained like a pair of stomped tomcats. Heavy odors of whiskey, tobacco, sweat, dirt, and a triple-deep layer of puke-soaked sawdust on the floor flooded my nose and made my eyes water as we crossed into the backwater tavern's waiting, interior gloom.

Soon as we'd made our way over the rustic liquor locker's threshold, Nate hooked a quick right and set up in a spot near the end of a coarse bar made of nothing more than rough-cut, two-by-twelve pine boards laid atop empty whiskey kegs.

Carl drifted to the corner on my left. He covered that entire side of the single, narrow, poorly furnished room with a wide sweep of his big blaster's open muzzle.

There were three tables along the wall opposite the bar, a fourth in the corner, and one more at the far end of the joint's makeshift serving counter. Place was hopping busy. Not an empty chair to be had. Not much available in the way of standing room.

Only nod to anything like decoration consisted of numerous stuffed animals, or their disembodied heads, hanging in a slapdash fashion on the walls. Joint even sported a stuffed rattlesnake sitting on the bar near the slick-pated drink slinger's right hand.

I shot a side-to-side glance around the room and almost laughed out loud. Only a single overflowing spittoon in the entire, depressing place, near as I could tell. Tobacco-stained pot was ten feet away, but I could smell it.

As soon as we came through the door, the crowd parted and I spotted the Coltrane boys and two other men. No way to have missed Benny's brother, Jesse, seated at the table in the farthest corner. Draped over the man, like a blond-haired human blanket, Daisy Cassidy had her tongue so far into his ear set me to wondering if she might be trying to lick a clean spot in his brain.

Bearded giant on Jesse Coltrane's immediate left and his dwarflike companion both pricked a familiar place in my memory. Figured the pair for Ennis Buckheart and his vicious little traveling companion, Egger Salt. Buckheart looked like a battle-scarred grizzly wearing a stovepipe hat. Salt brought a twelve-year-old child with the face of an ancient codger to mind.

I knifed a flint-eyed glance Carl's direction. Appeared he recognized Jesse and his friends as well. Could tell Carl had already assessed the situation and made a quick, calculated decision on how to handle it.

Guess our arrival didn't register on the Coltrane bunch, at first. Either that, or they were considerably stupider, and less attentive, than men carrying their kinds of reputations should have been. Or maybe the hundred-fifty-proof, who-hit-john skull pop they were throwing down had simply burned up enough brain matter to make them dim-witted in the extreme.

Managed to get near halfway across the room before most of the raw joint's other, more alert patrons realized that bony-fingered death had just shown up in the form of three hard-eyed men carrying shotguns. Of a sudden, that godforsaken roadhouse went to emptying out like water running over the lip of an overfilled rain barrel in a south Texas thunderstorm.

Heavy thump of booted feet on the boardwalk outside, and sound of animals leaving for parts unknown, quickly followed. In a matter of seconds, Hickerson's saloon got quieter than the inside of a dead horse.

As Carl sometimes liked to say, joint suddenly got so quiet you could hear amorous mice making wild-assed whoopee behind the wallboards. I would have sworn the air on every side of me crackled.

20

"BENNY GAVE YOU UP, BOYS."

PRETTY SURE DAISY Cassidy spotted me first. Couldn't have been more than ten feet away when the girl sliced a wicked, heavy-lidded glance my direction. She hopped off a hatless Jesse Coltrane's knee like the seat of her dress had somehow caught on fire. Girl brought the back of one hand up to twitching lips and sucked in air as if she had, unexpectedly, found herself at the bottom of a mile-deep lake.

Something about the Cassidy gal's steely, blue-eyed gaze had definitely changed since I last saw her back in the El Paso Hotel. Though no expert in such matters, by any stretch of the imagination, came to the immediate and inescapable realization that I stared into the face of madness. Madness so deeply entrenched as to be unfathomable. The change shocked and amazed me. Skin between my shoulder blades prickled. A cold chill ran down my sweaty spine as I returned her unhinged, glaring gaze.

Barely heard it when Daisy let out a peculiar, hacking giggle, batted her eyes at me as though flirting with a prospective lover, then, between fingers pressed against pouty lips, said, "Oh, my glorious God. I don't believe this."

His arm still draped around the swaying girl's waist, Jesse Coltrane appeared totally unconcerned. As if the grim-looking man a few feet away holding a shotgun didn't exist, he fiddled with a half-filled whiskey glass and continued jawing with the three other jokers at the table. I could see the hands of every man there, except those of Ennis Buckheart.

Her flabbergasted gaze still glued on me, Daisy Cassidy leaned over, whispered something into Jesse Coltrane's ear. Then she pointed me out with a finger that trembled.

Coltrane cast an insolent glare my direction, took a nibbling sip from his half-filled glass of brain-numbing panther sweat, then said, "Well, well, well. Just be damned, fellers. Look at what we've got here. Appears we're in the presence of the real and only Hayden by-God Tilden. And his famed companion Carlton J. Cecil. Pair of infamous Parker lawdogs and celebrated man killers."

Seated across the table from Jesse, a gent with a similar dark, lean, chewed-leather look, that I took to be his brother Leroy, shot a teeth-gritting gaze up at me. He dropped an acid-laced glance on Carlton, then hissed, "Think you're right, Jesse. 'Pears we've been corralled by the best known of all Parker's badge-wearin' bastards. Guess we must be famous, by God. Otherwise, Deputy U.S. Marshal Hayden Tilden and his favorite henchman Carlton J. Cecil wouldn't be here."

Egger Salt's nervous, weasel-eyed stare swept from Carl, to me, to Nate. He slapped Buckheart on the arm, then rocked his rickety, ladder-backed chair onto two legs. Little ferret said, "'Pears you law-bringin' sons a bitches is loaded fer bear today. Cain't remember last time I seen this many shotguns pointed my direction. Figure it best you know as how if you bastards've come a lookin' fer a fight—you're in the right place."

Man's voice sounded like glass breaking when Nate Swords snapped, "Won't be any trouble, Salt. Long as none of you make any sudden moves. 'Cause the first man as goes for his iron's gonna take the whole crowd of you to Hell with 'im on an outhouse door."

Buckheart torqued a tub-sized, bearlike head to one side as though he might bring a foot up and scratch his ear. "Ain't got no call to go botherin' us, by gar. This here's Tejas. Tejas, dammit. You bastards got no authority outside the Nations."

Think it surprised the whole bunch when I threw them a friendly smile, then said, "All too common misunderstanding on your part, Ennis. We're deputy U.S. marshals. Our authority extends to the farthest reaches of every state and territory. And today, we're here to arrest you boys for the crimes of bank robbery and cold-blooded murder."

Leroy Coltrane had assumed a lock-jawed look similar to that of a rabid dog. Slobbers dribbled from one corner of his mouth when he growled, "That's a steamin' load of horse manure, Tilden. Ain't got nothin' on us. Any of us. Even if'n you do, it ain't nothin' more'n a bag fulla dung, whatever it is. And whoever told you that windy whizzer's nothin' but a fork-tongued belly slinker and a son of a bitch."

Carl sounded like he just might fall down laughing when he said, "Benny gave you up, boys. Remember him? Little brother Benny Coltrane. Implicated all you skunks in the robbery of the bank in Winslow, the murder of a book peddler name of Marcel Cushman, along with the possible abetting in the murders of this girl's entire family."

"Benny?" Jesse said. "I don't believe that for a second."

"'Course your loving woman there added more fuel to the fires with what she went and did," I said.

Surprised me more then a bit when Jesse Coltrane shot an iniquitous look Daisy Cassidy's direction. Look of surprised understanding spread over his face when he growled, "You actually went and done it, didn't you? You crazy, lunatic bitch. That's why you showed up here like you done, ain't it?"

If looks could set fires, Jesse Coltrane would've gone up in flames like a burlap bag full of dried pine knots in a depot stove. Thought sure Daisy Cassidy was about to reach down, run a couple fingers up his nose, snatch his head off, then hang it next to the twelve-point buck mounted on the wall behind him.

"Shut it, Jesse," Daisy said. "Just keep your stupid mouth

shut. Ain't nothin' but a bunch of ignorant lawmen tellin' lies. They can't prove a thing."

"She's right, Jesse, up to a point anyway," I said. "But you might want to be aware that she's already set the law on you, and the rest of your gang, by telling everyone within a hundred miles of Dutch Crossing that you're the ones responsible for her entire family's unnatural departure from this life."

Jesse Coltrane's face flushed and eyes almost crossed. "You laid those murders off on me, Leroy, and the boys?"

"Three murders, as a matter of pure fact, Jesse," Carl said. "Includin' her entire family. Couple of them rubbed out with an ax. Gal's done made you an express appointment with the hangman."

Daisy Cassidy went into a kind of semi-crouch. Looked like a crazed, cornered animal when she shot me an overheated glare filled with enough lunacy and venom to kill a Montana moose. "Don't you listen to any of them, Jesse," she snapped. "They're lying. Lying like cheap throw rugs. Bet the truth's never had any place in either of these men's lying mouths."

"Better find another way to justify your crimes, miss," Nate called out. "Everyone here, including Jesse, Leroy, and their friends, knows that Hayden Tilden don't lie."

Leroy Coltrane rocked back in his chair and let out a disgusted grunt. Threw down a full shot of whiskey, then said, "If I tole you once, Jesse, bet I tole you ten times. Ten times, by God. This here gal's nothin' but bad news walkin'. Somethin' ain't attached and workin' proper in her thinker box. If'n you warn't doin' mosta yer thinkin' with yer crotch, from daylight till dark, you'd a seen the truth of it a long time ago."

With a glare of angry, squinty-eyed determination etched into his face, Jesse Coltrane got to both feet faster than I could have imagined. Red-faced killer grabbed Daisy Cassidy by the throat in a heartbeat. Couldn't believe my ears when he hissed, "Ain't nothin' I ever wanted more'n you, girl. Hell, I 'uz willing to do just about anything to have you. But, by God, they's some things that are just not acceptable no matter how good-lookin' a woman you are. Or how talented with that thang 'tween your legs."

Fingers clamped to the Cassidy girl's throat, Jesse shook her like a kid's raggedy doll. Think the three of us lawdogs yelled, "Let her go," at the same time. But he didn't hear a single word. Looking back on that day, from the vantage of time and some thought on the subject, the man might have been beyond hearing much of anything by that point.

Daisy Cassidy appeared in considerable distress when Jesse added, "Some behavior can't be tolerated when a feller lives the way I do. Rattin' a man out to the law, for somethin' he didn't do, heads a damned short list of such absolutely unforgivable transgressions."

Carlton might as well have thrown coal oil on a raging bank of head-high flames when he said, "She's been living with another man, too, Jesse. Young feller from back home named Jacky White. You know 'bout that? Yeah. She was shacked up with him in a hotel room in Fort Worth, until recently. Real cozy arrangement till she went and sliced his belly open and all his guts fell out on the ground. Probably blame that killin' on you as well, she gets the chance."

Coltrane's eyes went wild. His grip on Daisy Cassidy's throat tightened. Figured she'd be dead where she stood in pretty short order, when he growled, "What the hell'd you go and do? Who've you been livin' with, girl? What else have you blamed on me'n my boys?"

Dry, choked, gagging sounds filtered up from Daisy Cassidy's closed throat. Girl couldn't speak. Appeared to me she couldn't breathe either. Went to clawing at Coltrane's fingers and wrist. Her eyes rolled toward the top of her head.

Then, out of nowhere, Jesse's free hand came around and smacked her across the mouth so hard it made my own cheek burn. The lick rattled Daisy Cassidy right to the soles of her knee-high riding boots.

"Damn you," Coltrane yelped. "Who've you been sleepin' with, woman? What kinda lie'd you go and tell on me and my brothers? Best cough it on up, or, swear 'fore Jesus, I'll choke the life outta you right here, then piss on your corpse."

Guess those words had scarcely fallen from the eldest Coltrane's sneering lips when fate stepped in and took a hand in the situation. What happened next surprised and stunned the bejabbers out of me and everyone else there that day.

Not sure to this very instant how she came up with the knife. Stood no more than a dozen feet away from the two arguing lovers, and swear I just didn't see it coming. Neither did Jesse Coltrane. Suppose it's possible the pigsticker lay hid in one of the folds of Daisy's dress—my best guess anyway. Or maybe she had it strapped to her leg somewhere. Even after all these years, answer to the question's still a mystery to me. Doesn't really matter anyway, I suppose. Long, thin blade—second cousin to a flattened ice pick—flashed up under poor, dumb Jesse's ribs and snatched all the starch out of him, so quick, no one who witnessed the act realized what she'd gone and done—leastways, not at first.

Eldest living member of the Coltrane clan suddenly looked right surprised. He coughed, gagged, then grabbed at the gaping hole punched in his chest. Unbelieving, he shot a puzzled glance down at the wound, then made a retching sound like he might puke his socks up. River of blood filled the gaps between grasping fingers as he turned Daisy loose, went rubber-legged, stumbled, and fell backward into his recently vacated seat at the table.

Brother Leroy's chair flipped over and noisily bounced several times when he sprang to drunken, unsteady feet. A look of confused befuddlement sat on his face when he said, "What the hell's goin' on here? What's wrong with you, Jesse?"

"Oh, God," Jesse Coltrane gasped. "Think she done went'n stabbed me, brother. Jesus, think she might've . . . might've . . . gone an' kilt me."

Well, quicker than half of no time at all, the whole dance went straight to a sulfurous Hell. A pistol flashed into Leroy Coltrane's formerly empty paw. Unthinking idiot snapped off a shot that caught a still gagging Daisy Cassidy right between the eyes.

Least stable of the Coltrane brothers couldn't have been much more than six feet away when he fired that shot. The .45-caliber slug turned Daisy Cassidy's head into a blood-filled water trough. Opened a furrow in her skull of blasted bone, brain matter, hair, and chunks of scalp that exited in a hat-sized, misty wad of flying gore that splattered everything within ten feet around. Bullet rocked Daisy up on her heels, then she dropped like a sack of sand, thrown off the roof of a three-story Dallas bank building.

Carl and Nate responded to the stunning turn of events exactly the way I'd told them to. As a matter of pure fact, none of us hesitated. Daisy Cassidy's still warm body was on its way to the floor when we cut loose with six barrels worth of heavy-gauge buckshot.

Coltrane gang's table exploded in a dagger-filled cloud of flying wood splinters. Out front of a thunderous wave of sizzling black powder, our initial curtain of shotgun pellets swept through all four of those boys. Six-barreled blast shredded clothing and blew hats into the blood-saturated air.

Storm of shotgun pellets shattered several whiskey bottles and glasses sitting on the table. Sent riddled playing cards into the air like confetti. Chewed through muscle, flesh, and bone, then gouged dozens upon dozens of holes in the wall behind those boys. Smoking cavities filled with rivulets of blood and gore that splattered the wall and slid toward the floor like badly applied paint.

Hard to see much of anything a second after we dropped the hammers on that bunch. Thick, black, roiling cloud of acrid-smelling smoke filled the cramped corner and sent me to one knee. Knew Carl and Nate had likely got out of the line of fire by doing the same thing. Thank God, we didn't get so much as a single shot by way of return fire. Not surprising, actually, but I was sure as hell glad of it.

Smoke finally cleared on a scene of utter devastation. Limp, unmoving, shot-peppered bodies of Ennis Buckheart and Egger Salt sat upright in their chairs. Useless arms dangled at their sides. Caught straight on by the blast from my weapon, the pair of hatless men stared at the ceiling, empty-eyed, empty-handed. We later located their pistols on the floor beneath their chairs. Appeared to me both men had managed to draw their weapons about half a second too late.

Found Leroy Coltrane's shot-riddled body under the table.

He had fallen backward onto his overturned chair and reduced it to kindling, then rolled into a ball near Egger Salt's feet. One barrel of shot from Nate's big popper hit the poor goober in the left side, up under his arm. Man had a hole in his chest you could stick your fist into. Died instanteously. Alive one second, deader than Santa Anna and shaking hands with Beelzebub the next.

Near as we could figure it, most of Carl's twin barrels of buckshot slapped the right side of Jesse Coltrane's once-handsome face and instantly turned it into bloody smithereens. No way to identify the man from what remained of his vaporized head. Nothing left but eight or ten inches of exposed neck bone and a splintered piece of lower jaw that still sported a few teeth. Only way a body would have ever known, with any degree of certainty, it was Jesse was to have been aware of where he sat when the gunplay started.

We saw to the burials of the entire crew before heading back to Fort Smith. 'Course there was no undertaker available at Morgan's Cut. No way to get a coffin built, either, much less five of them.

Wrapped the bodies in blankets we bought at a half-assed mercantile near the saloon. Planted Daisy, the Coltrane boys, and the rest of them in what went for a cemetery atop a tree-shaded bluff overlooking the Brazos River. Had to dig the holes ourselves. Downright beautiful spot, to tell the God's truth.

Remember Carlton stuffed his hat on after the last shovel of dirt fell. He leaned on the short-handled spade, gazed around at the site's stunning natural beauty, then said, "You know, Tilden, not sure folks as evil as these deserve to rest in such a beautiful place. Hell, have trouble justifyin' the effort we're going to for these walkin' rattlesnakes."

Clapped him on the shoulder. Said, "Deserve doesn't have anything to do with it, Carl."

"I know," he said, then pitched the shovel aside. "But, if I'd of had my way, we'd a dragged 'em out into the big cold and lonely. Covered 'em with a pile of rocks to keep the coyotes off, way we done for that poor idiot of a kid Daisy

Cassidy left under the tree. Far as I'm concerned, it's all any of 'em should've expected—whether they deserved it or not."

And so, we made our way back to Fort Smith. I wrote my reports and waited. And, as usual, our actions and the outcome of the chase went unchallenged.

Truth be told, the whole mess turned out right profitable. Posted rewards on Jesse and Leroy Coltrane amounted to almost three thousand dollars. About a month after we made it back got word from Mr. Wilton's office that Ennis Buckheart and Egger Salt were wanted in Eureka Springs, Arkansas, for murdering the hell out of a farmer during the attempted robbery of a branch of the Elk Horn Bank located right in the middle of that picturesque downtown. Folks there wanted those boys bad enough that they put up two thousand apiece, dead or alive. Seems Eureka Springs' dead farmer had a lot of friends.

Couldn't do much but try to salve my conscience with such monetary good news, given the bloody outcome of the hunt. 'Course I never discussed that particular expedition with Elizabeth. Just couldn't bring myself to talk about it. Fact is, I don't remember ever mentioning the story to anyone, till now. But, you know, after the gunfight at Morgan's Cut, that beautiful gal of mine always allowed as how I was never exactly the same.

Had a lot of years to think about the whole ugly incident, and have to admit, I think Elizabeth was right.

EPILOGUE

GOT TO GIVE credit where credit's due. Martha Frances Harrison, appearing mesmerized, sat unmoving the whole night long. She listened to my lengthy yarn of lunatic behavior, gun smoke, and violent death like an awestruck child. Seemed as though as long as I talked, she had barely moved. Sometimes not even sure she breathed while I spun the tale out for her.

But when I finished, and after a few seconds of silence, she gazed up at me with misty eyes and said, "That's the most incredible story I've ever heard, Hayden. Exactly what you warned me to expect. Nothing like any western movie I've ever seen, that's for sure. A twisted, unrelenting, realistic tale of obsession, blood, murder, and as you warned before starting, quick death."

Outside the highly polished windows of our sunporch haven, off to the east, a snipped fingernail of sunlight sliced across the distant horizon. Muted light, filtered by a bank of thin, dark clouds, and reflected off the Arkansas River, bathed our hideout under the potted palm in a soft, reddish hue. Came damn near to being the exact color of blood.

Martye leaned my direction. She placed a warm hand on my leg. Squeezed, then said, "Had someone else told me that selfsame story, I would have dismissed it out of hand as being nothing more than a fanciful concoction designed to shock a tenderhearted listener. Truth is, I could never have brought myself to believe a man of your splendid conduct, and Southern cavalier refinement, ever took part in such brutal affairs. But having heard it directly from your own lips, well, I suppose the reality of those horrible events can't be denied."

Tried to smile, but couldn't. "You know, Martye, I do believe you're the best thing that's happened to me since Carl passed away. Right lonely around here till you showed up, darlin'. Really enjoy your company. Figured my experience with the devilish Daisy Cassidy would show you a side of me I've kept hidden from most people for more years than I care to remember. Pray I didn't say anything that would damage our friendship. One I sincerely hope lasts for some time to come."

She smiled. Grabbed my hand and stood. Pulled me out of my seat. Linked one arm in mine and started moving us down the hallway toward the cafeteria and a waiting breakfast.

We hadn't gone very far when she leaned against me and whispered, "Hayden, have you ever wondered what would have happened to Daisy Cassidy if you had managed to bring her back alive?"

Her question rang in my leathery old heart like a cracked church bell. "Yes. More times than I care to recall. More times than I care to think about."

"Would you venture a guess? Just for me."

Chin on my chest, I muttered, "Well, I'm pretty sure that after being found guilty, Judge Parker would have sentenced her to hang. And, very likely, her lawyers would have appealed that sentence."

"So, in your estimation, had the Cassidy girl lived, she wouldn't have been known to history as the first woman hanged by Judge Parker in Fort Smith?"

"Didn't say that. In the end, when all her appeals had justifiably failed, and the case had finally shaken out to its logical conclusion, in my estimation, Daisy Cassidy would have walked to her fate on the arm of hangman George Maledon. Climbed the steps of his Gates of Hell gallows in the little hollow not far from the courthouse. And, in all likelihood, Carlton and I would have been compelled to attend her hanging."

"My God."

"Indeed. It's an image that I'm eternally grateful had no chance to take root and add another scar on my heart."

Martye clung to my arm. Snuggled closer. Felt damned good having her next to me. And given the dangerous and deadly course of my past life, simply being alive and able to walk the halls of the Rolling Hills Home for the Aged felt good. Felt damned good.